Praise for
I LOVE YOU, BETH COOPER

"This book is laugh-out-loud funny."
—John Searles, NBC's *Weekend Today*

"This side-splitting novel of adolescence is a classic teen movie waiting to be made."
—*Entertainment Weekly*'s "The Must List"

"In his debut novel, *I Love You, Beth Cooper*, Larry Doyle . . . gives a twenty-first-century gloss to this familiar tale. . . . He is, as his credits suggest, wickedly funny. . . . When Doyle nails it, he's hilarious. . . . Reformed nerds will surely wince at Doyle's spot-on portrayals of Denis. . . . Denis and Beth are both rendered with sensitivity and depth. Doyle is especially good at revealing what lies in the heart of the popular girl; Beth is no vapid simpleton. And Denis has more going on than *Star Wars* and chaos theory."
—*New York Times Book Review*

"One of the 'best comedy books of the summer.'"
—*Time Out* (Chicago)

"The book is great. Those among us who will forever self-identify as recovering high school outcasts . . . will delight in this dark, absurdist, insanely funny send-up of a John Hughes movie. . . . Buy it."
—*New York* magazine

"Gleefully clever and adroitly sweet."　　　—*USA Today*

"Doyle takes his laughs when he can get them, which is pretty often, and his book has one major virtue: The story's action drives with beguiling speed to its conclusion. The reader never yawns waiting for something to happen. . . . What Doyle does best is depict the inner world of a cartoonishly nerdy nerd whose little nerd head is filled with hyperbolically nerdy thoughts. . . . A demonstration of the power of good comic writing." —*Weekly Standard*

"Larry Doyle's debut novel gets at the agony of adolescence in a way that will have people covering their faces with their hands, reading between their fingers to see what disaster will befall Denis next, and snorting with laughter the whole time."
—*Christian Science Monitor*

"Hilarious high school romp. . . . Doyle's insight into the mind of the smart but socially retarded Cooverman is nuanced and interesting. But the story, while somewhat predictable and episodic, never ceases to charm . . . unlike, say, P.E."
—E! Online's "Cool Stuff"

"Hilarious, suspenseful, and a little good-kind-of-sad, the novel is a smashup of a John Hughes movie, notes on white-bread suburbia, and a plausibly implausible plot." —*Blueprint* magazine

"This funny, hopeful novel is like a John Hughes movie in book form." —*Indianapolis Star*

"This slight, frenetic comic novel about a high school crush has all the cleverness and wit you'd expect from someone who used to be a writer for *The Simpsons*. . . . Complete with unexpected situations, colorful characters, and razor-sharp dialogue. . . . Darn funny." —*Salt Lake City Tribune*

"Doyle [injects] his own brand of insightful, engaging humor and convincingly re-creates the high school experience." —*New York Press*

"It's all outlandish fun, but what do you expect from a former *Simpsons* writer? The teens experience one *D'oh!*-worthy episode after another. As for the author, he's hit a homer." —Daily Candy (Los Angeles)

"*I Love You, Beth Cooper* is hip and hysterical, the kind of degenerative chaos theory of a comedy that could only be written by a writer who genuinely understands the high school experience, both from the awkward and stumbling perspective of a Denis Cooverman and from the lofty perspective of the 'in crowd.' Doyle has written a fun teen–coming-of-age story that never takes itself too seriously but resonates with genuine charm. It is, I think, must-reading for any teenager, or anyone who has ever been a teenager." —*Buffalo News*

"[An] outrageously funny novel. . . . Doyle has written for *Beavis and Butt-Head* and *The Simpsons*, making it no surprise that his first novel both celebrates and mercilessly satirizes all-things teen with outrageous, razor-sharp humor. . . . It's the nonstop jokes and wry, uproarious descriptions that set this apart, and like the shows Doyle has helped create, the text is filled with phrases ('benevolent cliquetator') and lines readers will savor." —*Booklist*

"It's high school hell. . . . Doyle has the scene down cold. Coldest (and best) is his wince-inducing master creation, ultra-nerd Denis Cooverman." —*Kirkus Reviews*

I LOVE YOU, BETH COOPER

AN **ecco** BOOK

HARPER PERENNIAL

NEW YORK • LONDON • TORONTO • SYDNEY • NEW DELHI • AUCKLAND

I LOVE YOU, BETH COOPER

A NOVEL

LARRY DOYLE

"Another Brick in the Wall (Part 2)," Words and Music by Roger Waters © 1979 Roger Waters Overseas Ltd. All rights for the United States and Canada administered by Warner-Tamerlane Publishing Corp. All Rights Reserved. Used by permission of Alfred Publishing Co., Inc.

A hardcover edition of this book was published in 2007 by Ecco, an imprint of HarperCollins Publishers.

P.S.™ is a trademark of HarperCollins Publishers.

HarperCollins books may be purchased for educational, business, or sales promotional use. For information please write: Special Markets Department, HarperCollins Publishers, 10 East 53rd Street, New York, NY 10022.

FIRST HARPER PERENNIAL EDITION PUBLISHED 2008. REISSUED IN 2009.

Library of Congress Cataloging-in-Publication Data is available upon request.

ISBN 978-0-06-173277-5 (tie-in)

09 10 11 12 13 RRD/WC 10 9 8 7 6 5 4 3 2 1

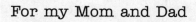

For my Mom and Dad

PREFACE

I LOVE YOU, BETH COOPER is the name of a novel.

I Love You, Beth Cooper is also the name of a movie, directed Chris Columbus from a screenplay by the book's author.

And *I Love You, Beth Cooper* is the name of this thing, a special expanded, illustrated version of the novel, containing stuff from the movie, stuff written for the movie but not used, stuff that occurred to the author while adding the other stuff.

All these *I Love You, Beth Cooper*s are all high-quality products that deserve your attention, but this is the one you need to buy right now.

THE ORIGINAL PREFACE I WROTE for this edition described the genesis of the novel and its journey from manuscript to motion picture, discussing the challenges inherent in adapting a literary work for a visual medium. As you might imagine, it was boring as shit. I couldn't even finish it, and it was mostly about me.

The biggest problem with that behind-the-scenes narrative, besides the absurd gravitas, was the utter lack of suspense.

I Love You, Beth Cooper was always a movie. The book is every teen movie ever made, the ultimate last wild night, as well as an affectionate dissection of the genre, exploring the myths and rituals of adolescence, an anthropological meditation if you will . . .

. . . *with lots of sex and comedy!*

The book reviewers seemed to appreciate that

> "This side-splitting novel of adolescence is
> a classic teen movie waiting to be made"
> (*Entertainment Weekly*).

and even those who did not

> "Less a novel than a novelization of a
> movie not yet made" (*New York Times
> Book Review*).

acknowledged it.

So now it's an actual movie. The End.

I'VE WORKED IN HOLLYWOOD for a dozen years now,
and I've faced my share of challenges, which come in
one of three forms: evil, idiots, and evil idiots.

True Hollywood story, illustrating the third kind:

I'm in the emergency room on a morphine drip, in
very special pain from an undiagnosed condition (kidney stones, turns out). My cell phone rings, in violation of hospital regulations. My wife answers. The
caller insists on talking to me. It's the producer.

PRODUCER

How are you doing?

ME

I think I may be dying.

PRODUCER

We really need that rewrite.

That happened on a different movie; I have no stories
from this one. And I would tell you if I did. As my
agents will attest, I delight in burning my bridges. But
unfortunately for this preface, nothing truly idiotic or
exceptionally evil happened during *I Love You, Beth
Cooper*'s journey from page to screen.

The script came together quickly, without any
shouting at all. The movie is faithful to the book, and
where it's not exactly the same, it may be better.

THE ONLY SIGNIFICANT CHALLENGE in adapting the book was commercial rather than creative. The movie had to be PG-13. Shot as written, the book is NC-17, and illegal in 38 states. Nevertheless, because none of the scenes require the comic misapplication of semen or menstrual blood, it was possible to translate without losing too much.* *Fucks* were changed to *shits, cunts* to *bitches*, full frontal female nudity to brief side boobage, and a male appendage with a loaded condom dangling off it to underpants. The characters no longer drink and drive. They drink, then drive.

These aren't my rules.

As it is, I suspect the movie is going to land an R its first time through the ratings board. A few *shits*, and beer sips, will have to go. Not tragic.

The lesson you should take away from all this: *The novel is much smuttier than the movie, with one word so filthy you won't even know what it means, and once you find out your innocence will be irrevocably lost, so you should just put this book down right now and buy the latest Junie B. Jones instead.*

FOR THOSE OF YOU skimming for Hayden Panettiere to make an appearance, here she is.

So, you drool, *what is Hayden really like?*

---

* For me, the one galling bowdlerization was the complete ban on smoking. Never mind that the one character in the book who smokes is a negative role model and is called on it by another character, abetted by a list of interesting statistics from the American Cancer Society; teenagers simply cannot be allowed to even *see* cigarettes anymore, on the theory that young prospective smokers will be scared away by their forbidden nature.

Nice kid. Sweet, smart. A pro. Doesn't squirm around when you snort cocaine off her like some actresses.

A joke, a thousand lawyers hasten me to point out. Ms. Panettiere so far has escaped the scum vortex that has sucked down many of her contemporaries. (That hasn't stopped the paparazzi from trying to catch her at it, of course. Once, during shooting, they managed to snap a picture of her frowning, which set the blogosphere ablaze.) She seems extremely level-headed, which is good because she is going to need it. *I Love You, Beth Cooper* is going to make her a gigantic movie star.

I hope.

THE ONE TRULY NEGATIVE ASPECT of this process was that in order to adapt *I Love You, Beth Cooper*, I had to go back and read it. I discovered, to my fleeting shame, that *parts of it weren't perfect*.

I would be dutifully cutting and pasting dialogue from the novel document into the script document, and the character would complain that they wouldn't really say that or, worse, they'd pipe up with a much better line.

It was very aggravating.

Goddamnit, I thought, *why didn't you say that before?*

Likewise, the director and producers and studio executives had all read the book, apparently, and made a number of suggestions that I must begrudgingly characterize as not bad.

I handed in the screenplay sick with the realization that the movie might turn out better than the book, and it would be partially my fault.

That's when I came up with the idea for this thing.

I'm told this is unusual, revising a novel after publication, and only reserved for masterworks that were butchered by evil, idiotic editors. However, I believe there is an argument to be made, using the words *Internet*, *transformative*, *rapidly*, and *impermanent*, and I welcome someone to make it for me. All I know is that this version of *I Love You, Beth Cooper* is 3 percent better than the original, and 12 percent funnier. And at least one X more obscene.

Not everything from the movie has been incorporated into this edition. I haven't included any of the actors' ad libs or the stuff Chris Columbus wrote, as much as I'd like to take credit for them. Nor have I included changes made for practical reasons, or changes that for whatever reason, I did not prefer to what was already in the book. Nothing has been cut from the book that didn't suck.

Most of the current additions were written for the movie but not used—they were *just too funny*, I was assured—and several embellishments came out the revision itself. Something now happens on page 154 that, had I included it in the first edition, might have convinced the studio the movie had to be an R. I would have paid to see it, at any rate.

Plus, kids, there's comics!

Sixteen pages of new Evan Dorkin comics have been sprinkled throughout the book, dramatizing incidents not included or only alluded to in the main narrative. There's even a four-page illustrated epilogue, showing where the characters might end up, for those who asked. We decided to do this because everybody loved Evan's chapter illustrations from the original, and also because, who doesn't like comics?

OH, AND DID I SAY, there's a movie coming out? I hear it's very good.

IT IS MY LADY; O! IT IS MY LOVE:
O! THAT SHE KNEW SHE WERE.

ROMEO DEL MONTAGUE

ERIC VON ZIPPER ADORES YOU.
AND WHEN ERIC VON ZIPPER ADORES
SOMEBODY, THEY STAY ADORED.

ERIC VON ZIPPER

I LOVE YOU, BETH COOPER

Cameron Alcott

David Bastable

Emily Jane Charlotte

Elisabeth Cooper

Denis Cooverman

Henry Giroux

Divya Gupta

Patricia Keck

Teresa Kilmer

Richard Munsch

Ian Packer

Jeffery Pule

Rebekah Reese

Gregory Saloga

Victoria Smeltzer

Angelika Steinke

Valerie Woolly

Stephanie Wu

1.

THE VALEDICT

JUST ONCE, I WANT TO
DO SOMETHING RIGHT.

JIM STARK

DENIS COOVERMAN WAS SWEATING more than usual, and he usually sweat quite a bit.

For once, he was not the only one. The temperature in the gymnasium was 123 degrees; four people had been carried out and were presumed dead. They were not in fact dead, but it was preferable to think of them that way, slightly worse off, than contemplate the unbearable reality that Alicia Mitchell's ninety-two-year-old Nana, Steph Wu's overly kimonoed Aunt Kiko and Jacob Beber's roly-poly parents were currently enjoying cool drinks in the teacher's lounge with the air-conditioning set at 65 degrees.

Ed Munsch sat high in the bleachers, between his wife and a woman who smelled like boiled potatoes. Potatoes that had gone bad and then been boiled. Boiled green potatoes. Ed thought he might vomit, with any luck.

Anyone could see he was not a well man. His left hand trembled on his knee, his eyes slowly rolled, spiraling upward; he was about to let out the exact moan Mrs. Beber had just before she escaped when his wife told him to cut it out.

"You're not leaving," she said.

"I'm dying," Ed countered.

"Even dead," said his wife, at ease with the concept. "For chrissakes, your only son is graduating from high school. It's not like he's going to graduate from anything else."

> *Tattoos of memories*
> *and dead skin on trial*

the Sullen Girl sang, wringing fresh bitterness from the already alkaline lyrics, her wispy quaver approximating a consumptive canary with love trouble and money problems. She sang every song that way. At the senior variety show, she had performed "Happy Together" with such fragile melancholy during rehearsals that rumors began circulating that, on show night, she would whisper the final words,

I can't see me loving nobody but you

then produce an antique pistol from beneath her spidery shawl and shoot Jared Farrell in the nuts before blowing her brains out. Nobody wanted to follow that. Throughout the final performance, Mr. Bernard had stood in the wings clutching a fire extinguisher, with a vague plan. Although the Sullen Girl didn't execute anyone in the end, it was generally agreed that it was the best senior variety show ever.

BEHIND THE SULLEN GIRL sat Denis Cooverman, sweating: along the cap of his mortarboard, trickling behind his ears and rippling down his forehead; around his nostrils and in that groove below his nose (which Denis would be quick to identify as the *philtrum,* and, unfortunately, would go on to point out that the preferred medical term was *infranasal depression);* from his palms, behind his knees, inside his elbows, between his toes and from many locations not typically associated with perspiratory activity; squirting out his nipples, spewing from his navel, coursing between his buttocks and forming a tiny lake that gently lapped at his genitals; from under his arms, naturally, in two varietals—hot and sticky, and cold and terrified.

"He's a sweaty kid," the doctor had diagnosed when his mother had brought him in for his weekly checkup. "But if he's sweating so much," his mother had asked, him sitting right there, "why is his skin so bad?"

Denis worried too much, that's why. Right now, for example, he was not just worried about the speech he was about to give, and for good reason; he was also worried that his sweat was rapidly evaporating, increasing atmospheric pressure, and that it might start to rain inside his graduation gown. This was fully theoretically possible. He was also worried that the excessive perspiration indicated kidney stones, which was less likely.

I hope you had the time of your life

the Sullen Girl finished with a shy sneer, then returned to her seat.

Dr. Henneman, the principal, approached the lectern.

"Thank you, Angelika—"

"Angel-LEEK-ah," the Sullen Girl spat back.

"Angel-LEEK-ah," Dr. Henneman corrected, "thank you for that . . . *emotive* rendition of "—she referred to her notes, frowned—" 'Good Riddance.' "

THE TEMPERATURE IN THE GYM reached 125 degrees, qualifying anyone there to be served rare.

"Could we," Dr. Henneman said, wafting her hands about, "open those back doors, let a little air in? Please?"

Three thousand heads turned simultaneously, expecting the doors to fly open with minty gusts of chilled wind, maybe even light flurries. Miles Paterini and Pete Couvier, two juniors who had agreed to usher the event because they were insufferable suck-ups, pressed down on the metal bars. The doors didn't open.

People actually gasped.

Denis began calculating the amount of oxygen left in the gymnasium.

Dr. Henneman's doctorate in school administration had prepared her for this.

"Is Mr. Wrona here?"

Mr. Wrona, the school custodian, was not here. He was at home watching women's volleyball with the sound turned off and imagining the moment everyone realized the back doors were locked. In his fantasy, Dr. Henneman was screaming his name and would presently burst into flames.

"Let's move on," Dr. Henneman moved on, mentally compiling a list of janitorial degradations to occupy Mr. Wrona's summer recess. "So. Yes. Next, and finally, I am pleased to introduce our valedictorian for—"

JAH-JUH JAH-JUH JAH-JUH JAH-JUH

Lily Masini's meaty father slammed the backdoor bar violently up and down. He turned and saw everybody was staring at him, with a mixture of annoyance and hope.

JAH-JUH JAH . . . JUH!

Mr. Masini released the bar and slumped back to the bleachers.

"Denis Cooverman," Dr. Henneman announced.

AS DENIS STOOD UP, his groin pool spilled down his legs into his shoes. He shuffled forward, careful not to step on his gown, which the rental place had insufficiently hemmed, subsequently claiming he had gotten shorter since his fitting. Denis had been offered the option of carrying a small riser with him, which he had declined, and so when he stood at the lectern barely his head was visible, floating above a seal of the Mighty Bison, the school's mascot. The effect was that of one of those giant-head caricatures, of a boy who told the artist he wanted to wrangle buffalos when he grew up.

Denis looked out at the audience. He tried to imagine them in their underwear, which was easy, since they were imagining the same thing. Denis sort of smiled. The audience did nothing. They were not excited by, or even mildly curious about, Denis's speech, merely resigned it was going to happen. He met their expectations.

"Thank you, Dr. Henneman. Fellow Graduates. Parents and Caregivers. Other interested parties."

Denis had left a pause for laughs. It became just a pause.

"Today we look forward," he continued. "Look forward to getting out of here."

That got a laugh, longer than Denis had rehearsed.

"Look forward to getting out of here," Denis repeated, resetting his meter before proceeding in the stilted manner of adolescent public speakers throughout history.

"But today I also would like to look back, back on our four years at Buffalo Grove High School, looking back not with anger, but with no regrets. No regrets for what we wanted to do but did not, for what we wanted to say but could not. And so I say here today the one thing I wish I had said, the one thing I know I will regret if I never say."

Denis paused for dramatic effect. Somebody coughed. Denis extended the pause to rebuild his dramatic effect.

He blinked the sweat off his eyelashes.

Then he said:

"I love you, Beth Cooper."

DENIS COULD THINK of no logical reason why he should not attempt to mate with Beth Cooper.

There were no laws explicitly against it.

They were of the same species, and had complementary sex organs, most likely, based on extensive mental modeling Denis had done.

They had both grown up here in the Midwest, only 3.26 miles apart, and could therefore be assumed to share important cultural values. They both drank Snapple Diet Lime Green Tea, though Denis had begun doing so only recently.

And while Beth was popular and good-looking—Most Popular and Best Looking, according to a survey of 513 Buffalo Grove High School seniors—Denis did have the Biggest Brain and wasn't repulsive, exactly. It was said that he had a giant head, but this was an optical illusion. His head was only slightly larger than average; it was the smallness of his body that made it appear colossal. He had the right number of facial features, in roughly the right arrangement, and would eventually grow into his face, his mother predicted. She also said he had beautiful eyes, though in truth, one more than the other. His teeth fit in his mouth now, and he did not have backne.

Denis could imagine any number of scenarios under which his conquest of Beth Cooper would be successful:

if Beth went to an all-girls school in the Swiss Alps, surrounded by mountains, hundreds of miles from any other guys except Denis, son of the maths teacher, and Beth was failing algebra, for example;

if Denis was a celebrity;

if Denis had a billion dollars;

if Denis was six inches taller, and had muscles.

Any one of those scenarios.

One also had to consider that there were 125 to 200 billion galaxies in the universe, each with 200 billion stars. Using the Drake equation, that meant there were approximately 2 trillion billion planets out there capable of sustaining life; the latest research suggested that one-third of them would develop life and one-ten-millionth would develop intelligent life. That left 1,333,333 intelligent civilizations created across the universe since the beginning of time, surely one of which was intelligent enough to recognize Denis and Beth were meant for one another.

Alternatively, if current string theory was correct, there were a googol googol googol googol googol universes, all stacked up with this one but with different physical properties and, presumably, social customs. In one of these, odds were, Denis Cooverman not only bred with Beth Cooper but was worshipped by ravenous hordes of Beth Coopers. Unfortunately in that universe

Denis had crab hands and inadvertently snipped each Beth Cooper to bits as she came ravenously at him.

This was but a small sampling of the thinking that went on in Denis's Biggest Brain prior to Denis's sweaty lips declaring his love for Beth Cooper in front of 3,221 hot, testy people.

For all its obsessive analysis, Denis's Biggest Brain had neglected to consider two relevant facts. Big Brains often have this problem: Albert Einstein was said to be so absentminded that he once brushed his teeth with a power drill. But even Einstein (who, according to geek mythology, bagged Marilyn Monroe) would not have overlooked these facts; even Einstein's brain, pickling in a jar at Princeton, would be able to grasp the infinitudinous import of these two simple facts, which now hung over Denis's huge head like a sword of Damocles— or to the non-honors graduates, like a sick fart.

The two incontrovertible, insurmountable, damn sad facts were these:

Beth Cooper was the head cheerleader;

Denis Cooverman was captain of the debate team.

THERE WAS A MOMENTARY DELAY in the reaction to what Denis had just said, because nobody was listening. While the adults contemplated cold beer and college tuition, and the graduates contemplated cold beer and another cold beer, their brains continued routine processing of auditory input, so that when Denis's mother yelped *Oh no,* they were able to rewind their sensory memory and hear, again:

"I love you, Beth Cooper."

Mrs. Cooverman had been following right along, syllable by syllable, and she knew something was up at syllable ninety-four, when Denis went off the script they had worked so hard on. Her *Oh no* was the release of tension that had accumulated in the subsequent twenty-nine errant syllables, building suspense for her alone. She did not know who Beth Cooper was, but she knew this was not appropriate for a graduation speech, and probably worse. Mr. Cooverman had been enjoying the speech until his wife yipped.

The bleachers echoed with confused murmurs, while down on the floor the graduating class retroactively grasped the tragic nature of what had transpired, and laughed. Dr. Henneman had been calculating how many dirty, dirty toilets required Mr. Wrona's lavish attention and had not noticed anything wrong until she heard the laughs; they seemed genuine, and that was not right.

Everyone who knew who Beth Cooper was—the entire class and several hundred adults—craned their necks to stare at her. She was near the end of the third row, next to an empty chair, the seat Denis himself was to return to once he was done humiliating her.

He wasn't done.

"I have loved you, Beth Cooper," Denis went on, his eyes clinging to his notes, "since I first sat behind you in Mrs. Rosa's math class in the seventh grade. I loved you when I sat behind you in Ms. Rosenbaum's Literature and Writing I. I loved you when I sat behind you in Mr. Dunker's algebra and Mr. Weidner's Spanish. I have loved you from behind—"

This got a huge laugh, one Denis should have expected, being a teenager. He also should have anticipated that Dr. Henneman would be looming up behind him, about to put her hand on his shoulder, but he did not and continued at the same measured pace.

". . . in biology, history, practical science and Literature of the Oppressed. I loved you but I never told you, because we hardly ever spoke. But now I say it, with no regrets."

DENIS MADE A NOISE, a dry click, as if resetting his throat.

"And so, let us all, too, say the things we have longed to say but our tongues would not."

He had returned to the approved text. His mother exhaled for the first time in more than a hundred syllables. Dr. Henneman decided intervention was no longer worth the effort, and sat back down. Denis also felt better, having disgorged his annoying heart, and so proceeded more confidently, with the well-practiced cadence of a master debater.

"Let us be unafraid," Denis preached, "to admit, *I have an eating disorder and I need help.*"

Fifty-seven female graduates, and six males, glanced around nervously.

"Let us," Denis chanted, "be unafraid to confess, *I am so stuck-up because, deep down, I believe I am worthless.*"

There were at least seven people Denis could have been referring to, and another four so low on the social totem their conceit was meaningless, but the clear consensus was that Denis was talking about Valli Woolly. Valli Woolly acknowledged the stares by baring her teeth, her version of a smile.

"Let us"—cranking now—"be courageous, truly courageous rather than simply mindlessly violent—"

Greg Saloga. He was definitely talking about Greg Saloga. It was so obvious that even Greg Saloga suspected he was being talked about, and this, like most things, made him angry.

"Let us stand up and say, *I am sorry for all the poundings, the pink bellies, the purple nurples . . .*"

Denis had received seven, sixteen and dozens, respectively.

"*I'm sorry I hurt so many of you. I am cruel and violent because I was unloved as a baby, or I was sexually abused or something.*"

Greg Saloga's big tomato face ripened as he erupted from his chair. He had not fully formed a plan beyond *smash* and *head* when something tugged the sleeve of his gown. He wheeled around, fist in punch mode, and came very close to delivering some mindless violence into the paper-white face of the diversely disabled and tragically sweet Becky Reese.

"Not now," Becky Reese said in a calming wheeze.

Greg Saloga felt stupid. She was right. He could kill the big-head boy *later.* He grinned at Becky Reese, much like Frankenstein's Monster grinned at that flower girl before the misunderstanding.

"You should sit down," Becky Reese said.

Greg Saloga sat down.

"In your seat," Becky Reese clarified.

DENIS MISSED his own near-death experience. He was busy expressing the regrets of fellow classmates who started *malicious, hurtful and totally unfounded rumors* (e.g. Christy Zawicky and her scurrilous insinuation that semen had been found in someone's fetal pig from AP biology) or who *chose indulgence over excellence* (e.g. most of the class but specifically Divya Gupta, Denis's debate partner, who drank an entire bottle of liebfraumilch the night before the downstate debate finals and made out with both guys from the New Trier team, revealing the entire substance of their argument even if she did not recall doing so). And Denis was just getting started, or so he thought.

"And let us not regret," he said, "that we never told even our best friend"—pause, then softer, slower—*"I'm gay, dude."*

Denis looked right at Rich Munsch, his best friend. This was unnecessary; everyone knew.

Rich Munsch, however, was flabbergasted. He mouthed, somewhat theatrically: *I'm not gay!!!*

Denis was about to respond when he felt four bony fingers dig under his clavicle.

"Thank you, Denis," Dr. Henneman said, leaning

across Denis into the microphone. "A lot to think about."

For a bright kid, Denis was not quick on conversational cues.

"I'm not done," he said.

"You're done." The principal moved decisively to secure the podium, driving Denis aside with her rapier hip.

She heard a *splish*.

She looked down and discovered she was standing in a puddle.

THE AUDIENCE SPATTERED ITS APPLAUSE as Denis shuffled off the stage.

"As I call your names," Dr. Henneman was saying, "I would appreciate it, and I think everyone would, if you came up and accepted your diploma quickly, with a minimum of drama."

The applause grew.

Denis felt good about the speech. He had let Beth Cooper know how he felt, after all these years, and had made some excellent points about other classmates besides. He wondered what Beth would say to him when he sat down beside her. He had prepared two responses:

"Then we agree"

or

"It's my medication."

Denis suddenly had a scary thought: *What if she tries to kiss me?* Would he politely demur, deferring such action to later, or would he accept the love offering, to the thunderous applause of his peers?

So Denis did not see the dress shoe that belonged to Dave Bastable's father that Dave Bastable had stuck in his path. Denis tripped, lurched forward, stomped his other foot onto the hem of his gown, dove across his own chair and sailed headlong into Beth Cooper's seat, where, fortunately or unfortunately, she no longer was.

2.
THE 10-MINUTE REUNION

YEAH. WE GRADUATED HIGH SCHOOL.
HOW . . . TOTALLY . . . AMAZING.

ENID COLESLAW

DENIS GRABBED a Diet Vanilla Cherry Lime-Kiwi Coke from the cafeteria table. He forwent the selection of Entenmann's cookies that was also available for graduates and their families, because his stomach hurt. He could not tell whether this was because he was overheated and dehydrated, or because he had not defecated in the week leading up to his speech, or because he had just done either the single greatest or most imbecilic thing he had ever done in his life.

In any case, the Diet Vanilla Cherry Lime-Kiwi Coke didn't help.

As he had every thirty seconds since he arrived, Denis surveyed the cafeteria. Fresh alumni, a few still in caps and gowns, most in caps and jeans, caps and cutoffs, caps and gym trunks, or, in the case of members of Orchesis, caps and orange Danskins, clustered in the same clusters they always had, in almost the exact spots they once ate lunch, even though none of the tables were there. Yet they all talked about how hot it had been in the gym and what they planned to do that evening, which was pretty much the same, only in different clusters.

She was not there.

ON THE REFRESHMENT TABLE a silver cube blasted the platinum thrash rap of Einstein's Brain,

> *Fuck this shit*
> *Nuff this shit*

The song captured the essence of adolescence and expressed it in easy-to-understand language, while simultaneously managing to aggravate adults, no mean feat these days. (Sales of the clean version were poor, however.)

What you can do wit
All this shit
Just fuck it!

Although Denis didn't like thrash rap, he was feeling a little outlawish and this song, he decided, would serve as his own personal theme song, saying in rhyme what he had said in rhetoric. He moved closer to the table to facilitate others in making the connection.

"Oh, dear God," Mr. Bernard said, rushing past Denis and picking up the music box, searching for a way to turn it off, or failing that, destroy it. Mr. Bernard did not like modern music or its devices, his primary qualifications to head the Music Department. He shook the box, but it only seemed to get louder:

Fuckitfuckitfuckitfuckitfuckit

Mr. Bernard started to raise the box over his head.

"Let me, Mr. Bernard," Denis said, taking the cube from his twitching fingers. He pressed a nonexistent button on the metallic surface and the music changed to that Vitamin C song that wouldn't go away. Lulled by the classical string opening, Mr. Bernard wandered away.

He could have at least said *Thank you*, Denis thought, or *Awesome speech*.

And so we talked all night
about the rest of our lives

Denis did his reconnaissance. He did not know what he would do if he found her, only that he needed to do it.

Closest to the exit were clumps of parents who hadn't been dissuaded from attending (Denis's own father and mother—who thought his speech was an "interesting choice" but were "still so very proud" of him, respectively—seemed only too happy to wait out in the car, where the Sunday *New York Times* was). Mothers chatted up the teachers, hoping to squeeze out one last compliment about their children, while fathers checked their iPhones for weekend business emergencies.

Rich Munsch fidgeted beside his parents as his father interrogated Ms. Rosenbaum, his English teacher.

"I mean," Ed Munsch said, gesturing with his third complimentary Coca-Cola beverage, "is it really worth all that money to send him to college?"

"Everyone should go to college," Ms. Rosenbaum answered.

Ed Munsch chuckled. "Well, not *everyone*."

BETH COOPER WAS NOWHERE.

Denis began strolling, ostensibly checking things out but also providing an opportunity for the things to check him out. He was prepared to accept the accolades of his peers with good humor and a humble nod he had been practicing.

He stopped at a twenty-foot orange-and-blue banner hanging on the wall. It read "Congrats to BGHS CLASS OF '07" and featured a Mighty Bison painted by Marie Snodgrass, who would one day go on to create Po Panda, star of *Po Panda Poops* and *Oops, Po Panda!*, two unnecessary children's books. The bison wore a mortarboard and appeared to be drunk. Other graduates stood around the banner, signing their names to heartfelt clichés and smartass remarks.

No one took note of Denis.

Denis pretended to read and appreciate the farewell messages while searching for his name. The only entry that came close was:

I'm Gay, Dude, signed Richard Munsch

Just below this was affixed:

stu 𝒦

This was Stuart Kramer's "tag"—which he used exclusively in bathroom stalls and on his notebooks—placed there to ensure proper credit for this witticism. Denis was annoyed; that was *his* line.

Denis considered seeding the banner with a few anonymous hosannas to his *awesome speech,* just to get the ball rolling, but he was afraid he might get caught, and he didn't have a pen.

WHERE WAS SHE?

Denis was thinking about just leaving, and then he was thinking about just staying, when he felt those familiar authoritarian talons dig into his soft upper flesh.

"Mr. Cooverman." Dr. Henneman had snuck up on him again.

"Oh, Dr. Henneman," Denis said, with hopeful bonhomie. "Or I guess now I should call you Darlene."

"No," Dr. Henneman said. "You should not."

She fixed Denis with the look, the look she had fixed many thousands of times before, but which she had never imagined she would have fixed on this particular boy.

"Mr. Cooverman," she lectured, "I've never known you to do anything so reckless. At *all* reckless."

And then came the part of the upbraiding familiar to legions of Buffalo Grove High School malefactors, jokers, and stunt-pullers, an interrogatory also familiar to disobedient children and husbands throughout the English-speaking world.

"What," Dr. Henneman inquisited, "*what* were you thinking?"

DENIS COULD NOT THINK of what he had been thinking. He knew that what he had been thinking had been carefully thought, and would surely satisfy Dr. Henneman. But he was having trouble accessing his brain. Every time he tried going in there, the view of his vast hypertextual data matrix was obscured by one insistent memory. All he could see was the replay of a few minutes in his room a week before, when he decided to go ahead with the speech. It was the image of Rich Munsch bobbing around in front of his face.

"You gotta do it!" Remembered Rich was saying, in full dramatic flower. "It'll be like—"

Rich puckered his lips and scrunched his nose, and began yelling in a nasal and New York-y accent.

"*You're out of order! You're out of order! The whole trial is out of order!*"

Denis said what he usually said when Rich went into another of his inscrutable celebrity impressions: "What?"

Rich's response, in the standard format: "Al Pacino in . . . *and Justice for All*, 1979, Norman Jewison."

Rich bounced up and down a couple of times.

"Unforgettable speech. Like *yours* is going to be!"

There was nothing there to quench Dr. Henneman, Denis decided. He also concluded that the sociology of alien civilizations and implications of infinite universes might be too esoteric for the discussion at hand. And he probably shouldn't bring up *mating*. He began composing a creative plausibility, what in debate they referred to as *bullshit*, when Rich's face came bobbing across his brain again.

"You will *never* see her again!" Rich declared with awful finality. "*Nunca*. After graduation she will be *gone*! Until like maybe the tenth reunion, if you both *even live that long*."

Rich enjoyed having an audience, even of one, and took a little strut before delivering his next, tragic line.

"And she'll be so very pregnant—baking someone else's DNA—she'll have this big cow grin and *she won't even remember who you are!*"

"She'll remember me," Denis said. "I sat behind her in almost every class."

"*Behind her. Behind* her. Be-*hind* her," Rich incanted, like a poorly written television attorney. "She never *saw* you."

Rich stepped back for his close-up.

"*You don't exist.*"

This was a persuasive argument. Denis knew what it felt like to not exist, and didn't much care for it. He doubted it would hold much sway with Dr. Henneman, whose existence nobody doubted. He scanned his memory again, for even the slightest scrap of logic behind this monumental blunder, and there was Rich again.

"If you don't do this," Rich said, pausing to imply quotation marks before croaking out of the side of his mouth in a quasi-tough-guy voice:

"*You will regret it, maybe not today, maybe not tomorrow, but soon and for the rest of your life.*"

"What?" Denis said.

"*Bogart,* dude!"

"I 𝘿UNNO," Denis told Dr. Henneman.

Denis had upon his face that sheepish but super-cilious grin only found on a teen male in trouble. He had never deployed it before, but Dr. Henneman had certainly seen it, and she was trained to wipe it off. "Not the behavior I expect from someone going to Northwestern University." And then, oh so coolly: "You know, one call from me and you're going to Harper's . . ."

That smile wiped right off.

"Oh. Don't do that."

Harper Community College, located just five miles away in once lovely Palatine, offered credit courses in:

Computer Information Systems;

Dental Hygiene;

Certified Nursing Assistance;

Heating, Ventilation and Air Conditioning;

Hospitality Management; and

Food Service.

It was where young lives went to die.

"That would be . . . *unimaginable*," Denis said, even as he was extravagantly imagining it. "I, I don't know what I was thinking . . . I was . . . I was under an in-fluence!"

The phrase *under an influence* triggered a series of autonomic responses in Dr. Henneman: check eyes, arms, grades. But wait, this was Denis Cooverman. Valedictorian, debate champion, meek, quiet, perhaps too quiet, socially isolated . . . She studied Denis for Goth signifiers: pale, check; pasty, perhaps; eyeliner, no; hair, ordinary; piercings, none visible. His gown: there could be any number of semiautomatic weapons or sticks of dynamite under there.

But, c'mon: *Denis Cooverman.*

If Dr. Henneman had been one of those evil robot principals you keep hearing about, she would have started repeating IRRESOLVABLE LOGIC CONFLICT as smoke poured from her optical sockets and her head unit would have sparked and then exploded, just like in Mr. Wrona's sweet custodial dreams.

Instead, she bowed her head and whispered, "Drugs?"

"Oh? *No*," Denis flustered, "not drugs. They're whack," quoting a health education video that could use some updating. "No, by influence, I meant my thinking process was influenced, negatively impacted, by which I mean . . . Rich Munsch."

Dr. Henneman smiled. This would be perfect for her blog, The Uncertainty Principal, the twelfth most popular high school principal blog in the state.

"You really shouldn't be taking romantic advice from Richard Munsch," she said.

Denis—and this will be a recurring theme—didn't know that now would be a good time to shut up.

"But he was *right*," Denis insisted. "I had to do something. I would have been forgotten. Not even. I'm not there." Denis pointed to his head, and because he was Denis, he pointed precisely to his hippocampus. "She has no memory of me. No dendritic spines in her cortex that whisper: *Denis*."

(Denis knew that dendritic spines did not whisper, but he could be poetic, too, in his own way.)

"So I *had* to," Denis continued his pleading. "To *stimulate dendrite growth*. I mean"—and this is where he thought he had her—"Dr. Henneman, haven't you ever been in love?"

Dr. Henneman had been in love, and was in love, with her husband, Mr. Dr. Henneman, who was standing not more than fifteen feet away but remained invisible to all of her students because it required them to acknowledge that she had feelings and plumbing. The plaintiveness of Denis's cry, however, rekindled in

Dr. Henneman the heartache of Paul Burgie, the brown-eyed demon who took her to second base (then above-the-waist petting and not a Rainbow Party) and reported back to the other seventh-grade boys that Dr. Henneman's nipples were "weird"—*as if he had a representative sample!*

Dr. Henneman caught herself crossing her arms tightly across her chest, as she had through junior high. Such silly, everlasting pain. She answered Denis with something approaching empathy.

"There's another Beth Cooper out there," she told him. "One just for you. The world is full of Beth Coopers."

Dr. Henneman began to walk away, already filing Denis under STUDENTS, FORMER and composing additional summer projects for Mr. Wrona. *The grooves between these floor tiles could use a good tooth-picking . . .*

"Dr. Henneman?"

"*Yes,* Mr. Cooverman?"

"You won't call Northwestern."

Dr. Henneman chuckled. "As if I have any actual power," she confessed, as she often did to graduates. "Denis, with your SAT scores, you'd practically have to kill someone to not get in."

ALONE AGAIN, Denis decided to assume a cool pose against the wall, in case anyone chose to reference him while discussing his now infamous speech. It was a pretty good pose: casual yet defiant. But no one was talking about his speech; few even remembered it. At the end of the ceremony it had flown out of their heads like trigonometry, gone forever.

Denis canvassed the room, a cruel smile playing across his lips, he thought.

Rich's father was at the snack table, filling paper

napkins with cookie remains. Rich was performing for his mother and Ms. Rosenbaum, both laughing despite obviously having no idea what he was doing. Miles Paterini and Pete Couvier, the junior ushers, were acting like they were already seniors, scoping out where their lunch table would be, temporarily forgetting how unpopular they were. And there was Stephen Gammel guzzling a Coca-Mocha, the horrible new carbonated coffee beverage, and Lysa Detrick showing off the chin she got for graduation, and:

There she was.

BETH COOPER WAS less than thirty feet away. Twenty-seven floor tiles. She was chatting with Cammy Alcott and Treece Kilmer, fellow varsity cheerleaders and Table Six lunchers. Chatting about *him*, Denis suspected. Remarkably, he was about to be correct.

Cammy, who had a preternatural sense for when she was being stared at, noticed Denis first. Denis jerked his face to the side—universal body language for *Yes, I was staring at you*—while maintaining his casual yet defiant pose against the wall. It made him look like a male underwear model, except not. Out of the corner of his rapidly darting eye Denis saw Cammy point. Treece, and then Beth, turned in his direction.

Denis considered yawning to underscore his indifference to the attention, but he was afraid a scream might come out, undermining the effect.

Cammy made a short remark, with either a slight smile or a slight frown. Treece whinnied like a frightened mare, a thing she did in situations where other people laughed.

Beth Cooper began walking toward Denis.

WHEN DENIS WAS EIGHT, he read a story about a boy who discovered he could render himself invisible by turning at a precise angle. Young Denis spent several days systematically rotating himself until he, too, knew the exact angle of invisibility.

Right now Denis could not fathom how he could have forgotten such important information.

3.

HERE SHE COMES

"HOLY SHIT! IT'S THE MOTHER LODE!"
TOMMY TURNER

"HERE SHE COMES," as it so happens, was playing on the iCube as she came.

This was not the "Here She Comes" by the Beach Boys or the "Here She Comes"es by Boney James, Bonnie Tyler, Dusty Springfield, Android, Shantel, Mardo, Joe, the Eurythmics, the Konks, the Mr. T Experience or any of 238 other bands. Nor was it the Velvet Underground's "Here She Comes (Now)" or U2's "Hallelujah (Here She Comes)" or Hall and Oates's "(Uh-Oh) Here She Comes," which is actually called "Man Eater."

Had any of these "Here She Comeses"es been playing when Beth Cooper came it would have been a spooky coincidence (especially "Man Eater"); the fact that this "Here She Comes" was also Denis and Beth's unofficial song (pending Beth's notification and approval) made it, well, also a spooky coincidence, but spookier and more coincidental.

Beth Cooper's coming was accompanied by the latest and therefore greatest song to be called "Here She Comes," by Very Sad Boy,* off his new album, *Third Time's a Charm*, a reference to his upcoming suicide attempt.

> *Here she comes*
> *But no, not for me*

Denis tried to retract his entire head into his body cavity but it wouldn't go.

Graduation cap set at a provocative angle, Beth Cooper came. She seemed to be moving—nay, *sashaying*—in slow motion, as all around her blurred and the song became a sound track.

> *Here she comes*
> *No never for me*

*Née Judah Weinstock.

In the music video Denis spontaneously halluci-
nated, a sudden breeze kicked up. Beth's long brown
hair flew about her face promiscuously.

> *Here she comes*
> *Oh, she comes for me*

Her gown clung to her skin like a damp nightie. It
was apparently quite cold in the cafeteria.

> *Here she comes*
> *And there,*
> *there I go*

BETH STOPPED. She was twenty inches from Denis,
and, for perhaps the first time, facing him. She was
about his height, and this for some reason both startled and delighted Denis. They could walk down the
hallway with their hands comfortably tucked in each
other's back pockets. They could wear each other's
T-shirts. They could kiss ergonomically.

"You embarrassed me," Beth said in the flat, mid-
western voice of an angel.

Denis's mouth went dry.

It hung open a bit.

Death was imminent.

Then she smiled.

"But it was so sweet, I'll have to let you live."

Only a fool would have read this gesture as anything other than kindness. Denis was such a fool.

"Great," Denis said, clarifying: "That's great."

Then, a pause. A terrible, multisecond pause.

Denis panicked.

Beth didn't notice.

"So," she said, "Henneman must've given you major
shit."

At that moment, Denis realized he hadn't planned
for his plan to lead to conversation. Violence, sex, either

way he had a plan (both defensive). But *chitchat.*
So, Henneman must've given you major shit.
RESPOND.

"Some shit," Denis responded, with simulated indifference. "Little shit. A modicum of excreta." That didn't come out as cool as his brain told him it would. Before he could damage himself further with *a fecal smidgen,* Beth changed the subject.

"Was it like eight hundred degrees in there?" She scrunched her brow, as she did all things, intoxicatingly. "Like boiling?"

Denis chuckled dryly. Or that was the general idea. He kind of snorted.

"Actually, the boiling point—of water—is two hundred and twelve degrees. Fahrenheit," he said, adding casually, "One hundred Celsius."

Denis instantly knew that was hugely geeky, what he said, and further he knew his brain knew how geeky it was even before he said it; he suspected his brain was out to sabotage him, perhaps fearing that an exterior life would cut down on his Sudoku time.

Fortunately, Beth wasn't listening.

"I am so hot," she said.

Right there, inches from Denis, Beth did this: She bent over and lifted her gown over her head. She was not naked underneath, as Denis imagined, but somehow even better, she wore tight cutoff jeans and a sweat-soaked belly shirt. The shirt pulled up with the gown, revealing the underside of a lacy, clean, perfect and pink brassiere.

Denis had an overwhelming, inexplicable, perhaps primal urge to eat that brassiere.

"I can imagine," Denis swallowed, "that you're hot."

"I'M NOT GAY, DUDE."

Rich interloped, oblivious, it seemed, to the historic presence of Beth Cooper.

Rich was more than a foot taller than Denis, which always gave their conversations a cartoonish cant. Now, with Rich's flamboyant indignation and Denis's twitchy anxiety, they constituted a bona fide classic comedy duo, like the ones on those black-and-white DVDs Denis's father insisted he watch.

"I am so *not* gay," Rich snipped, hands perched on his hips.

Denis kept flicking his head in Beth's direction, in long and short flicks. Rich didn't know Morse code but eventually got the gist.

"I didn't realize there was a line."

Beth, on the other hand, was a master of the segue.

"That's okay," she said. "I have to get back—"

"Halt!" Denis blurted. "I mean, wait."

Beth waited.

Two hundred and fifty million nanoseconds passed.

Denis formulated a plan. Quite a good one, considering the quarter second that had gone into it.

"I'm having a little soiree at my house tonight." A smirk twitched along his lips. "Of course, that's redundant. *Soirée* means 'evening.' In French."

Rich was mad at Denis, but he wasn't going to leave his friend hoisting on his own petardness like that.

"A party," Rich translated. "More of a party than a French thing. Music. Drinks. Prizes. And drinks."

"That sounds fun," Beth said with merely anthropological interest.

"It *is* fun," Denis ejaculated. "Will be, in the future. And you're invited. Officially."

"Okay," Beth said.

"It's 706 Hackberry Drive. Zip code 60004 if you're Mapquesting—"

"I Google Map."

"Who doesn't? Mapquest blows." He rolled his eyes so emphatically they became stuck up there, fluttering in the grand mal fashion.

Beth waited for Denis to fall down, and when he didn't, said, "Wow, thanks," her voice dripping courtesy. "We do have this other thing we have to do—"

"What time?" Denis said, much too quickly.

"Whatever time parties start," Beth shrugged. "Nine?"

"Great!" Denis improvised, "Because ours starts at six-thirty."

"It's a pre-party," Rich jumped in. "For getting pre-trashed."

"Well," Beth said, surrounded, "maybe we can stop by . . ."

Denis nodded the Cool Nod, the mere feint of a nod, but too quickly and too often, making him look like a bobble-head doll.

"That's coo—"

A mammoth paw engulfed Denis's face and slammed his head against the cinderblock.

THE PAW WAS HUMAN, Denis surmised, from the way its thumb was opposed deeply into his throat.

Greg Saloga, Denis thought. *This has to be Greg Saloga, killing me.*

And yet these did not smell like Greg Saloga's fingers, of Miracle Whip and Oscar Mayer all-meat bologna, a reliably pungent bouquet that sophomore year had temporarily rendered Denis a vegetarian. Denis hypothesized that Greg Saloga must have washed his hands for graduation, a minimum of one thousand times.

Unbeknownst to Denis, Greg Saloga's bologna fingers were miles away. After the ceremony, Becky Reese's family invited him out for ice cream. Greg Saloga liked ice cream. It was cold and creamy.

Denis could not see whose hand was buckling the plates of his skull. One eye had a clear and intimate view of the cafeteria wall, which was not beige at all but white with a fine misting of yellow grease. The outward-facing eye had a forefinger in it, doubling whatever image was unobstructed, and so all Denis was able to make out was a slab of angry red meat with at least one orifice.

"You wooed my girl," the angry red meat said.

Denis did not recognize the voice, or the accent, a brassy southern drawl with swampy undertones. But he deduced the *gull* to which the voice referred had to be Beth Cooper, since she was the only one he had ever wooed. That would make this extremely humungous furious person . . .

Impossible.

Beth Cooper did not have a boyfriend. She had broken up with Seth Johansson in November, after he hit a deer with his car and refused to take it to the hospital. Since then, she had not been seen with any other guy on more than three successive occasions. Jeffery Pule, her prom date, had been a Make-a-Wish type situation; even though there were reports that Pule had felt Beth up under the guise of a fit, he was dead now and so completely out of the picture.

Beth Cooper did not have a boyfriend.

"YOU MUST BE BETH'S BOYFRIEND," Rich said brightly, extending his hand in hopes of tricking the meat into releasing his best friend's face.

The meat swiveled in Rich's direction. Its jaw was massive and appeared to have extra bones in it.

"I have to go to the bathroom," Rich excused himself.

The meat returned its attention to Denis. A slight shifting of its grip allowed Denis a better, albeit more terrifying, look.

The meat was a handsome young man whose army green jacket and army green trousers and army green beret and assorted patches, pins and epaulets suggested he was somehow affiliated with the United States Army.

The Army Man leaned in, putting his full weight on the hand clamped to Denis's face.

"Are you prepared to die?" he asked.

"Not really," Denis smush-mouthed.

"Kevin!"

Denis would not have guessed Kevin. Animal, Hoss, Bull or Steve. Not *Kevin*.

"Kevin, stop!"

Kevin turned to Beth, casually leaning on Denis's face.

"Return to your friends, Lisbee," he said, courtly like. "I will rejoin you shortly."

Beth made a petulant, defiant sound. "I hate to repeat myself," Kevin said less courtly. Beth did as Kevin requested.

Denis called after her: "Eight(ish)—"

Kevin squeezed Denis's head, silencing it. He moved in very close. Steam vented from his nostrils, hot beer vapor and a lemony smoke Denis could not immediately place. His lips brushed Denis's cheek.

"You demean her," Kevin drawled all over Denis, "and insult me."

Guys much braver than Denis would have simply apologized here.

"Actually," Denis countered, "she said it was 'sweet.'"

Kevin began choking Denis, just a little bit.

"You move in on my girl," he said, squeezing ever so slightly more, "even as I am fighting for your freedom and safety with my very life."

"Appreciate your sacrifice," Denis squeaked.

"Now over there," Kevin twanged on, "a moral

transgression of this order would dictate the severing of your head. Or some other relevant part."

Denis quickly ascertained the relevant part.

"But we're a civilized people," Kevin said, abating his strangling as evidence. "So I am going to give you ten seconds to convince me I should let you live."

"You mean persuade, not convince," Denis said.

Denis was about to discover if the human head could pop.

"IS THERE A PROBLEM HERE?"

Dr. Henneman delivered her catchphrase with Rich standing to her left. Behind and to her left.

Kevin released Denis.

"No, ma'am," Kevin said. "My hand slipped."

"We were debating my speech," Denis explained, rubbing his throat. "In the negative, this gentleman argued—"

Dr. Henneman ignored Denis and addressed Kevin.

"I can't allow you to kill him on school grounds."

Kevin nodded and walked away.

Dr. Henneman contemplated Denis. Half his face featured a port-wine stain shaped like a giant hand.

He wasn't her problem anymore, Dr. Henneman decided.

"Good luck in all your future endeavors, Mr. Cooverman," she said. "You too, Rich."

She left.

Denis checked for his Adam's apple.

"On the bright side," Rich said, "Beth Cooper talked to you."

DENIS DID NOT SEE ANY BRIGHT SIDE. Beth Cooper had a boyfriend, and he was going to kill Denis. Neither of these were promising developments. The very best Denis could hope for was that Kevin would only *almost* kill him, causing Beth to break up with Kevin in disgust and, overcome with guilt, visit Denis in the hospital every day, discovering what a tremendous person he was and, perhaps, sponge-bathing him.

The fantasy quickly collapsed in a cascade of hospital regulations and other improbabilities.

Denis watched horror-struck as, across the cafeteria, Kevin was introducing Cammy and Treece to two of his army buddies.

Oh no.

Beth and Kevin were being officially inducted into a social circle. Soon they would become Beth & Kevin, then Beth'n'Kev, and eventually Bevin.

It did not look good for Deneth.

Denis's woebegoneness somehow penetrated the penumbra of Beth's happiness. She turned in his direction. She crinkled her upper lip, tilted her head approximately fifteen degrees, and then, quite clearly, mouthed:

Sorry.

It was the most beautiful word that Denis had ever seen.

The gesture also attracted Kevin's attention, unfortunately. He pivoted, evil-eyed Denis, and then, using the hand not cupping Beth Cooper's silky belly, made a slicing motion across his pelvis.

Denis's testicles ducked into his abdomen. They huddled there, trembling.

Rich was puzzled. He imitated the crotch-chopping gesture.

"What is that," he asked, "an army thing?"

4.

WHAT THE FUN

MAYBE I'M SPENDING TOO MUCH OF MY TIME
STARTING UP CLUBS AND PUTTING ON PLAYS.
I SHOULD PROBABLY BE TRYING HARDER
TO SCORE CHICKS.

MAX FISCHER

A MOTLEY COLLECTION of serving dishes were arranged in some intelligent design on the kitchen table:
a large cornflower blue plastic bowl,
a stainless steel mixing bowl,
an old ceramic ashtray, a Bento Box, and
a chip bucket from the Ho-Chunk Casino in Baraboo, Wis.
They contained, respectively:
Natural Reduced-Fat Sea-Salted Ruffles,
Jays Fat-Free Sourdough Gorgonzola Pretzel Dipstix,
Triple Minty M&Ms,
Quattro Formaggy Cheetos, and
"Wasabi Lime Soy-tato Chips?" Rich read from the bag.

"My mom says if you're going to eat junk, it doesn't have to be crap."

"She's trying to kill you, dude."

Denis sat at the table, very still, and Rich sat opposite him, rolling his chair back and forth.

This was the party thus far. It was 7:30 p.m.

"She's not going to come," Rich said.

"She might. She said she might."

"I'm still mad at you."

"I know."

Rich reached for a chip. Denis was upon him.

"Let's save the snacks."

DENIS HAD BEEN OBSESSIVELY PLANNING this party ever since he'd told Beth about it that afternoon. He made his parents stop at the grocery store on the way home from graduation. They were only too happy, since Denis had never hosted a party before, and only had that one friend.

Denis's mother even allowed poison into the house she otherwise forbade. For someone who shunned anything processed, preserved or tasty, she seemed to know a lot about the relative merits of the various brands of poison.

"I *lived* on these in college," she said, putting them back. Instead, she nudged her son toward the more sophisticated crappy snacks, contending they would train his palate. She had been training Denis's palate since he was a baby, spiking her breast milk with pureed asparagus and later serving him *croque-tofu,* like grilled cheese only terrible, and homemade chicken nuggets made from actual chickens. Denis was the only toddler on his block who referred to *basgetti* as *bermicelli.*

Years later, Denis's mother felt guilty when she read in her alternative health magazine, *Denial,* that junk food was linked to an early onset of puberty. At fourteen, Denis's puberty had yet to onset, and his mother feared his trans-fatty-acid-and-bovine-growth-hormone-deficient diet was to blame for his pubic postponement. Denis's doctor assured her that boys mature much later than fat girls, and that the stool sample she had cajoled out of her son was unnecessary, and extravagant.

Speaking of which, Denis spent forty-five minutes in the bathroom when he returned home, evacuating seven days of excess stress and its biochemical byproducts. A MacBook perched on his knees, Denis diagnosed himself with post-traumatic stress disorder and irritable bowel syndrome. He was half right.

Denis spent another half hour in the shower, deepcleaning the entire assembly, going back to hit the trouble spots again and again. He rinsed, lathered and repeated, and for the first time in his life, put conditioner in his hair and waited the requisite two minutes.

During his final rinse cycle, Denis set the showerhead to PULSE and let the rhythmic jets massage the same three inches of his scalp while he replayed the best minutes of his life so far.

"You are so sweet," she says, smiling. "I guess I'll have to let you live."

"I guess you will."

"Henneman must've given you major shit."

"Little shit," he coos in a suave French voice.
She giggles.
"Was it like 800 degrees in there? I was so hot."
"You're still hot."
The blood rushes to her cheeks, and elsewhere.

The human brain is an amazing organ, versatile and loyal. Denis's five-pounder, which could recall Klingon soliloquies with queasy accuracy, could also creatively misremember recent events if it felt its owner needed a break. Rest assured, the brain had an unedited master of the scene in question and could evoke it at will, as it would later that night and seventeen years from now, with Denis walking down the street feeling pretty good about himself until his brain sucker-punched him with evidence to the contrary.

Denis's brain also had Big Green Kevin tucked away in the dark recesses of its Reptilian Complex, with the other monsters. It was keeping sight and smell samples on file in case it needed to activate the system's Fight-or-Flight Response, or as it was known around Denis's brain, the Flight Response.

With Unpleasant Memory Repression set on FULL, Denis tilted his head back and let the hot water ripple over his eyes and lips, like in a soap commercial or an otherwise not very good movie on Cinemax.

His memory fogged over with steam.

"Hey," he says, so cool. *"I'm having a little thing later. Music. Drinks. Prizes."*

"Wow, that sounds fun!" She bites her lip. *"I have this other stupid thing I'm supposed to go to . . ."*

A mischievous glimmer in her eye.

". . . but maybe I can stop by for a few minutes."

He cocks a brow. "We won't need more than a few—"

"DENIS, ARE YOU OKAY IN THERE?"

Denis dropped the conditioner.

"Just getting out, Mom."

Denis dried, rolled on some X-Stinc Pit Stick, followed up with several clouds of his father's deodorant powder, brushed his teeth and gargled with X-Stinc Breath Killaz, formulated for the male teen mouth. He tried on some corduroys, some cargo pants, brushed his teeth again, and pulled on a brand-new rugby shirt that was pre-grassed and muddied to look as if some serious rugby had already been played in it.

"You look cute," his mother squealed. "Supercute."

Denis was devastated.

"She doesn't mean that," Denis's father said. "You look fine. You might want to pull the waist of those pants down a bit."

THE STREET LIGHTS CAME ON outside Denis's house.

It was 8 p.m.

Denis sat, hands folded on the kitchen table. Rich continued rolling back and forth, in longer and longer swaths.

They had spent much of their lives this way, at this kitchen table, in front of the TV, lying around in Denis's room, not saying anything. Of the more than 20,000 hours they had logged since bonding in kindergarten over their mutual ostracism, Denis and Rich had spent perhaps 8,500 of those hours, almost an entire year, doing nothing at all, except being together.

Rich picked up the conversation exactly where it had left off a half hour before.

"I should punch you."

"Please do."

Rich was not going to punch Denis. Every time he did—when they were five, nine and thirteen—he was the one who ended up crying. Instead, he decided to agitate Denis, something he had become exceedingly good at over the past fourteen years.

"Hey," he brought up in casual conversation, "what if she comes and brings her Army Man and he cuts your nuts off?"

Denis's Reptilian Complex scurried under a rock.

"That's gonna be messy," Rich observed.

"He wasn't really . . . it was a metaphor."

"Though it would make it Party of the Year."

"She won't bring him."

"She might. She said she might."

Denis touched his neck, tracing the raspberry thumbprint on his windpipe. He gulped, and gulped again, but the cold, hard loogie of dread stubbornly inched up his throat.

Rich grinned.

Then felt awful.

Those two seconds neatly encapsulated their entire friendship.

RICH LOOKED FOR SOMETHING to get Denis's mind off what he had just put it on. He reached across the table and plucked an iPod from its cube.

"New?"

"Graduation present," Denis hocked out.

Rich fingered the smart new design and interface that made all previous iPods look like gleaming turds.

"I hear this one vibrates for her pleasure," he moaned, slowly shaking the device down his pants.

Denis snatched the iPod back from the brink of befoulment.

"*You* vibrate for her pleasure."

Rich laughed. "That's not even an insult, dude."

Denis sniffed the iPod before returning it to its dock. He rotated the cube seven degrees counterclockwise, then two degrees clockwise.

Sensing something had gone awry with his party's feng shui, aside from the total lack of guests, Denis began fiddling with the two-liter bottles of

soda on the kitchen island, or "bar area." He harmo-
nized the carbonated beverages with a plastic bowl
filled with ice and a box of Dixie Krazy Kritter
cups.

"You know what I got for graduation?" Rich said,
swiveling in his chair. "A bill. My dad says I owe him
two hundred and thirty-three thousand, eight hundred and fifty bucks."

(Rich's father was a dick.)

"*A quarter of a million dollars? They don't even
buy you shoes.*"

"That includes fifty grand for 'wear and tear' on my
mom," Rich said, acknowledging, "She is pretty worn
and torn."

Denis reached out to put his hand on Rich's shoulder, but misjudged the spinning rate and had to settle
for his friend's ear.

"I'm sorry your dad sucks."

Rich seemed philosophical about it. "It *was* completely itemized. Very detailed."

He looked up at Denis.

"Who knew he was paying attention?"

THEY WERE QUIET AGAIN. Denis began to re-
arrange individual chips in the casino bucket.

"You shouldn't be so nervous, dude."

"I'm not nervous. I'm particular."

Rich occasionally claimed to know things about the
opposite sex. Such as: "They can smell fear."

This terrified Denis. "No, they can't."

"*I* can smell it."

Horrified, Denis sniffed his armpit.

"Oh, no," he cried. "*Fear.*"

Denis headed for the sink, removing his shirt.

"Why didn't you tell me?"

"What are you talking about? That was *me*, just
now."

Denis ran water through a sponge and shoved it under his arms, bitterly.

"Puberty has done nothing but screw me."

THIS WAS TRUE. Puberty had come late to Denis Cooverman, but it had come with a vengeance. Thick curly hairs and sebaceous secretions everywhere. Virulent erections in organic chemistry, mysterious in origin, certainly not attributable to his lab partner, Martha Warneki, whose breath smelled like dead things (Denis suspected she was hitting the formalin). His own smorgasbord of odors, unresponsive to traditional cloaking methods, so ghastly they sometimes awoke him in the middle of night, forcing him to shower just to get some sleep. Robust and succulent acne that in his junior year required medications so mutagenic that the packaging warned Denis not to touch any woman who was pregnant or thinking of ever becoming so. (This was not a problem.)

In the past six months, Denis had gotten his adolescence more or less under control—he could often identify why his erections wouldn't go away, though he remained powerless to stop them—but his hormones still reserved the right to rage at inopportune moments, such as the present one.

"Goddammit," Denis said, twisting a freshly soaked sponge into his pits, hoping to drown the fear.

"Don't worry," Rich said. "She can't smell you. She's miles away."

Denis sniffed his rugby shirt. Perspiration, not the sexy kind. He began flapping the shirt in the air, keeping his elbows up in order to dry his armpits. One might say he looked like a frenzied chicken, but even chickens have their dignity.

This was the kind of moment when Denis's parents would usually walk in, and they did.

"Looks like this party is well under way," Denis's father remarked cheerfully.

Denis clutched the shirt to his bosom.

"Spilled . . . something colorless."

Denis's parents were accustomed to finding their son in awkward poses like this, and let it pass.

Rich swiveled to Denis's mother, who resembled Denis but in a much hotter way.

"*Hola,* Mrs. C."

"Don't call me Mrs. C," Mrs. C said. "I mean it."

She turned to her son, fussing with his shirt buttons.

"Denis Petey Cooverman, look at *you!*"

She stepped back, soberly surveying the whole, then suddenly grabbed his trousers and adjusted the waist up four inches, killing several million grandchildren.

She frowned.

"You're not wearing those awful underpants, are you?"

Those would the briefs she had begged Denis to burn: inelastic and threadbare with three or more holes conspiring in the rear. At least they were white(ish) and not star-spangled or Spider-Manned, styles he retired sophomore year after the Geometry Incident. He had worn this lucky pair to every debate tournament except State, when he let his mother pack, and look what happened there. He had worn them for his graduation speech, washed them, and put them on again with his party attire, feeling they would boost his confidence and possibly perform miracles.

His mother began fiddling with the buckle of his belt.

"Mom!" Denis shrieked, wresting his crotch from her control.

"Gotta side with your mom," said Denis's father. "What if you do get lucky? Once she reaches the underpants. . . . That's a deal breaker."

"They are not nice underpants," Rich agreed.

His mother rejected both sides of the proposition. "He is not wearing those ratty things. And he is not getting lucky, not like that. Not on my watch."

Denis looked to his father in abject desperation, their usual signal.

"So," Denis's father transitioned away from the underpant discussion, "How many guests are you expecting at this shin-dizzle?"

"Not too many," Denis said.

"None," Rich clarified.

"Well," Mr. C said, "don't trash the place or commit any major felonies."

"We'll be home at eleven," Mrs. C said.

"And not *one minute before*," Mr. C further joshed, opening the refrigerator door. "And it wouldn't be a graduation party without . . ." He withdrew a large bottle in a festive CONGRATS gift bag. ". . . champagne!"

"Whoa! That is *so negligent*," Rich exclaimed, his highest compliment. His own father once let him have a sip of his beer, but that was only to get him to take his nap.

Denis looked to his mother.

"You sure?"

This was an argument Mrs. C had lost. She was magnanimous in defeat. "*One* glass per guest. And nobody who drinks, drives."

"And," Mr. C said, "I know exactly how many bottles are in my wine rack. Twenty-three." Denis's father had become a wine enthusiast after watching an award-winning film about a couple of drunks who drank fine wine. Denis's father drank the finest wine that Jewel-Osco carried and placed on sale.

Denis's mother gave Denis the disaster drill she gave any time she left the house.

"Here are our numbers," she said, pointing to the well-pointed-at sheet on the wall next to the phone, "if . . ."

She could never bring herself to complete the conditional, for fear of giving it life.

"If someone's dead or on fire," Mr. C added, "call 911 first."

Mrs. C fixed her husband with a look that said, *You've just killed our son and set him on fire.*

"What?" Mr. C responded. "Bad advice?"

"I'll be in the car."

She kissed Denis on the cheek.

"Have fun. But not too much fun."

"Not much danger of that, Mrs. C," Rich said.

"And no more ill-considered schemes."

"That was a great speech," Rich disagreed. "All-time great."

"No more all-time great schemes," Mrs. C said with a smile, though what she meant was, *Soon my son will be on to better things and you will be gone.* She plucked a chip from the blue bowl. "Sea Salt! Yum!"

DENIS'S FATHER DROPPED the joshing shtick the moment his wife was out of earshot. He only did it to annoy her, and to seem cooler than she was. For some reason this was important to him, even if the only witness was his son's loser friend.

He sat down next to Denis, suddenly extremely earnest.

"Son," he said, "this is your last summer before college. That accelerated program isn't going to leave much time for toga parties . . . or whatever. So I want you to enjoy this summer—"

"I know, Dad."

"As a reward for all your hard work."

"I'll do my best."

Denis was a great kid. Perfect, according to the Educational Testing Service. His father couldn't help feeling this was his fault.

"Just get out there," he pressed on, "do all those 'teen' things you haven't had a chance to do yet."

"That's gonna be hard," Rich said. "He hasn't done any of them."

Denis shrugged. "The whole 'teenager' . . . 'coming of age' . . . it's a relatively recent construct."

"You know," Mr. C. said, slipping a paternal arm around his son. "It's okay to just have fun sometimes. Sometimes, you just have to say, *What the F.*"

"Curtis Armstrong in *Risky Business*," Rich cut in. "1983, Paul Brickman. Except he didn't say 'F.' "

"*Fuck,*" amended Mr. C, under cross-generational peer pressure.

"Yay!" Rich mini-cheered.

Mr. C squeezed his son's upper arm and rose. He stood there, allowing his message to sink in. Then he said:

"There's condoms in my bedside table."

"Do you know exactly how many there are?" Rich asked.

Denis's father alarmed himself by responding in a completely uncool and absolutely fatherly fashion.

"They're not toys," he said.

5.

THE L WORD

IF YOU GUYS KNOW SO MUCH ABOUT WOMEN, HOW
COME YOU'RE HERE AT LIKE THE GAS 'N' SIP
ON A SATURDAY NIGHT COMPLETELY ALONE
DRINKING BEERS WITH NO WOMEN ANYWHERE?

LLOYD DOBLER

IT WAS ALMOST NINE. Little had changed. Denis was currently standing, scratching something on his pants. Rich fingered Denis's new iPod.

"Hey, so: I'm not gay, dude."

The iCube began playing "Girls Just Wanna Have Fun." Rich danced to it momentarily. Realizing this did not support his argument, he turned it off.

"It's okay if you are," Denis said, trying to determine whether the crusty crud he was scraping had come from inside or outside his pants. "Really."

"Well, really, I'm not," Rich insisted. *No soy homo.*

"Okay." Denis smelled his finger. The empacted crud, whether foreign or indigenous, had a barely discernible odor. He headed to the bathroom.

Rich was used to Denis wandering off like this, and did what he usually did. He followed.

"What makes you think I'm gay?" Rich asked, standing in the doorway, absentmindedly twirling a salmon-colored guest towel into a long, tapered cylinder.

His arms soaped to the elbows, Denis systematically scrubbed downward.

"Everybody thinks you're gay."

"They don't know me. You know me. What makes *you* think I'm gay?"

Denis gave it some thought, rinsing under each fingernail.

"Everything," he concluded.

Rich snapped Denis's ass with the tip of his soft, pink sword.

Exhibit A, Denis didn't say. He took the towel from Rich and methodically dried between each finger. "I mean, you just, I don't know, you seem gay to me."

"Is it because of drama club?" Rich pressed him as they returned to the kitchen. "Because you know, a lot of actors aren't gay. More than half!"

This was a difficult subject. They had never seriously discussed Rich's sexuality before, even when they were eleven, after Rich had the idea to reenact the climactic light-saber battle between Luke Skywalker and Darth Vader using their boners. Especially after that. But Denis felt he owed Rich a fuller explanation, having outed him and all.

"Rich, all during high school, and before, you've never once had a girlfriend."

"Neither did *you.*"

It was going to get ugly.

"I *tried*, at least," Denis argued. "And I did . . ." His voice trailed off. ". . . have one."

"Patty Keck!" Rich yelled. "Your secret shame!"

Rich had agreed to never mention Patty Keck, Denis's secret shame.

"Yeah, well," Denis grumbled. "My point is. I had one."

"Making out with a girl like that—" Rich shook his head with deep sadness. "I'm not sure that's not gay."

This brought about a lull in the conversation. Rich plucked a pretzel from the bucket. Denis did not stop him.

"You know she's not going to come."

"I can construct at least nine scenarios where she comes."

"Stop constructing scenarios, dude. School's *out.*"

"1)," Denis enumerated, "her 'other thing' gets cancelled; 2), it's too crowded and loud . . ."

"She'd hate that."

"You don't know her."

"Yeah, I don't have six years' experience smelling her hair."

It was ugly.

THEY TOOK TURNS glaring at different parts of the room, anywhere but directly at each other.

SEVEN YEARS EARLIER...

YOU CANNOT HIDE FROM ME FOREVER, LUKE...

I WON'T FIGHT YOU, FATHER. I WILL NOT YIELD TO THE DARK SIDE OF THE FORCE.

THEN YOU WILL DIE!

OKAY, SO COOL... I'M SKYWALKER AND YOU'RE VADER...

AND WE GET YOUR DAD'S CAMCORDER...

AND WE DO A SHOT-FOR-SHOT RE-CREATION -- ANGLES, EVERYTHING...

OF THE CLIMACTIC LIGHTSABER BATTLE...

Rich's glare roved to the festively wrapped bottle that was still sitting on the table where Denis's father had put it down.

"Or maybe she'll hear we have a whole bottle of champagne."

"You mock," Denis said, "but you know nothing of chaos theory." Denis wasn't sure how chaos theory applied here, exactly, but he knew that Rich did know nothing of chaos theory, or much else, unless it was in a movie. Denis often used his superior intellect to score points on Rich, but like here, they were hollow victories.

"*Nobody's* coming," Rich said. "They're all going to Valli Woolly's. Maybe we could go there. Oh, no, wait— you called her a stuck-up bitch in front of the whole school."

"*You* wrote that."

"I didn't say it in front of the whole school."

"That was *your* idea!"

"It wasn't my idea to gay me!"

Denis was unrepentant. "It was in keeping with the theme."

"*Theme.*" Rich cringed. "Even when you're breaking the rules, it's through assmosis."

Another lull.

"You know," Rich said eventually. "Gay guys don't say, 'dude.'"

"Lame gay guys do," said Denis, still mad about the Patty Keck breach.

"So what's that say about you?" Rich asked sarcastically. "Your only friend is a lame gay guy."

Lull.

"Which I'm not." Rich defiantly scooped up a fistful of snacks and fingered them in his mouth. He crunched once, stood up, and returned to the bathroom.

706 WEST HACKBERRY DRIVE went dark.

"Hold still."

"Stop wiggling your butt."

The porch lit up anew, revealing Denis on Rich's shoulders, having successfully replaced the 65 watt bulb with a 300 watt halogen lamp, much better to read the house number from the street, or the next street over.

It had been forty-five minutes since Rich and Denis had questioned the very foundation of their relationship, and so they were friends again.

"You know," Rich said as Denis crawled down his back, "when we go to college we won't have to be this way."

"What way?"

With thumb and forefinger, Rich branded an *L* on his forehead.

"We're not—" Denis started to protest.

He conceded the point.

Denis snuck down the driveway to check for traffic, which so far this evening had consisted of two girls on bikes, neither of whom was Beth Cooper nor had seen her nor had any interest in alerting Denis if they did see her.

Rich tailed Denis, working himself into one of his production numbers.

"Nobody else from B-G is going to Northwestern, and U of I is a huge school. We can reinvent ourselves!"

He sang:

I can be whoever I want to be.

Denis did not recognize:

"Lesley Ann Warren in Rodgers and Hammerstein's *Cinderella*, 1965, Charles S. Dubin, director."

"*That* is somewhat gay," Denis said.

"It's Leslie Ann Warren, not Audry Hepburn," Rich scoffed, flicking his wrist in dismissal. "Okay. First, we gotta change your name. Denis is . . . unfortunate."

"Not as unfortunate as *Dick Munsch*."

"D-E-N-I-S? You're a vertical stroke from penis, dude."

Rich drew a *D* in the air and appended the stroke.

"Thank you for bringing that to my attention," Denis said.

"And my name is not Dick. It's not gonna be Rich either. I'm gonna go by Munsch. Or maybe 'The Munsch.' Now, *you*: Denny, El Denno, Deño, Den-Den . . . Your middle name's Pete . . . DP? Nope. D-Pete? *Eh.* Cooverman . . . *Coove!*"

Denis grimaced. "Sounds . . . vagina-ish."

Rich waggled his eyebrows and opened his arms to welcome:

"The Coove . . . *master!*"

Denis looked at his watch. "It's ten o'clock."

"Hurray. Let's open the champagne."

"We can't open it until she gets here."

"Or," Rich said, "we *can*," and sprinted up the driveway toward the house.

Denis squeaked and gave pursuit.

Rich was running more for show than speed; Denis caught him in the foyer with a flying tackle to the knees that failed to bring the Skinny Red Giant down.

"Don't drool on the shoes," Rich said, shuffling into the kitchen with Denis dangling from his ankles.

Rich grabbed the champagne bag. Denis popped up and grabbed back, directly above Rich's hand. Rich wedged his left hand above Denis's right. Denis clawed the top of the bag. Rich released the bottle, conceding defeat.

Denis fell into a chair. He placed the champagne back on the table, not even in its correct spot. He snatched a handful of M&Ms and began glumly tossing them into his mouth.

"Hey," Rich said, smiling too broadly, "who needs girls? *This* is a party!"

Denis moved the champagne to its correct spot. He spun the pretzel bowl, hoping the reactive centrifugal force would create an attractive Fibonacci spiral.

A size-13 foot banged onto the table, bouncing twenty-one pretzels out of the bowl.

"Check out the new *zapatos*," Rich said. "Two paychecks. Very Gene Kelly, circa 1945, don't you think?"

Denis lifted Rich's dancing shoe and dropped it off the edge of the table.

She's not coming, he realized.

Rich seemed okay with that. He swiped a pretzel from the table and dangled it on his lip like a smoking Frenchman. "So your parents use *condoms*." He took three seconds to say the last word.

"Not a topic for discussion."

"Do you think they're lubed or—"

"Your sister's sports bra," Denis cut him off, and effectively.

The boys sat, quietly eating fancy crappy snacks.

Chewing thoughtfully, he asked, "You ever jerk off with a condom on?"

"No," Denis replied.

"Just asking."

Rich flossed with a forefinger.

"Probably not that great," he speculated.

And then the doorbell rang.

DENIS HOPPED UP SO FAST he banged his knees on the table. He hobbled excitedly to the front door.

"I *told* you."

Rich loped behind him. "It's probably just the police telling us to keep it down in here."

Denis pressed himself against the door, peeking out through the sidelight. The waterglass produced an ethereal image, luminous, gossamer, a dream. On

Denis Cooverman's porch floated the celestial figures of Beth Cooper, Cammy Alcott and Treece Kilmer.

Denis could not talk, leaving it to Rich to speak for them both.

"Dude. It's the Trinity."

6.

A YOUNG MAN'S PRAYER

SHE'S GOING TO SHOW HER BOOBS! THANK YOU JESUS!

ROLAND FAYE

I believe in the Trinity (One in Three, Three in One) Beth the first, Cammy the Second and Treece the Third.

I believe that Beth Cooper is an Angel and that She was made human by the power of God. God chose Mary, the wife of Randy, to be the mother of his most Awesome Creation.

I believe that Beth Cooper is the one True Angel, and that Cammy Alcott and Treece Kilmer are merely Sidekicks, who through their chosenness by Beth have attained social oneness with Her.

I believe that Beth Cooper is a gift of God that proves that He loves us without condition.

I believe that Beth Cooper is the One and Only Savior of my Wretched Adolescence and it is through Her that I may achieve Salvation.

7.

LIVE NEW GIRLS

MAYBE IT WAS A DREAM, YOU KNOW,
A VERY WEIRD, BIZARRE, VIVID,
EROTIC, WET, DETAILED DREAM.
MAYBE WE HAVE MALARIA.

GARRY WALLACE

"HOLY CRAP!"

Denis couldn't believe he just said "Holy crap." Or that he was twittering his hands and pivoting indiscriminately as he yammered.

"Holy mother of crap!"

For all his posturing about plausible scenarios, Denis hadn't truly expected Beth Cooper to show up at his house, and had no real plan beyond continuing to hope that Beth would show up at his house. Now that she had, he had nothing. And the prospect that she might enter his home, and see how he lived and what kind of person he was, scared the holy crap out of him.

"What are we going to do?"

Rich leaned in close to Denis's face.

"RUN AWAY!!!!" he whisper-screamed.

Denis staggered, startled, but also thinking *good plan*, and was already dithering about which way to run when Rich started laughing.

The doorbell rang again.

Denis looked through the sidelight. Luminous Beth checked her watch, while ethereal Cammy made exasperated gestures and watery Treece fidgeted.

"They're discussing leaving!" Denis said, as if watching a horrific car accident and being powerless to stop it.

Rich flung open the door.

"Ladies!" he proclaimed.

THIS WAS THE DIFFERENCE between Denis and Rich.

To outsiders, meaning everybody else, they seemed very much the same, and were often mistaken for one another even though they shared about as much DNA as either one shared with a chimpanzee. One was short and slim and the other was tall and skinny, one was topped with a thick pelage of dark curls and the other with fine reddish tufts that looked temporary, one had had braces and the other should have had braces but his father wanted to give it a few more years to see if it would work itself out. Yet the main and signature difference between the two was not physical but metaphysical; they lived in alternate realities.

Denis lived on Planet Fear and Rich resided in Hollywoodland.

Denis was afraid of many things. A very long list of them could be found in a manila folder in the office of Dr. Maple, the phobophilic lady psychiatrist Denis had seen from the age of five until twelve as a result of his parents having too much disposable income (Denis's therapy was completed successfully at age thirteen, a typical outcome for Dr. Maple, who suffered from ephebiphobia, a fear of teenagers). But of the myriad things Denis feared—which included, briefly, a fear of misusing the word *myriad*—the thing he feared most often and most enthusiastically was the future.

Based on a close reading of current events and a misapplication of the third law of thermodynamics, Denis believed that the universe tended toward tragedy. Since his own life had been free of anything genuinely tragic, Denis figured he was due. He feared that if he did anything that was "adventurous" or "unscheduled" or "fun," it would end tragically. Statistically, it almost had to.

Rich had had a much less tragedy-free life. We needn't go into the details, since it's a long, sad and ultimately unoriginal story, but as a result Rich had developed a coping mechanism by which all of the terrible things that happened to him were merely wacky complications that would, before the movie of his life was over, be resolved in an audience-pleasing happy ending. He occasionally worried his life might be an independent film, or worse, a Swedish flick, but he chose to behave as if the movie he lived was a raucous teen comedy and he was somebody like Ferris Bueller or Otter from *Animal House,* or, worst-case scenario, that guy who fucked a pie.

And so Rich threw open the door and proclaimed "Ladies!" knowing that no matter what happened next, or after that, or subsequently, eventually he would be loved and vindicated and everybody would be dancing to a classic song from the seventies.

Denis, meanwhile, thought he had finally met his doom.

BETH COOPER SAUNTERED through the door, swinging the tartan pleats of her Luella Bartley strapless plaid dress, $39.99 at *Targét.* She wore her party face, not unlike her real face, but with the hue and contrast dialed up. Her hair, too, was subtly tarted, with spontaneous ringlets happening strategically around her head. She still smelled like Beth Cooper, only more so.

"Hey," she tossed off, entering Denis's house with such cool authority he wondered if he was the one who lived there. So this was Afterschool Beth. Denis couldn't tell how much he liked this version. At least a lot, he decided.

Cammy catwalked in behind Beth, working a white vintage-wash Abercrombie skirt and black Fitch Premium beaded racerback top, $119 retail, bought on super sale for $71. Nearly six feet and bone blond, she had the gait and mien of a fashion model, to go with the legs and teeth, yet there was something in her slate green eyes, something disturbingly out of place: thought.

"Nice place," Cammy said, her flat contralto displaying no affect while projecting disdain.

Last and slightly least, Treece bounced over the threshold in a red leather bustier that displayed top, side and bottom cleavage and a black nano mini that might have been a rubber band. The semi-ensemble, with the Choo boots, easily cost more than $1,000, though she clearly neither knew that nor cared. She was wide in ways boys and men don't seem to mind, with overdone hair that encircled her face like a toilet seat, and plump brown eyes and pillowy lips that brought to mind a cute cartoon cow. Very cute, but cartoon, and cow.

"I've never been in this house before," Treece chirped with a baby lisp she was unlikely to outgrow.

DENIS WAS PARALYZED. Adrenaline, epinephrine, seratonin, corticosterone, testosterone and several more exotic hormones squirted from various glands or were being synthesized like crazy throughout his body, in far beyond prescription strengths, and so all nonessential functions such as thinking had been shut down.

Rich stepped into the hosting breach.

"So," he inquired cordially, "where's our boy in uniform?"

Denis's testes began climbing their vas deferens again, until Beth uttered those three beautiful words:

"We're hating him right now."

(Denis could count; he just stopped listening after the first three.)

Beth explained, "One of his army buds was getting all date-rapey with Treece."

Treece was clearly annoyed by this. "It wasn't like he wasn't going to get a blow job at the end," she said, making a *duh* face. "I mean, if he was nice."

Cammy rolled her eyes without moving them at all. "And so thanks to Miss Manners here, Graduation Night's crapped."

Treece's mouth popped open. "You're *blaming the victim!*"

"Guys"—Beth stepped in—"it'll be okay. They'll go looking for us at Valli Woolly's, and when they don't find us they'll go to that strip club they tried to drag us to, and then we'll go to Valli Woolly's, just later."

Rich whispered to Denis out of the side of his mouth. "Which scenario was that?"

"Variation on Four," Denis side-whispered back.

Cammy took in her surroundings, looking for a reason to go on living. "So? Until just later?" she asked. "We sit around sucking each other's Suzy Qs?"

If Denis's eyes could have fallen out, they would have. They would have bounced around crazily on the floor, made *yipe yipe yipe* sounds, skedaddled up the stairs and hid under Denis's pillow.

"Thank you, Cammy," Beth said. "Like I'm going to get that image out of my head."

(Like anyone was. Denis's brain had fast-tracked that image into permanent storage, accidentally overwriting some early flying-car sketches.)

Beth made a sudden movement in Denis's direction; he flinched.

"So?" She had a bright and shining smile. "Where's the party?"

Denis almost said *What party?* Even that would have been preferable to what he did, which was blink several times.

"Here," he eventually said, in the dazed, detached manner of a crime victim. "This is"—he gestured to his general vicinity—"it."

"Are we the first ones here?" Beth asked.

"We are *never* first." Treece chirped gravely, adding with alarm, "This doesn't *smell* like a party."

Cammy, half-lidded: "I *told* you they were going to kill and eat us."

"Oh, no. Of course not." Denis choked out a laugh. "I don't even eat *red meat*, let alone human flesh, which tastes like veal, only sweeter. Supposedly."

"You're a little early," Rich transitioned smoothly. "We weren't expecting anyone until . . . eleven. Right, Coove?"

"Oh, right," Denis blinked. "That's when my paren—"

"*La fiesta es* this way, *mi bonitas . . .*"

Rich pinched Denis's upper arm and led him toward the kitchen, whisper-singing,

> *Dreams really do come true,*

and whisper-citing: "Judy Garland in *The Wizard of Oz*, 1939, Victor Fleming, director, additional scenes by King Vidor.

"You're not in Kansas anymore, dude." Rich placed his hands on Denis's cheeks, signaling he was about to say something of profound importance.

"Follow the Yellow Brick Road," he said, adding slowly, emphatically, deep meaningfully, "Follow. The. *Yellow Brick Road.*"

Denis was dumbfounded. "Is that like . . . *treasure trail?*"

"What? No, God, *no*," Rich revulsed, "It's a metaphor for *life*, not Dorothy's . . . *yick!*"

BACK WHERE WE LEFT THEM, Cammy was glaring at Beth. The glare said, *Why are we in this strange-smelling house alone with Your Itty-Bitty Stalker and his Gay-And-Not-Even-Fun-Gay Friend, no doubt about to be drugged and undressed and violated in uninteresting ways when we could be getting drugged and undressed and truly violated by members of the United States military?* That's a rough translation.

"Be nice," Beth admonished the glare. "He's the valvictorian."

"And he *loooovs* you," Cammy added in a geek voice that sounded nothing like Denis but sufficed.

"From behind!" Treece bleated, then began whinnying, because anal sex was hilarious, in the abstract.

Beth Cooper was a benevolent cliquetator. She allowed her subjects free rein and even the illusion of equality. Occasionally, though, she needed to reassert her absolute authority, and this was one of those occasions. She did so in the traditional teen-girl manner, through superior attitude and psychological terror.

"It's nice to be loved," Beth said. "You two should try it sometime."

Beth walked away. Cammy achieved a smirk, but her heartless wasn't in it. Treece pouted.

"I try it all the time," she said.

IN THE KITCHEN, Denis stood at attention, like a waiter in an unfun restaurant, as the girls entered. Rich was acting like a waiter, too, but from a José O'Foodle's, the unbearably fun restaurant he had been fired from for exactly this behavior.

"Hi, I'm Rich," he said with high theatrical cheer, "I'll be your cohost this evening. On the central table you will find assorted snackables, sweet 'n' salty *comidas* for your comesting . . ."

The girls considered the crap on the table.

"The pretzels are fat-free," Denis suggested. "A healthful alternative."

Beth scowled. "Are you saying I'm fat?"

"Oh," Denis said. *Goddammit,* he thought.

Denis had not yet learned to preload appropriate responses to fat-related queries (i.e. unequivocal denials) so they could be automatically delivered without hesitation. Instead, he appeared to be processing the question, which can be fatal.

"You, *fat*?" Rich intervened. "Why would he say that? Come on. He's not *retarded.*"

Beth frowned more definitively. "My brother is retarded."

Rich froze. There was no appropriate response when somebody played the retard card. Now both he and

Denis stood at attention, condemned dorks, without blindfolds.

Cammy snickered, causing Treece to unleash a single whinny and Beth to finally release her smile.

Denis exhaled; he would not, after all, have to move to Europe. Rich let out the laugh he had been choking on.

"That's cold," Rich said. "Damn cold. You probably don't even have a brother."

"No," Beth said. "He died."

Rich guffawed.

Beth did not.

"I'm so sorry," Denis said.

This was a nervy move on Denis's part. If Beth didn't have a dead brother, he would be a double dork. Fortunately for him, she did.

"It was a long time ago." Beth looked directly at Denis. "But thank you."

The raw emotion of the moment unnerved Rich, sending him into a fit of impression. He stretched his face lengthwise and fluttered his fingers over his chest.

Well, shut my mouth,

he enunciated in a British-ish accent. "Stan Laurel in *Way Out West,* 1937, directed by James W. Horne."

"What was *that*?" Cammy asked.

"It's something he does," said Denis, as if it were an unalterable fact of life, like the wind or tragedy.

"*I'm* fat." Treece joined the conversation from earlier. She threw a potato chip in her mouth. "But it's good fat." She did a quick shimmy, and her good fat shook like bowls full of jelly.

THE FIRST THREE BARS of "Here She Comes" by Very Sad Boy played in a tinny synthesis. Beth pulled a cell phone from her purse. She was displeased by the caller ID, but answered anyway. "What do you *want*, Kevin?"

She walked out of the room. She didn't seem very happy to talk to him, Denis thought. Maybe she'll just tell him to go blank himself, she's having such a wonderful time over at Denis Cooverman's house, 706 Hackberry Dr—

Denis got that old testicular feeling again.

"**I NEED BEER**," Treece announced.

"Yes, you do," Rich agreed. "*¿Dónde está la* beer, Coovemaster?"

"Um," answered Denis, distracted. "My dad doesn't drink beer."

"How is that possible?" Treece asked.

Rich remembered:

"We have *champagne!*"

He whisked the gift bag off the table, where it had been sitting unrefrigerated for the past ninety minutes, and pressed it into Denis's chest.

"*¡Tienes le champag-nah!*"

"Could you please mangle one language at a time?" Cammy requested.

Treece wrinkled her nose. *"Champagne."* She uncurled the word as if it were French for *excessive and frequent evacuation of watery feces.*

"Same alcohol as beer," pitched Rich, selling hard.

"More," Denis said. "Two-point . . ." He quickly calculated:

$$A_{(beer)} = Avg[.04 \rightarrow .06] = .05$$

$$A_{(champagne)} = Avg[.08 \rightarrow .14] = .11$$

$$\Delta_{(alcohol)} = \frac{A_{(champagne)}}{A_{(beer)}} = 2.2$$

". . . two times as much alcohol, on average."

Rich could only shake his head in admiration at his friend's determination to be true to himself, no matter what the cost. Rich himself was willing to be anybody anyone wanted and would keep trying on personalities until one of them became popular. For some reason, his most recent persona spoke a lot of half-assed Spanish.

"Let's pop this *pupito, rápido!*" habla Rich with insouciance, belied a bit by the way he was clawing at the gift bag Denis was clutching.

Denis removed the bottle from its bag.

It was Freixenet, one of the finer sparkling wines in the under-$10 category.

"Cristal," Rich said. "Black Label."

"Cristal seems to have changed its logo," Cammy said. "And spelling."

Treece bit her pinkie. "Champagne," she said, "makes me do . . . *things.*"

Denis would never hear the word *things* the same way again.

Cammy, dry: "*Water* makes you do things."

"Not regular water."

If Rich were a paper-and-ink cartoon rather than a flesh-and-blood one, a lightbulb would have appeared above his head.

"*Uno momento.*" He raced out of the room and romped up the stairs.

"*Un momento,*" Cammy said.

THE SPECIFIC MECHANICS of the champagne bottle were alien to Denis. "Seems self-explanatory," he mumbled as he propped the bottle on his thigh and began peeling the foil back slowly, sweat speckling his forehead, as if dismantling a party bomb.

Beth reappeared in the kitchen, pissed.

"Yeah, well, *Kevin,* maybe, *Kevin,* maybe I'm busy right now."

She looked up and pointed at Denis's lap.

"I want some of that."

She meant the champagne, but neither Denis nor his lap immediately figured that out.

Beth started out of the room, her voice rising.

"I'm not going to tell you where I am! *Or* who I'm with! But I will tell you *this*, Kevin: I'm having *champagne!*"

She wants champagne. Denis flailed away the foil and furiously twisted the wire, ten or fifteen times, stopped, then started to untwist it.

"Champagne coming right . . . *Yi.*"

His fingertip was bleeding. He pressed on with no concern for his own safety. Cammy and Treece watched with morbid fascination.

Denis placed both thumbs under the cork and applied steady pressure, suavely at first, desperately thereafter. He leaned against a wall for leverage, clasping the sweaty, slippery bottle between his forearms and applying insufficient force accompanied by girlish exertions. Blood dripped over his knuckles.

"This is . . . odd," he she-grunted. "The internal pressure is 90 psi. It should just—"

In walked Beth, screaming into the phone.

"Don't you *dare* GPS me!"

Denis couldn't even begin to analyze the health ramifications of that, because at that exact moment, Rich appeared behind Beth. He raised his arm and opened his hand. A ribbon of condoms cascaded behind Beth's head.

Ribbed, Rich mouthed lubriciously.

Denis's eyes widened just in time for the cork to pop and ricochet off his cornea.

HE OPENED HIS MOUTH TO SCREAM. A foaming column of lukewarm champagne geysered into the back of his throat. He gasped, gulped, and gurgled in various combinations. That it was not school milk but champagne that came out his nose did not make Denis feel any more sophisticated.

This, as it turned out, was exactly the kind of thing Cammy found amusing: the pain and suffering of others. Her laugh was surprisingly husky, somewhere between a chortle and a guffaw. Treece was too nice to laugh, but not nice enough to offer help.

Beth snapped her phone shut and rushed to Denis's side.

"You all right?"

"Yeah, I'm great," Denis claimed. "Oh, *ow.*"

He cupped his bloody hand over his bludgeoned eye, and without even realizing he was doing it, slid down the wall to the floor.

"Yee," he said.

"We need ice." Beth turned to Rich, who was tucking the last of the prophylaxis into his shirt pocket. *"Ice?"*

Rich hurried to the kitchen island "bar area" and stuck his hand in the plastic bowl of ice. It came out wet.

"Frozen peas," Beth ordered, snapping her fingers at Rich and directing him toward the refrigerator.

Rich resented being snapped at. This dickhead from Stevenson High School did that at José O'Foodle's once, and Rich spat in his O'Salsa, nearly killing him. Apparently the guy had a peanut allergy and Rich had been eating only Snickers bars that month. No one ever found out how peanut and cocoa traces made it into a salsa made only from fresh tomatoes, chiles and beer, but it cost the Dining Thematics Corporation nearly $2 million.

"What are you *doing*?" Beth yelled at Rich, who had been reminiscing the above paragraph. "This is *your* friend down here!"

Rich abandoned his reverie and went to the refrigerator. He opened the freezer door and began picking through the contents.

"Frozen peas . . . Frozen *peas* . . . Fro-*oh*-zen pa-puh *peas* . . ."

"*Anything* cold!"

Rich hurled a box across the room.

"Stat!"

Beth snatched it out of the air.

"Frozen waffles?"

Rich peered in the freezer. "Either that or Lean Cuisine."

"Whatever," Beth said, meaning *whatever*.

His mission completed, Rich took out a pint of ice cream and went looking for a spoon. He singsang to himself:

> *I scream*, you *scream* . . .

WITH PARAMEDIC SPEED, Beth ripped open the box and extracted two frozen waffles. She dropped to her knees, straddling Denis's thighs, a bodily juxtaposition Denis had only experienced with Greg Saloga prior to a belly-pinking.

Beth took his hand and lifted it off his injured eye. She tenderly pressed the waffles against it.

"Agh," Denis said.

"It's okay," Beth soothed. "This will help."

Why was Beth being so nice to him? Was it because she was so nice, or because it was to him? Either way, she sure was nice. Denis gazed at her through his surviving eye.

"I'm sorry I'm so pathetic," he thought, and then realized he had also said it.

Beth laughed, so lightly and so kindly that Denis felt it in his chest, not his stomach.

"Can I tell you a secret?"

Yes, tell me all your secrets, Denis kept to himself.

Beth leaned in, whispered: "All boys are pathetic."

THIS WAS NEWS TO DENIS, perhaps the best news he had ever heard. If Beth thought all guys sucked, he didn't need to not suck, only to suck *less.* This was doable. Possibly.

Denis relaxed for the first time since the previous Sunday. He became the smart, sweet, moderately clever and only medium pathetic boy he usually was.

"On behalf of all boys, then," Denis said, "I apologize."

Beth made a serious face. "Accepted."

"It's 150,000 years late, but it needed to be said. And sorry for all those wars and stuff."

"You're funny."

"Sometimes even when I'm trying to be."

Beth took Denis's hand and led it back to his eye, transferring responsibility for the waffles.

"Gentle pressure."

Denis twisted a flinch into a grin. "Thanks, Lisbee."

The moment vanished.

"Don't call me that," Beth said. "I hate that."

"But Kevin—"

"That is one of the privileges that Kevin enjoys," Beth explained coldly.

Cammy concurred. "Kevin has many privileges."

"Front door privileges—" Treece began, working into another sodomy whinny.

Beth raised her hand, silencing them.

On the opposite side of the kitchen island, Rich was upside-down spooning ice cream onto his tongue, waiting for such a conversational opening. "So, Beth," he said, "you think your Army Man has triangulated your signal and is on his way over? Because we might need more waffles."

"Never mind him." Beth waved dismissively. "He thinks just because he's killed some guys, he can kill anybody he wants."

That didn't help.

"Let's see under there," Beth said. Denis whimpered as softly as he could as Beth removed the waffles. The blast area was already purple en route to black and beyond.

"Open."

The eyelid stuttered as it retracted.

"Pee-yuke," Treece noted.

"Dude." Rich grossed out. "That's NC-17."

It looked worse than it was, since it looked like Denis was at least blind, perhaps dying, and possibly a brain-eating zombie.

From the inside, it looked: bloody. Denis tried to focus on Beth's face, which he knew was only inches away. What he saw, swirling in a red sea, was a blurry pink mass with two darker circular areas in the upper half and a small horizontal smear in the middle of the lower half. If that was a face, then:

"MY CONTACT!" Denis gasped.

Beth snapped her fingers again.

"Contact down!"

Treece and Cammy initiated contact-retrieval maneuvers, dropping to squats and sweeping the floor with their fingertips in long, overlapping arcs.

"Don't worry," Beth told Denis. "We'll find it. We always do."

"You wear contacts?" Denis asked, enthralled by this defect they apparently shared. "What's your prescription?"

Before either could comprehend the deep geekitude of the question, and before Denis could compound it with whatever he might say next:

"Found it!" Treece said.

She held up the champagne cork. A gelatinous dollop clung to the metallic cap. Quite proud of herself, she marched over and presented it to Beth.

"What do I win?"

"The thanks of a grateful nation," Rich said, presenting her with the half-eaten pint of ice cream.

Treece held the container like an acting award.

"Chubby Monkey!"

Beth peeled the sticky contact off the cork, rolling it around on her fingertip.

"Gucky."

She stuck her finger in her mouth and sucked the lens off.

As she swished it around, salivating, her luscious lips pursed, pulsating. Her pretty pink tongue unfurled and there on the wet tip, bathed in Beth Cooper's juices, was Denis's sense of sight.

Beth Cooper had invented a whole new sex act: the eyejob.

She tilted Denis's head back and gently pried open his swollen eyelids.

"Ohhhhhh." He moaned with pain and pleasure, which is how all the weird fetishes start.

"There."

Denis blinked. His contact was back in. Beth came into focus, framed by a velvety crimson swirl.

"How's that feel?"

Denis didn't have to answer. Beth could feel for herself.

Denis grinned shit-eatingly.

"Pretty good, I guess," Beth said.

Beth bounced from her knees to her feet in a single cheerleading move. Denis's ascent was graceless by comparison, hindered by the need to keep a forearm wedged between his legs. He clutched the counter and hauled himself up. Leaning against the kitchen island, hips inward, he twisted his upper torso in the direction of the girls, and smiled. He was fooling almost no one.

"You hurt your back?" Treece asked.

Cammy pointed at the ice cream.

"Chubby Monkey."

Treece looked at the ice cream, then at Denis's crotchal contortions and back at the ice cream. The creamy banana taste in her mouth helped her put it all together.

"Oh," it dawned on her. "The monkey is *chubby.*"

During the polite silence all around, Denis scooted the perimeter of the kitchen island, placing it between his erection and judgment. Rich slid the frozen waffles across the counter. Denis lowered them out of sight.

"You might've scratched your cornea," Beth said. "Maybe you should go to the hospital."

"Oh," said Denis, who had been thinking the same thing, "Let's not spoil the party."

"What party?" Cammy wanted to know.

Denis's tendency to answer sarcastic questions sincerely was short-circuited when he realized he was still gripping the bottle of:

"Champagne!"

"*La bebida de los* gods!" Rich yelled in support. He grabbed a stack of the Krazy Kritter Dixie cups and attempted to set up five in a row. This took a few tries.

"Delicious champagne," Denis said, buying Rich time.

"*Delicioso,*" Rich agreed. He finally accomplished five upright cups, and stepped back with a hand flourish, as if he had just done a magic trick.

Denis filled the first cup. The second cup started strong but quickly faded to a dribble. Denis considered filling the remaining three cups with squeezings from his rugby shirt, but took the high road.

"Even things up a little . . ."

Denis poured from the first cup into the final three, then some from the fourth cup into the second cup, and then a little bit more from the first into the third, producing five Dixie cups with approximately no champagne in them.

He distributed the cups, making sure to give Beth the one with Ally, the pretty giraffe, on it.

Treece squinted suspiciously. "Why'd I get the hippo?"

"It's *good* fat," Cammy said.

"That's racist," Treece jabbed at Cammy.

"It's not *race*-ist," Cammy mocked.

"It's fattist."

"*You* said you were fat. Two minutes ago. And every two minutes before that."

"I was *owning* it."

Beth sighed. "You're not fat, Treece."

"I *have* fat," Treece said.

"Everybody has fat."

"Not everybody," Cammy said.

"A toast!" Denis yelled.

Usually when one proposes a toast, one has a toast to propose. This was one of the details Denis had neglected based on its infinitesimal probability of coming up. And yet, here he was, toasting Beth Cooper with a paper cup of champagne. He improvised.

"To the future!"

Rich had his friend's back. "To the future—and beyond!"

"Go future!" Cammy exclaimed with a tiny swing of her fist, suggesting less than complete sincerity.

"*Go,* future!" Treece exclaimed with the same tiny swing, signaling true enthusiasm.

"The future," Beth simply said.

The girls micro-chugged their champagne splashes. Rich sipped his urbanely. Denis, who had left his own cup empty, made a show of guzzling it.

Treece crushed her cup and looked for someplace to shove it. She noticed something sticking out of Rich's shirt pocket.

"Party balloons!" she squealed, extracting the unfolding ribbon of ignominy.

"Um." Rich raised a finger. "Those aren't—"

"I *know* what they are," Treece said, tearing a foil pouch open with her teeth. She popped the condom into her mouth, breathed in deeply, and blew out a ribbed rubber bubble.

Beth turned to Denis, amused but also a little disappointed.

"What exactly," she wondered, "did you have planned for this evening?"

"Oh," Denis said, sort of maybe pointing toward the contraceptive Treece was inflating. "Those are my dad's."

Treece stopped blowing. "Your dad's not hiding in a closet or something? I hate that."

Beth then said with polite finality:

"Well, this was fun."

Treece tied off the party balloon and flicked it at Rich.

HIS LIFE HAD CHANGED, in some potentially tragic but no doubt important way, and Denis didn't want it to end.

"Not yet," he said. "You can't go . . . yet."

He needed a reason for them to stay. He had a hundred-dollar bill in his wallet, a graduation present from Aunt Brenda, but it might be awkward trying to split it three ways. Also, potentially insulting. His Diamond Series Extra-Extended Special Edition *Lord of the Rings* Trilogy Blue-Ray HD Box Set? If they started watching it now . . .

"We haven't drunk the wine!" Rich declared.

Of course! The forbidden wine!

"Twenty-three bottles!" Denis added, parallel-processing how much time it would take them to drink that much wine and how much trouble each successive bottle would get him into.

Treece frowned. "Wine reminds me of Jesus."

In four years of debating at the highest secondary school levels, Denis had never encountered such a perfect rebuttal. He was struck dumb by the twisted beauty of it.

"We could make coolers!" suggested Rich, unencumbered by logic and the rules of argumentation.

Denis hoisted a two-liter bottle of Diet Blackberry Sprite above his head. "Let there be coolers!" he said triumphantly, as the sweaty bottle slid out of his sweaty hands and exploded on the kitchen floor.

Goddammit.

Rich again lept into the social abyss. "And music!" He handed the iCube to Denis. "Wine, women, and 10,000 songs!"

"Well, I haven't loaded that many yet," said Denis, shaking soda off his shoes. "But I did put together a special playlist for the occasion. A 'Commencement Mix'—"

"DJ C's Slammin' Graduation," Rich quickly saved.

"Or that." Denis pushed ▶. From the iCube came 53Hz to 16kHz of seventies mellowness:

> *Life, so they say, is but a game*
> *and we let it slip away*

"Slammin'," Cammy said.

"That's more for chilling," Rich said. "Ironic chilling."

Denis pressed advance. Out came languid fifties harmonies:

> *There's a time for joy, a time for tears . . .*

"My mom helped me put this together," Denis explained.

A time we'll treasure through the years . . .

Denis ripped the iPod out of the cube and started scrolling through the list. "There's real music on here," he said, spinning. "That Einstein's Brain song, Happy Talk, the Licks . . . you like Very Sad Boy, right?"

Beth touched his elbow. He looked up. She gazed into his good eye.

They really could have kissed ergonomically.

"We do kind of have to go," she said. "Thanks. It was a great party."

She moved in to kiss him, hesitating.

Was it the smell? The smell of fear and pathos?

No, it was she didn't want to hurt him. She kissed the other, uninjured cheek.

"Bye."

The simultaneous bursting and breaking of Denis's heart was drowned out by a tremendous roar. Blinding lights engulfed the front of the house. Denis's first thought was it had to be the Apocalypse, but it was something much, much worse.

8.

MORE WAFFLES

BIFF WILCOX IS LOOKING FOR YOU,
RUSTY JAMES. HE'S GONNA KILL YOU,
RUSTY JAMES.

MIDGET

"SHIT," Beth said. "Kevin."

9.

PARTY MONSTERS

NUNCHUCK SKILLS, BOWHUNTING SKILLS,
COMPUTER HACKING SKILLS . . . GIRLS ONLY
WANT BOYFRIENDS WHO HAVE GREAT SKILLS.

NAPOLEON DYNAMITE

DENIS WAS DEAD. This much was certain. The only real question was whether, as he was dying, would Denis cry, or beg, or scream like a girl, or lose control of his bowels, or in some other way abase himself, robbing his demise of the tragic gravitas he felt it deserved. Denis considered hitting the bathroom as a precaution, but Rich and the girls had already rushed to the front of the house, leaving him standing there alone, looking silly without even the simple dignity of being dead.

And his face hurt.

Reflexively, Denis reached up to touch his battered eye and poked it with the iPod he was holding.

"*Yiye!*" he said in response to this relatively minor amount of pain. He was not going to do well, being stabbed, or stomped, or whatever cause of death his killer had chosen.

Denis looked down at his iGouger.

Goodbye to You
Michelle Branch
The Spirit Room

So now his possessions were mocking him too. *Goddammit*, Denis muttered as he dropped the iPod in a pocket, *goddammit*, and joined the party to his execution.

THEY WERE GATHERED in the living room, in violation of house rules, squinting out the front window at a blinding white noise. Denis slunk up and peeked out around Treece.

The source of the terrific sound and vision was a five-ton H1 Alpha Hummer, with 300 horsepower, 520 pound-feet of torque, a MSRP of $140,796 and seating for five assholes. The earth-killing machine was painted *black diamond*, murkier than pure black and slightly more frightening, named for the insane ski slopes and not, as Denis might have guessed, for the moon gem Eclipso used to possess Superman in Action Comics #826 (Denis no longer collected comic books, and hardly ever went through his sixteen boxes of meticulously Mylared back issues, arranged by publisher and title, but AC #826—who wouldn't know that?).

The Hummer was currently off-road, in the middle of the Cooverman lawn, on top of a Beauty of Bath apple tree Denis and his father had planted together that Arbor Day. Its 6.6 liter engine gunned in martial glory, enhanced by two side-mounted external loudspeakers blasting what Denis recognized from Act III of Wagner's *Die Walküre* but which every other teenage boy on the planet would have known was really from the fucking sweet chopper attack in *Apocalypse Now*.

The monstrous vehicle snarled a final time and fell dark and silent. Three doors snapped open and corresponding military figures disembarked synchronously. They wore civilian clothes, but identical civvies, a habit that was apparently hard to break. The uniform of the night was black khakis, black polos and black loafers, making the trio look like an elite unit sent into a downtown club to terminate a rogue DJ. None of them had enough hair to gel, but their heads glistened menacingly nonetheless.

Treece waved happily at her date-rapist. "Sean!"

Denis had hoped to go out with some class.

"Shaw-on!" Treece yelled much louder, waving in wide semaphoric arcs, signaling *I'm here! I'm here! Oh, and here's that guy you promised a penilectomy!*

The lights went out on the upper floors of Denis's brain, leaving the lizard in charge.

"Get down!"

Denis hugged Treece and threw them both to the floor. Treece's body recognized this as foreplay and her lips parted in Pavlovian response.

"*Everybody* down!" Denis screamed in a barely audible squeak.

The three left standing regarded him with odd curiosity.

"Why?" Beth asked.

"He's going to kill me!"

"So?" asked Cammy.

"He's not really going to *kill* you." Beth sighed. "He just likes to be scary."

"He's scary," Denis confirmed.

"The *most* he's going to do is maybe beat you up a little."

Denis had been beaten up a little, thrice by Greg Saloga and once by Dawn Delvecchio, whose premature chest he had slightly ogled in the fifth grade. Being beaten up a little meant bruising but no breaking, twisting but no tearing, and loss of less than a tablespoon of blood. Denis suspected Kevin would not adhere to these guidelines, or even, based on news reports, the Geneva Convention. Given what the military did not even consider *abuse,* Denis shuddered at what might constitute a *little beating* under the U.S. Army Code of Conduct:

27–3. Procedures applicable to 'Beating, Light'

a. Splatter zone limited to 10 feet (3.048 meters)

b. No detachment or removal of extremities or organs;

c. Extremities or organs inadvertently detached or removed must be left with original owner for possible reattachment or implantation;

d. Extremities or organs inadvertently detached or removed and not returned to owner cannot be

(1) Fashioned into a necklace, or

(2) Devoured to gain the owner's power, unless approved in writing by commanding officer;

e. Derisive pointing at genitals prohibited, except to aid owner in locating of same.

As usual, Denis was letting his imagination run wild, shriek and knock things off shelves. Also as usual, he was allowing this to distract him from more immediate practical concerns.

"The door!" Denis eventually realized. "Secure the door!"

Denis scurried across the floor, frantic commando crawling, looking less like a Navy SEAL than an actual seal.

"Is he always like this?" Cammy asked.

"This is new behavior," Rich observed. "But not surprising."

"I think it's kinda cute."

Cammy looked at Beth as if she had just insisted that *Zuma* was still a decent show.

"It is. He is," Beth said. "Kinda."

"Yeah," Treece agreed, squeaking her nano mini back into place. "Like when a puppy gets so excited he pees all over everything. It's cute and funny, but then there's pee over everything."

BY THE TIME HE REACHED THE DOOR, Denis had two severely lacerated forearms (the sisal carpeting was environmentally friendly but otherwise vicious) and something wrong with his pubis, a hairline fracture perhaps or a hip dislocation. He pushed aside his everyday hypochondria in deference to the greater goal of surviving to obsess another day. He lunged upward, grasping the deadbolt and turning it with what could only have been a moment to spare.

Denis fell against the door, dry heaving with relief. He sat there, eyes closed, still breathing.

He opened his eyes.

He had a perfect view of the back patio door, which was presently sliding open.

Kevin did not look very happy.

A hand appeared in front of Denis's face. It was small and downy with sea-mint-lacquered nails; it wasn't holding a knife. It still gave Denis a heart cramp.

"Hey," Beth said.

She was reaching down for him. Her hair fell over her face in two silky sheets, swaying; it was lightly brushing against Denis's face. This was the most intimate he had ever gotten with a girl, if you didn't count Patty Keck, his secret shame, and Denis didn't. It was obviously the worst time to be thinking about sex, but Denis hadn't been given the choice.

"Don't be afraid," Beth said, correctly reading his expression but not its cause. "I'll handle this."

Oh, yes, this, Denis was reminded. *My assassination.*

Denis took Beth's hand and she pulled him to his feet—with ease, he noticed.

"I wasn't afraid," Denis wanted to explain. "I was . . ." All the words his brain offered up were rough synonyms for fear, from *pusillanimous* to *shitting bricks,* and including *epistaxiophobia,* fear of nosebleeds, and *rhabdophobia,* fear of being beaten with sticks, two of Denis's more reasonable phobias, and ones he was soon to have the opportunity to face (along with his agliophobia, gymnophobia, athazagoraphobia, and a few others).

"Prudent" finally popped out. "I was just being prudent."

"Well, c'mon, Prudence," Beth said, pulling him toward the kitchen.

KEVIN WAS A MAN IN A HURRY. He needed to get this killing done and not let it eat up his whole evening. He was flanked, in the strategic sense, by Sean, who had a bigger body but a much smaller head, and the other one.

Beth entered leading Denis by the hand.

Kevin snarled. A real snarl, like the kind a dog might make, right before biting your eyes.

Beth let go of Denis's hand. He didn't mind. It freed him to tremble on both sides of his body.

"Congratulations, you found me," Beth said, asserting control of the situation with sarcasm. "Now let's just—"

"Shut up, Lisbee."

"Kevin," scolded Beth. "Have you been doing coke?"

"Shut your goddamn mouth!" he responded, louder than necessary.

In a high, tiny voice, Denis said: "He's coked up!"

Treece shook her head sagely. "That is *not* one of the good drugs."

Kevin was not only coked up. He had also been drinking: vodka, bourbon, rum and a red liquid from Cambodia that came in a handblown bottle with a human tooth on the bottom. Since cocaine is a stimulant and alcohol is a depressant, the twin intoxicants should theoretically cancel each other out, but it never seems to work out that way.

The only sound in the room was Kevin's breathing. It probably could've been heard even if everyone hadn't shut his or her goddamn mouth. As it was, the seething hiss of a known killer, inhaling fear and exhaling hate, proved to be an effective mood setter.

Kevin picked up the champagne bottle on the counter and slowly upended it, tilting his head as he did so. He grunted. Denis half expected him to use a stick to try to extract ants from it. Concluding that the champagne had been consumed, and that this was an attempt to lubricate his mate, Kevin became 25 percent more furious. His cobalt eyes swept the kitchen for more anger boosters, and found one on the person of Rich, who was holding a large milky balloon with a reservoir tip. Kevin stopped breathing altogether.

Later, in Denis's dreams, Kevin's hair bristled like the hackles of a demonic dog, and venomous saliva streamed from his canines, burning a hole in the kitchen floor. In reality, Kevin pointed a disconcert-ingly muscular finger at Denis and shouted:

"PREPARE TO DIE!"

Rich lived for openings like this. "Mandy Patinkin in *The Princess Bride*, Rob Reiner, 1987," he rattled off. "Also, the same line was used by Emperor Zurg in *Toy Story 2*, 1999, John Lasseter, and by Marshall Teague in *Roadhouse*, 19—"

A heavy black object grazed Rich's skull and em-bedded in the wall behind him. (For an affordable sparkling wine, Freixenet sure made strong bottles.)

"*Kevin Patrick*," gasped Beth, ratcheting up to the first-and-middle maternal reprimand. "Just *stop*."

Denis stepped in to aggravate matters. "This is *completely* inappropriate," he said. "We just had this kitchen painted."

Ba-GOOSH Ba-GOOSH Ba-GOOSH went two-liter bot-tles of Ocean Spray Cranberry Fizz, Blood Orange Faygo and Salted Mountain Dew as they burst around Denis, vividly staining the linen white walls cran-berry, blood orange and morning urine.

"I need to warn you," Denis continued in defiance of common sense, "this is willful damage to property; that's a legal term."

Having exhausted his supply of hurlable beverages, Kevin picked up the next available object.

Denis finally shut up when he noticed a midsize mi-crowave oven coming at his head. He felt something hook the back of his neck and pull him to the floor. The microwave, a week out of warranty, crashed through the plasterboard above him. A dry rain of gypsum dust fell upon Denis, followed by the microwave itself, which bounced nonfatally off his head.

"Ow," Denis said. (He did not make a sound like "ow"; he said the word *ow*.)

Denis was crouched, lightly powdered, facing a lightly powdered Rich, who three seconds earlier had yanked him from the path of a speeding appliance. Rich offered some advice.

"This time, truly: *RUN AWAY!*"

Denis ran away. Rich stayed behind briefly, covering his friend's retreat by heaving the inflated condom at his attacker. Kevin caught the balloon with one hand and began squeezing it slowly. Presumably he thought it would pop at some point, adding to his cool menace. When it did not, he took the thing in both hands and crushed, contorted and clawed it with diminishing menace.

Cammy to Treece, genuine interest: "What brand was that?"

Treece tasted her lips. "Durex."

Kevin's jaw rippled. He backhanded the condom away and marched forward.

DENIS REACHED THE FRONT DOOR only to discover some moron had locked it. He stood for several seconds, blinking rapidly, formulating how he might pick the lock, or failing that, combine common household products into a plastique. Rich arrived at his side. "Dude, just—" he said, and reached for the deadbolt.

"Too late," Denis mumbled, and ran up the stairs.

"You don't run up the stairs!" Rich yelled up at him. "Have you never seen a movie? You run up the stairs, you *die!*"

Rich was about to cite specifics when he saw Kevin marching toward him. Kevin growled, smashed an overhead light fixture with his bare fist, then kept coming in the ensuing darkness.

Rich ran up the stairs.

"*¡Arribame!*"

RICH BURST INTO DENIS'S ROOM and crashed into a squadron of X-Wing Starfighters, not for the first time. He thrashed in the tangle of suspended *Star*

Wars collectibles and, for the very first time, did not hear Denis pissing and moaning that this or that one was made specifically for the Chinese market, making it extremely rare except for the 37 million other ones in China.

Denis was preoccupied. He was rifling through his closet, tossing out *Journals of the American Medical Association* and *Juvenile Oncology,* his snorkel, copies of *Famous CGI Monsters* and *Celebrity Sleuth: Women of Fantasy 15,* an old diving mask, Hobbit Monopoly and 3-D Stratego, and a pair of big, floppy, noncombat swim fins.

Wielding the impotent fins, he whined, "Why didn't I play baseball?"

Kevin arrived at the doorway. Sean and the other one fell in behind him.

Denis thrust his hands back into the closet, praying they would reappear holding anything resembling a weapon. A loaded revolver would be ideal, though unlikely (his mother felt hunters should be tried for war crimes and his father drove a Prius); a stick with a nail in it would be acceptable. What Denis retrieved certainly resembled a weapon; it was a 1:1-scale replica of the original Skywalker light saber with electroluminescent polycarbonate blade and ten motion-controlled digital sound effects.

Kevin barked with amusement. His troops barked exactly the same amount. A martial grin spread across his face as he reconnoitered the room: a medical school skeleton wearing a "BGHS Debate Team" T-shirt; the original *Star Wars* poster of Luke, light saber aloft; further charts of human muscular and circulatory systems; a poster of Professor Stephen Hawking posing with a poster of Marilyn Monroe; *Futurama* figurines . . . (In Denis's defense, a girl hadn't been in his room for more than ten years.)

"What a Eugene." Kevin chortled. The laughter triggered an endorphin rush that broke his fragile concentration, and he lost his homicidal focus. Why, he wondered, did he even consider this easily snappable geek a threat, instead of an amusing nuisance to be swatted away, or lightly stepped on?

And then he saw it.

On the ceiling above Denis's bed: Beth Cooper beaming down, kneeling in her cheerleading uniform. Denis had scanned the yearbook squad photo, Photoshopped the others out (digitally re-creating the portion of Beth's skirt obscured by Treece's knee), enlarged the image 7,000 percent, printed it in tiles, joined the tiles with an X-Acto blade and rubber cement, affixed the assemblage over his bed with wallpaper paste, and moved his bed three inches to the right to center the image. It had taken him five hours, not counting buying and setting up the scanner.

Kevin didn't appreciate all the effort. He grabbed the pelvis of the medical skeleton and tore it off the spine.

"Dr. McCoy!" Denis gasped.

Kevin took a femur in each hand and ripped them free of the pelvis.

"Now," Denis admonished, "that used to be a person."

Fiendish glee best described Kevin's expression as he approached Denis, slowly spinning the skeleton's lower legs around the knee joints.

"That is very disrespect *foo*—"

Twenty-six foot bones kicked him in the ear.

Denis lifted his light saber to fend off the human nunchucks, but Kevin's bone-fu was unstoppable. Flying phalanges of fury booted him about the face and neck.

"Dude!"

Denis turned to see that Rich was at the open window, on the other side of it, beckoning him.

"Don't just—"

Denis took a calcaneus to the temple. He staggered backward into a corner, trapped. So this was it: boned to death in his own room. Not exactly the tragedy he had always dreamed about. He thought of his mother finding his bloody pulped remains, and then he thought of that copy of *Celebrity Sleuth: Women of Fantasy 15* on the floor, lying open to topless shots of Kristanna Løken, the Terminatrix. Embarrassing. If he had time, he would try to eat the magazine before he died.

KEVIN SEEMED TO BE DECIDING. To kill or not to kill? Or how slowly? How excruciatingly? Whichever, he was relishing the decision-making process.

Something splintered against his skull. As it turned out, it was another skull. Beth stood behind Kevin, holding the jawbone of Dr. McCoy. "Calm down! Remember what the chaplain said!" she pleaded, grabbing his shirt.

Beth was allowed to touch Kevin in places he didn't even allow the army doctors to touch, but his shirt was not one of those places.

"You want some of this?" He raised a femur to her.

"Kevin." Beth backed away, releasing the shirt. "Let's just—"

"*Do* you?" Kevin asked again, in a dead, calm voice.

Beth said "No" very quietly.

She glanced past Kevin, who wheeled around to see the last of Denis going out the window. He turned back with a look of confused revulsion.

"You *like* this dork?"

Beth's failure to vomit at the suggestion was taken as a yes.

"I *am* going to kill him," Kevin said, dropping the bones and heading for the window. His compatriots followed.

Beth looked around Denis's room, shaking her head. When she saw her poster, she smiled so hard she almost cried.

10.

DUMB MONKEYS

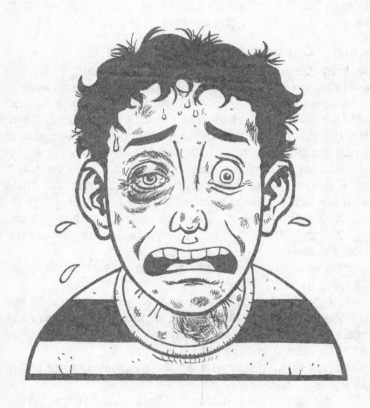

HE'S JUST DOING IT TO GET A RISE
OUT OF YOU. JUST IGNORE HIM.

CLAIRE STANDISH

AS HE WAS DEFENESTRATING HIMSELF, Denis observed that the eaves outside his window were only eighteen inches wide and sloped down at a 45-degree angle. This was the sort of detail he had surely noticed before, saw every day, but didn't attach any real importance to until it turned out to be really important. Like, for example, now.

His trajectory was going to take him past the eaves and another dozen feet straight down onto some lawn furniture that wasn't comfortable even when you sat on it properly. Denis would have to take death-evading measures. Using his sophisticated knowledge of physics and aerodynamics, he spazzed about and managed to save himself by wedging his face into the gutter.

"Hey!"

Denis coughed up the leaves he had promised to clean out the previous fall. Rich was twenty feet away, humping the far corner of the house.

"What are you *doing?*"

"Drainpipe," Rich grunted. "Shimmying."

Rich gave Denis a thumbs-up. The drainpipe *jinked* as it disengaged from the gutter, and Rich held his increasingly ridiculous pose as the pipe fell away, slowly at first and progressively faster in accordance with the laws of gravity, and into the darkness.

Denis squirreled it down the eaves and peered over the edge.

"Rich!"

Ca-chunk.

A rivet popped on the section of the gutter he was leaning on.

The gutter *ca-chunked* again, and then *ca-CHANKed.*

Denis plummeted. Just below were bushes planted to commemorate Denis's First Holy Communion, since the jujube was the source of the thorns in Jesus's crown. (Denis's parents treated their Catholicism not so much as a religion as an anthropological teaching opportunity.)

Denis fought his way through the thorns of Christ, his clothes pierced and skin scratched where it wasn't already contused (there too, but harder to make out). He ran over to Rich, who was lying on his back clutching the drainpipe between his legs.

"I'm paralyzed," Rich said with remarkable calm. "I'm a paralyzed virgin."

"Sorry," Denis said.

Above them, the gutter rattled.

Denis watched in shock and awe as three studly silhouettes leapt from the roof in unison and landed on the grass, tumbled together, and seamlessly rose to perfect commando formation.

Denis looked down at Rich. He was gone.

"Yo!"

Rich was standing in the next yard.

"Run, you dumb monkey!"

A very large dog appeared out of the shadows and swallowed Rich.

THE BEAST WAS ALL OVER HIM when Denis arrived. Rich was thrashing his arms and legs wildly, tossing his head from side to side and squeaking and squawking, suggesting the dog was up to no good.

"Kimberly, down!" Denis commanded, yanking the dog's collar. Kimberly backed off Rich and sat, panting happily.

"And now I'm partially eaten." Rich sighed. "The *chicas* don't go for half-eaten guys."

Kimberly was a big dog, a rottweiler-Lab-and-possibly-black-bear mix, but she was no man-eater. She was merely playing with Rich, and maybe tasting him a little.

"Kimberly?" Denis scoffed. "She's just a puppy

d-*ahgoo!*" Denis sneezed, and remembered why he didn't play more often with this big fluffy sack of dander and mites.

He sneezed again, and felt his open eye start to swell closed.

He sneezed again, and there was Kevin.

"Listen, Kevin," Denis began diplomatically, and then, where the abject apology should have gone, he sneezed in Kevin's face.

Kevin wiped off the snot particulates and, looking for a place to dry his hand, settled on Denis's face. He reached out and very nearly got his fingers bitten off.

Puppy Kimberly's large and sharp teeth glinted in the moonlight as she snapped and snarled, lunging at Kevin's body parts. He backed into his backup, feeling, what was it—*fear?* Roadside bombs and sniper fire barely got Kevin's attention anymore, but there was just something about fangs.

"Good dog!" Denis said. He reached down to help Rich up and discovered his friend had once again run off without him. *"Good doggie,"* Denis reinforced, and fled.

DENIS RAN LIKE A DUMB MONKEY through the backyards of Hackberry Drive:

through the Deters', whose son Lawrence went to Notre Dame on a football scholarship but decided to become a priest instead, breaking his father's heart;

through the Lemleys', whose daughter Lucia had once sold Denis fudge and lemonade made from recipes contained in the rhyme *milk, milk, lemonade, around the corner fudge is made;*

through the Cobes', who always gave out full-size candy bars on Halloween;

through the Schmidts', whose twenty-two-year-old daughter Shauna got undressed every night at nine, and took her time about it;

through the Snelsons', who always went out of town on Halloween, leaving a bag of cheap peanut butter kisses hanging off their doorknob, until that one Halloween;

and into the Confers' yard, under which nine cats were buried, and where Denis finally caught up with Rich, who was doubled over and breathing hard.

"Coach Raupp was right," Rich winced. "We are total pussies."

Denis tapped Rich on the back. They both saw:

Kevin and his troops marching at them double time, in a cadenced trot. They hurdled a four-foot chain-link fence without breaking stride.

Rich mulled this. "We may be dealing with cyborgs."

Denis took off toward the front yard.

"Hey!" Rich yelled, betrayed.

ACROSS THE STREET there once was a playground equipped with the monkey bars that Justin Cherry was briefly the king of, before tumbling off and becoming stupid. The Park District had taken the unpopular legal position that Justin was already stupid; as part of the ensuing massive settlement, the playground had been torn down and replaced by "Justin's Jungle," a rain-forest-themed Safeplay™ space, built on a Tiny-Turf™ seamless safety surface and constructed from EnviromenPal™ recycled plastic play components. Children seemed to enjoy it, despite its safety.

Denis ran up a monkey tongue and into its manic head.

"Have you learned *nothing?*" Rich complained, climbing the structure after him.

The boys clattered across the SynTeak™ Suspension Bridge and through the Eco-Go™ KnowFun™ Pagoda.

"Is there a point to this?" Rich asked. "Is there a plan here?"

Denis dove into a crawl tunnel that was mercifully free of theme, except for being banana yellow.

"Oh," Rich said. "The *hiding* plan."

Denis curled up near the midpoint of the tunnel, positioning himself between two of the Comfortholes™ that dotted the structure, allowing children to smile and wave at their parents and allowing parents to never ever lose sight of their precious, precious children. Rich didn't fit quite as nicely as Denis; his head and neck pressed against the top of the tube and knees jammed into the opposite wall.

Moonlight filtered in the ends and holes of the tunnel. A warm wind whistled through almost imperceptibly. The boys' panting slowed to heavy breathing. If Rich and Denis were ever going to make out, this was the time.

Rich grinned.

"Beth Cooper was *straddling* you," he said, vastly expanding the meaning of *to straddle*. "*Excellente.*" Rich chortled lasciviously and may have winked; it was too dark to tell.

Denis was raising a finger to shush Rich when a massive limb shot through the hole next to his head. He first mistook it for a leg; the toes grabbed his nose and he realized it was a heavy-duty arm.

About the same time another arm sprang from an opposing hole, took hold of Rich's collar and began whipping him back and forth, slamming his head into the tunnel wall.

Denis freed his nose from its attacker and scooted away, and into a third arm, which wrapped around his neck and began choking him with a definite purpose.

Rich made all the expected sounds as his head spanged off the hard yellow plastic. Denis made no sound at all because there was no air getting in or out of his lungs. Instead he steadily turned the color surrounding his injured eye, which had passed indigo and was entering aubergine.

Based on the rate of his progression to unconsciousness, Denis concluded that he was being *both* suffocated and strangled, in effect overkilled, and that his death would arrive shortly. He wondered where the requisite premortem flashing-before-his-eyes of his life was.

Ah, here it came:

The back of Beth Cooper's head, and then the right side of her perfect face, as she turns to talk to Kate Persky . . .

Neon parrot fish swarming around him, wanting his wet bread, as he scuba-dived in the Great Blue Hole off Belize with his parents . . .

Beth cheerleading on the gym floor, from high in the bleachers, glimpsed around somebody's fatty tattooed head . . .

In his room, reading The Man Who Mistook His Wife for a Hat, *lying on his bed next to Rich, watching* The Valachi Papers *on a portable DVD player* . . .

The back of Beth's head again, turning slightly as she reaches over her shoulder to return a pencil she had borrowed from him.

That about summed it up.

Denis heard celestial trumpets. The tunnel filled with a brilliant light.

White light, Denis thought, *that's a bad sign.*

I'm dead.

In a plastic yellow tube.

Just as quickly, Denis wasn't dead anymore. The arm released him. Air streamed into his lungs and blood flowed to his brain. The sound of celestial trumpets resolved into a high-pitched car horn, and the beckoning light bobbed and veered away from the mouth of the tunnel.

Denis was confused, and then flabbergasted, when a happy face appeared in one of the Comfortholes™.

"Hi!" Treece said.

OUTSIDE THE TUNNEL, a white 1996 Cabriolet convertible had Kevin pinned against a giant laughing giraffe. Beth was leaning on the horn. Under the circumstances, Kevin was conciliatory. "Lisbee?" he said, like a boyfriend who had done something awfully wrong and was so sorry even though he wasn't certain what it was he had done.

And then: "Lisbee!" he screamed, slamming both fists on the car hood, like a guy who was too coked up to wait three seconds to see if the first strategy worked.

Beth responded by easing the brake and tapping the gas, causing the vehicle to gently lurch into her boyfriend.

INSIDE THE TUNNEL, Denis crawled over to Rich. After being yanked to and fro and having his head slammed into a durable plastic enclosure a few dozen times, Rich was a bit discombobulated.

"I'm a shaken baby," he said.

A hairy hand continued to grip Rich's shirt, but was only halfheartedly whipping him back and forth in a distracted manner. Denis got the hand's attention by biting it, hard.

Sean yanked his arm out of the tunnel, yowling.

Denis nudged and shoved and finally shoveled his semi-conscious friend out the tunnel. With Treece's help, he folded Rich into the backseat of the Cabriolet. Beth threw the car in reverse, and Denis hurled his torso over the front door as it backed away.

The Cabriolet was doing minus 40 mph when Beth spun it 180 degrees and Denis's lower body did an impressive demonstration of centrifugal force as he clung to the interior door handle. The car tore forward down a grassy incline with Denis struggling to remain attached, and then hit the curb, throwing the boy aboard.

BETH SWUNG on to Arlington Heights Road without stopping or signaling in accordance with the Illinois Rules of the Road, or without yielding the right of way to the Volvo XC-90 that was already on Arlington Heights Road. This resulted in some sudden brakeage on the Volvo's part.

Rich bounced around in the backseat, more than dazed.

"You okay?" Treece asked. "Is your brain dead?"

She stuck her finger in his ear.

"No blood," she pronounced happily.

Denis was up front, in a position that might unfortunately be described as fetal, on top of Cammy, who did not appreciate it. She shoved the boy mass off her lap and down into the passenger legroom space that the Cabriolet wasn't known for.

Denis rocked from side to side on the floorboards as Beth swerved around any object doing less than twice the speed limit.

"We got away," Denis pointed out from his cubby. "You can stop escaping."

Cammy shrugged at him. "She always drives like this."

In the back, Rich stared into infinity.

"I was in driver's ed with her."

DRIVER'S ED WAS TAUGHT by Coach Raupp, who resented having to do it and was incensed that physical education class time was wasted on such an *ass-spreading activity*. This was reflected in his teaching style, which was screaming. He screamed on the test course, *If that cone was a BABY GIRL, you would have KILLED it!* He screamed on the road, *Pull over NOW so I can SLAP you!* The only time he wasn't screaming was when he was showing *Wheels of Tragedy* (1963), and its sequel *Highways of Agony* (1969), two films that had been dropped from most driver's ed curricula because their incorporation of real accident footage of dead, mangled and dismembered teens led to more crying than learning. But every time that imprudent hippie was scooped off the roadway and his stoned brain casually slid out onto the pavement, Coach Raupp could be heard cackling in the back.

He screamed at Beth Cooper only once.

Rich was in the backseat then, too, with Victoria Smeltzer, when she still weighed over a hundred pounds. Coach Raupp was in his typical instruction pose, one fist balled in his lap and the other rhythmically pounding on the dashboard. Beth was driving with blissful confidence, as she always did, unaware she was about to kill them all.

"Yo, Munsch," Coach Raupp snapped, "what is the speed limit on Illinois highways?"

"Sixty-five," Rich answered, for once almost certain he was right.

"Then can you tell me *why the hell* Mizz Cooper is doing over *seventy*?"

Rich's hopes of ever answering two consecutive questions correctly were dashed.

"I'm not doing seventy," Beth responded. "I'm only doing—" She stared down at the speedometer: 71. "The flow of traffic." The vehicle meanwhile drifted off the highway and onto the loose gravel shoulder; Beth tugged the wheel and popped the car back into its lane, more or less.

"Pull over!" Coach Raupp screamed. *"Now!"*

Beth pulled over, now. She neglected to signal or to decelerate. Coach Raupp overcompensated for this by slamming on the instructor brake, sending the car into an uncontrolled skid. Beth tried to steer back onto the highway. The car slid sideways and began to roll, tumbling side over side several times before erupting into an enormous fireball.

"It did not," Denis said at lunch that day, as Rich related the story. "You'd be covered in third-degree burns. Your nerve endings would be exposed. You'd look like this." Denis held up his slice of school pizza. "Only more sauce."

Rich took the slice, folded it lengthwise and funneled the grease unto his tongue. "I was thrown clear. Everybody else got crispy creamed."

"Victoria is right over there." Denis nodded furtively, so as to not attract her attention. Victoria was sitting with Patty Keck, his secret shame, eating her Diet Coke while Patty finished both of their lunches.

"Half of Beth's face is . . . just gone," Rich said. "Like Mel Gibson as the eponymous *Man Without a Face*."

He held the pizza over one eye.

"Is it this? Is this what you see? I assure you it is human. But if that's all you see, then you don't see me."

Would Denis still love Beth if she were *The Girl Without a Face?*

"Which half?" he asked.

"The good half."

Denis decided he did not have to decide. "And this has been another Richard Munsch dramatic presentation."

Rich swallowed the last of Denis's pizza. "Car did almost tip over."

RICH WAS IMAGINING he was in the scariest, goriest, least educational driver's ed film ever made:

In it, Rich played himself. Treece was played by Shanley Harmer, the actress who starred in *Bitches* on the CW, and then went on to movie fame in *Holy Mallory* and that Internet mp4 with Licks' front man Brent Koz. He was mentally casting Denis—that kid from *Geek Camp?*—when he suddenly flew forward, bounced his face against the front seat and slammed back next to Treece.

"I'm the least notable person in this car," Rich observed with quiet, final clarity. "When we all die, I'll be 'fifth student.'"

"They always spell my name wrong," Treece complained.

Beth had overshot the red light by a couple of car lengths. Black SUVs coming in opposite directions very nearly crashed into the front passenger and rear driver's sides, tearing the little Cabriolet in half like two wolves fighting over a plump bunny. Beth gave a cursory *my bad* wave and rapidly backed out of the intersection, coming within five-eighths of an inch of hitting a third black SUV behind her.

Denis crawled out of his hole. The last few seconds

had brought back Rich's Driver's Ed Tales (there were several) and so he was currently struggling with the conflicting emotions of:

1) intense joy that Beth had just saved his life, choosing him over a former boyfriend;

2) fear.

"That was . . . with the car back there, but—"

"That wasn't for you," Beth cut him off. "I don't want you to get the wrong idea. Kevin can't have another incident. One more, and it's court-martial for sure."

Joy left and fear reigned.

"One more *what?*"

THE LIGHT TURNED GREEN and Beth floored it. Denis, perched between the two front seats, was thrown into the back.

"So," Treece said when he landed next to her. "That was fun."

"Some fun," added Rich, now partially recombobulated. His head lolled in Denis's direction. "Your dad would be so proud."

Denis thought of the champagne bottle lodged in the wall, the Technicolor gooshes, the dead microwave and mutilated lawn. He leaned back through the front seats.

"Can I borrow your cell phone? I left mine—"

"Good catch," Beth said. She pulled her cell phone from her purse and tossed it out of the car. "GPS that, asshole."

The phone flew through the window of a passing Honda Civic and hit Harold Angell, a thirty-four-year-old nurse practitioner who had no ironic connection to anyone in the car.

Denis sank back into his seat. He bounced off Treece and then Rich as Beth swerved along her merry way.

"Her driving's gotten a lot better," Rich commented.

Denis felt around behind him for the middle seat belt, finally pulling out something that appeared to have been chewed on by several packs of dogs. The buckle fell off.

"You can use my phone," Treece said, reaching into a pouch that cost more than Denis's entire wardrobe. "Not this one." She dropped a silver flip-phone back in. "My mom has it tapped"—meaning only that her mother scoured the bill for calls to men her mother dated. "Here."

Treece handed Denis a hot pink phone encrusted with jewels and dangled charms that looked as if it had been decorated by a three-year-old but which had been custom junked up in Japan at considerable cost.

"Tell your parents I said hi," Cammy remarked from the front seat.

"What makes you think I'm calling my parents?"

"Because you're you," Treece said, much nicer.

DENIS'S FATHER WAS DRY-HUMPING Denis's mother in the back of the Prius when his phone began buzzing.

"You're vibrating," Mrs. C said.

"You *bet* I am!" Mr. C moaned, grinding into her.

Mrs. C did not grind back. "It might be Denis."

Mr. C sighed. Yes, it might be Denis. Their son could be calling to ask permission to download a movie off iTunes. Or perhaps to tell them to pick up some milk or a *Scientific American* on the way home. Some emergency of that sort.

Mr. C pulled a cell phone out of his shirt pocket. The screen read CALLER ID BLOCKED.

"Telemarketer," he said. Mr. C slipped the vibrating phone down the front of Mrs. C's slacks.

"Mr. C!" Mrs. C growled.

ON HIS END, Denis, thankfully, only heard the usual leave-a-message-at-the-beep and then the beep.

"It's me," he told the phone. "Rich and I . . . went out. But we're okay. I can explain the kitchen. You can call me at . . ."

He looked to Treece. She grabbed the phone away.

"That's my *stealth* phone!"

Up front, Beth turned on the radio. In a quavering depressissimo, a future lesbian sang:

I learned the truth at seventeen . . .

Beth frowned. She pushed SEEK. Synthetic drumbeats and electro-boops accompanied a future cartoon composer:

Makin' dreams come true
Living tissue, warm flesh—

Beth turned the music off.

"Radio sucks," she pronounced.

Denis remembered. He pulled the iPod from his pocket.

"Tune to 87.1."

There was much groaning. Undeterred, Denis leaned between the front seats and turned the radio back on. "No, seriously, you'll like this," he promised, tuning and hoping.

Music equally ancient but not the least bit objectionable began blasting out the speakers, a man named Alice repeating the words of a playground chant:

No more pencils,
No more books,
No more teacher's dirty looks.

Beth's head banged to the olden beat. Denis was hugely relieved. Ordinarily, the declaration that school was out for summer made him anxious. But this summer, he thought, might be all right.

School's out forEVER!

Beth sang along, with heavy emphasis on the last two syllables. Here, Denis begged to differ. School was not out *forever*, just until—

School's been BLOWN TO PIECES!

screamed Beth, taking both hands off the steering wheel and waving devil horns above her head.

"I *love* this song," yelled Treece. "Who doesn't want to blow up their school?"

Denis was happy his song selection was a success, but he'd have been much happier if Beth was steering her vehicle. The car drifted toward the center line, toward oncoming traffic and into physics equations too complicated for Denis to work out on the fly.

Denis decided that if Beth didn't feel like steering she wouldn't mind if he did. He reached for the wheel, planning on nudging it just enough to prevent death. He got two fingers on the rim.

With one hand, Beth matter-of-factly executed a nearly perpendicular right turn at full speed.

Denis toppled forward and fell face first between Beth's legs.

11.

ESTRANGED BREW

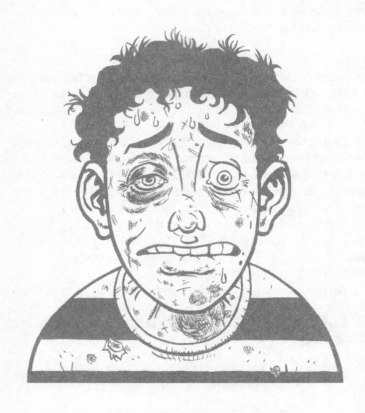

I BET YOU'RE SMART ENOUGH
TO GET US SOME BREW.

DEBBIE DUNHAM

THE CABRIOLET CAREENED into the White Hen Pantry parking lot and skidded into the only available space, bouncing off the concrete wheel stop.

Denis's face remained lodged in Beth's thighs. The moment when he could have withdrawn his head without incident had passed. He couldn't get out now without a good exit line, and he was without one. He imagined Beth was appalled, hurt, violated, furious, fed up and, *oh, no, was she sobbing?*

Beth was chuckling.

It was dark down there, Denis guessed. He took no chances and kept his eyes shut. He couldn't close his nose, however. It smelled musky, a little like butt, less pungent, more floral, and—was *spicier* the right word?

It took Denis a surprisingly long time to realize he was sniffing Beth Cooper's vagina.

His eyes opened involuntarily. It wasn't nearly dark enough down there. Beth's panties were white. They spoke to Denis. They said,

$$\textit{Hello.}$$

The lettering was hot pink. It clashed with the blue-green plaid of the skirt, yet somehow it worked.

Outside Denis's newly discovered universe, time was passing and, for Beth, the amusement of having a socially inappropriate boy's head between her legs was waning.

"Crack him like a walnut," Cammy suggested.

Denis felt a hand tugging his hair. He wanted to stay.

I love you, he whispered as Beth lifted his head out of her welcoming center.

"I'm sorry," Denis said.

"Let's get some beer," Beth said.

Beth hopped out of the car and Denis crawled after her. "Two minutes," she called back to the others, reaching the door before Denis and opening it for him.

"Snacks," Treece yelled. "Everybody wants snacks!"

"Everybody," Cammy said flatly.

Treece acknowledged the insult with a grotesque lip formation. "And a bucket for Cammy!" She mimed bulimic fingers and then turned to Rich, palm up, awaiting her high five.

Whoa, Rich thought, *catfight!*

"LISTEN," BETH SAID, once they were inside.

Denis had not yet formulated a plausible explanation for the amount of time he had spent in her genital environs.

He went with implausible.

"I lost consciousness briefly, back there. I wasn't looking or smelling . . . your person."

Beth had no idea what he was talking about. "I don't want you to think I'm a bitch or anything. What I said. I mean, I didn't want to see you get hurt, obviously. But I just wanted to be clear, you know, about my motivations."

"Oh, sure," Denis said. "I figured as much."

They reached the beer display. Beth turned toward Denis, brightly, and then not.

"God."

The convenience store fluorescence brought out the colors of everything that had befallen Denis's face so far that evening:

ruby-rimmed right eye tucked in a billowing of black, violet and yellow flesh;

newer plummy bruises on his ears, forehead, cheeks and chin;

across the whole face a delicate lattice of crimson scrapes.

"Maybe you *should* go to the hospital," Beth said.

"Your eyes aren't blue," Denis responded. He had been staring at her as she gaped at him, and seeing things.

"What?"

"There's green in there," he said. "And around the pupil, there's a hazel"—the scientific term came first—"corona . . ." He sprung open his hand: "Starburst."

"Yeah," Beth acknowledged. "My grandmother said they were a real 'dog's breakfast.'"

"Lucky dog," Denis said, and on purpose.

Beth's lips twitched upward even as her eyes cast downward. She tilted her face away, and came back with a huge, sanitary smile.

"What kind of beer do you like?"

THE CATFIGHT WAS DISAPPOINTING. Treece and Cammy traded a couple of cryptic remarks, references to previous and ongoing grievances, and fell into an uneasy détente. Rich figured that if it was not for Beth, these two wouldn't be friends at all.

Treece was texting on her stealth phone. "How do you spell 'fiasco'?"

"F-I-A-S-C-O" spat Cammy.

"I'll just put a frowny," decided Treece.

"So," Rich said, seeing if he could get them scratching again, "how long have you two been going out with Sean and—what was the other one?"

"That's weird." Treece screwed up her face. "Something." A few moments later Cammy laughed, and Rich knew what was coming was not going to be funny. "Could you ever imagine, Treece, that we would be spending our graduation night with Dick Muncher and the Penis?"

Rich flipped the bird at the nape of her neck. "You have nicknames, too, you know."

"*Really?*" Cammy said.

"Yours is Cunty," answered Treece, flipping her cell closed. "Mine's *really* rude."

"Fuck a duckling," Cammy said, changing the subject.

Approaching the car were Henry Giroux and his buddy Damien, the only two guys from BGHS that Cammy wanted to hang out with less than Denis and Rich. Henry was the local purveyor of aftermarket pharmaceuticals, not quite a drug dealer though he played the part, replete with an embroidered urban dialect spoken only in the suburbs. What made Henry's lily-white gangsta act all the more sad was that he was African-American. He was a black whigger.

"Yo, yo, beautiful ladies!"

DENIS DID NOT KNOW what kind of beer he liked. As far as he knew, he did not like beer.

"Microbrew," he answered.

"What kind?"

"Any kind."

Beth reached into the cooler and pulled out a six of Molson Dark, followed by a twelve of PBR tallboys. She dumped both in Denis's arms.

"Snacks!" Beth said.

Denis followed Beth through the salty fat aisle as she piled on, with seeming indiscrimination, bag upon bag of what his mother cleverly called Muerto Chips and Deadlios.

"I don't want to alarm you, but I'm seeing a lot of sodium and partially hydrogenated oils here . . ."

Beth looked puzzled for a moment, then suddenly clutched her chest.

"Erk!" she said.

Denis smiled. "Okay, maybe I—"

Beth dropped to the floor, dead.

Oh no, Denis thought. *Oh no, oh no. Oh, no!*

A crowd gathered around the body, pushing Denis back.

"The poor girl," an old lady said. *"She was so popular."*

Denis realized what he must do. He threw the beer and snacks to the ground with much crashing and crunching. He pushed through the crowd.

"Please," he ordered, "stand aside. I'm a life-guard . . . and pre-med."

He knelt by her side. Quickly triaging the patient, he tore open her dress.

The old lady clucked.

"This is a medical procedure," Denis hushed her, in a rich baritone.

Denis gazed down at Beth's still, lifeless but nevertheless pretty amazing chest. She wore the same pink brassiere he had seen earlier and filed into memory for just such a situation.

"Chest," Denis said. He placed his hands, with some reluctance, between her breasts.

"Aren't you supposed to kiss her first?" a little girl asked.

"Right. Mouth."

Her lovely, probably still warm mouth. He leaned over to kiss her so full of life she would never be able to be respirated by anybody else again.

"No. Chest then mouth," said Dr. Beverly Crusher, really filling out that Star Fleet uniform.

Denis started to sweat. He glanced back at Beth's chest.

Then her mouth.

Her chest.

Her mouth.

His mouth on her mouth, her lips quivering, returning to life.

His mouth on her chest . . .

"HEY, SPACE BOY!"

Beth snapped her fingers, turning Denis's eyeballs back on.

"Remind me not to have my real heart attack in front of you."

"No," Denis protested. "I'm *trained*."

Beth was already at the end of the aisle. She pointed to the left and went that way. Denis waddled after her, the eighteen beers and eight bags exceeding his carrying capacity. In the next aisle, ten packages of sweet, fatal snacks awaited Denis's abiding arms. Beth had a preference for chocolatey coating, he noted.

"Suzy Qs! *Yum!*"

Beth held up a package of the Hostess snackcake that would be forever dendritically entwined in Denis's brain with the verb phrase *sucking each others'*. Seeing the labial cakes oozing creme only strengthened the connection, as did the way Beth flicked her tongue when she overpronounced the word *yum*. This freely associated with his mother's *yumming* earlier in the day, creating a gooey endocrinal mess.

"My mom says 'Yum.' Not like that."

Beth licked the outer flesh of her *labia oris* in a slow, elliptical pattern, then repeated *yum* as a kind of a moan, with a short, sharp breath separating it into three parts, Denis observed.

Was Beth consciously trying to pop his pituitary gland? Or was this kind of sexual sabotage purely instinctual, or was it all a figment of his anterior hypothalamus? One thing was certain: Denis knew too much about biology and not enough about women.

"How much money you got?" Beth asked.

"Oh," Denis said, blinking back into the real world. "I, my wallet . . ." He nodded over his shoulder, to suggest he could not presently reach his back pocket, not that Beth should stick her hand in there.

Denis barely felt it, unfortunately.

"Money, money, money," Beth said as she flipped open his billfold. Denis's mind flashed on its terrible contents:

his school ID, taken during a severe acne storm;
a Photobooth picture of Rich and him that could easily be misconstrued;
a video-game token; and,
goddammit.

"Wow," Beth said, very impressed. "I never met a certified member of the Starfleet Academy before."

"That's expired."

Beth slipped the official identification card back and plucked out the hundred-dollar bill.

"Thank you, Denis Cooverman!" she sang, and then noticing the lavender glitter pen inscription, "And thank *you*, Auntie Brenda!"

Or that.

"GO AWAY, HENRY."

Rich was pleased with the cold shoulder Cammy was giving Henry Giroux. There was a limited niche for "characters" in the high school ecosphere, and Rich felt his Smooth-Talking Film Aficionado was going underappreciated due to unfair competition from Henry's Retro Ghetto Jivist. Rich chalked this up to the fact that Henry possessed drugs, albeit lame ones, and that he was nominally black. (The only other black person in their class, Lisa Welch, was in band and therefore invisible.)

Henry did not go away. He leaned a hip against the car and stylishly tipped the porkpie off his head and sent it rolling down his arm. The hat bounced off the crook and tumbled to the pavement. Henry turned to Cammy with the same cocky expression he would have used had the hat rolled effortlessly into his hand.

"What do you *want*, Henry?" she asked.

"*Bumboklaat*, girl," Henry shucked. "Jes' seeing if you wants to partay."

"No."

"Whaddya got?" Treece asked.

"We got the Ritz," Henry said, using his own slang for Ritalin. "And some sweet 'D.'"

"That would be Claritin D?" Cammy supposed.

"Das right; check it!"

Henry opened his pleather coat. The pockets were crammed with various pharmaceuticals, many labelled *Free Sample.*

"Break into your Dad's office again?"

"Lemme hook you lily self up with some kickin' Mercedez."

"You don't have any Benzedrine," Cammy said.

"*Adderall*, beeyatch!"

Treece was disappointed with the selection. "Don't you have any real drugs?"

"Fo shizzle my pizzle!" Henry said.

"Why do you talk like that, Henry?" Cammy asked.

"Jes' representin'."

"You live in Terramere. Your dad's a pediatrician and your mom runs 'Curves.' Why don't you represent that?"

"Salty!" interjected Damien, who looked like a pig with hair.

Henry was not about to let some ho dis him like that. "Why are *you*"—pointing ten fingers at Cammy—"rollin' with Prick Muncher and Da Penizzle?"

"I can't answer that."

Rich did not like the direction this conversation was taking.

"You too fine for candy cracker ass scrubs."

"You'll get no argument from me."

Rich stood. "I'm going to go check on the *cervezas*."

"*Adios, muchacha*," Henry dismissed Rich, and returned to Cammy and Treece. "Why don't you ice the bustas and kick it with a brutha?"

"Sure," Cammy said. "You just go back to 1992 and I'll meet you there."

Henry was undeterred.

"Come on over to the Dark Meat Side.

"I don't believe that's gangsta, Henry," Cammy said. "I believe that's geeksta."

Treece giggled, but Henry was unbowed. "Once you go black," he Courvoisiered them, "you never-fo'ever go back."

"That's not true," Treece said with some authority.

RICH WAS MAD AT HIMSELF for not going mano a mano, mouth to mouth, with Henry Giroux back there. At first, he had seen no need; he was enjoying, admiring, the way Cammy dismantled that little minstrel showoff. But then she turned and sided with Henry against him. Rich prided himself on not caring what the popular kids thought, feeling that their very popularity demonstrated their inferiority, somehow, but it hurt him that Cammy agreed he was a *candy cracker ass scrub*, whatever that meant, exactly.

And *Dick Muncher and The Penis*? Was that common usage? Rich had been called *Dick Munch* since the seventh grade and he himself had called Denis *Penis* earlier in the evening, but it never occurred to him that people would put the two together, turning them into the gaynamic duo or something. *Dick Muncher and The Penis*. More like supervillains.

Well, at least he got first billing.

Beth was at the candy rack, standing next to a giant pile of junk food with legs. Beth spotted Rich's approach and shooed him away. He kept coming.

"*¡Muchas snackaballes!*"

"Back to the car," Beth ordered.

"Why?" he asked.

Beth was unaccustomed to having her orders countermanded. It became very cold in there.

"I guess you are the boss of me," Rich said, backing away.

On his way out, Rich stopped to look at a magazine,

mostly for spite. He picked up a copy of *American Man*, the Magazine for American Men. On the cover was a lustrous male chest with impossible pectorals and a brightly feathered fishing lure dangling from one nipple.

Cut Bait!
POWER FISH TO FITNESS

read the coverline. "Cocktail Music: Which Tequila Goes Best with Beck?" was also promised inside, along with "Have You Forgotten Your Glutes?" As a matter of fact, Rich had forgotten his glutes, along with his abs, pecs, lats, and all three types of ceps.

"*Hola, Ricardo.*"

Standing next to Rich, perusing that month's *Details*, was a middle-aged man in a white jogging outfit. He was in decent shape for his age, but not for terrycloth shorts.

"Oh, hi, Mr. Weidner," Rich said, shoving his *American Man* back in the rack. "I mean, *hola, Señor Weidner.*"

Sr. Weidner closed his magazine, leaving a finger inside to mark his place. He smiled. "You can call me Cal, now."

"Okay. *Muy bien. Hola, Cal.*"

"You're keeping up your Spanish."

"*Todo las veces.*"

"*Todo el tiempo.*"

"Right," Rich said, pointing to his head. "*Soy retardo.*"

Sr. Weidner smiled again, a little pained. "So, listen, *cenemos alguna vez. Si te gusta. ¿Comeremos tapas y hablaremos Español?*"

Rich had no idea what Sr. Weidner was saying. Guessing it was a question, and reading hopefulness in his former teacher's expression, he replied, "Yeah. *Sí.*"

"*¡Maravilloso!*"

"*Excellente,*" Rich agreed. "But I should probably go. I've got two *chicas calientes* waiting for me in the *autobus.*"

"*Bien,*" Sr. Weidner said. "*Llámame,*" he added as Rich walked away. "I'm in the book."

BETH LED DENIS to the checkout counter. As she unpacked him, she whispered, "Follow me." Denis nodded. He would follow her.

The clerk behind the counter was a loser, and a pretty sizable one. His hair looked as if it had been washed far too often but not for the last month or so. He had a skinny head and narrow shoulders and spindly arms and a truly humongous ass. He looked to be anywhere between twenty-eight and forty-three, as is often the case with losers.

Beth plunked the beer on the counter with a bored look.

The loser started scanning the snacks, staring at Denis. He sneered more than usual. "What's with your boyfriend?"

"My little brother," Beth corrected.

Denis winced. He understood the exigencies of the situation, and knew he did not look twenty-one (ticket takers would occasionally ask if his parents knew he was seeing this movie, which was rated PG-13 and contained scenes of intense action that might give him nightmares). And yet, the only thing worse than a girl thinking of you as a brother was her thinking of you as a little brother. Brothers, at least, got long hugs. Little brothers got head pats and lollipops.

"What happened to his face?" the loser asked.

My injuries, Denis thought, *must add a certain weathered maturity.*

"Dad beats him," Beth said.

The loser picked up the Molson and swung it toward the scanning plate, only to jerk it back at the last second, returning it to the counter.

"I need to see some ID."

Beth looked surprised. She shrugged, a tad much, and produced a small coin purse. It was stuffed with bills, Denis noticed. She fished out her driver's license with two fingers and flicked it at the clerk.

"You've lost weight, Patricia," the loser said, examining the ID. "And you certainly don't look thirty-seven."

"Thank you."

The loser handed back the ID, slid the beer away from the snacks, and hit the total button. "That'll be $56.72."

Beth dropped the pretense. "C'mon," she pleaded. "It's graduation night."

"Con-*grad*-ulations."

"You're a cool guy," Beth cajoled. "Be cool."

"I could lose my shitty job."

Denis began working on a Plan B. Appeal to reason. *Rejected.* Smash loser over head with beer, grind jagged bottle neck into his throat. *Rejected.* Grab beer and run. *Analyze.*

Beth already had a Plan B. She smiled shyly at the loser.

"I'll touch your dick."

"AND THEN SHE TOUCHED HIS DICK."

Denis sat in the back of the Cabriolet, a six-pack of Molson Dark in his lap.

"Ew," Treece opined. "Even I wouldn't do that. Unless the beer was free."

Up front, Beth and Cammy were sipping tallboys,

heads shagging to DJ C's unexpectedly slammin' graduation mix:

> You're my one, baby, yes you are
> My sweet hot secret cherry tart
> We've been playing in a minor key
> But you've finally reached majority

"She touched his dick," Denis repeated.
"So there's hope for you," Rich said.
Treece qualified, "*If* you've got beer."

> You're legal
> Oh my oh my oh my
> You're legal now
> Oh my oh my oh my

"Inside or outside?"
Denis pretended not to understand.
"The pants. Inside or outside?"
Treece did a little clap. "Good question!"

INSIDE, FOR LESS THAN A SECOND, and then out.

Inside, a moment's grope, and then out, her fingers splayed apart.

Denis's brain rewound again.

Inside, her sea-mint fingers curled around his unwashed
grease pole,
cheese stick,
night crawler,
chancre factory,
Jergened gerkin,
rancid flaccid fetid flesh appendage,
dick, dong, dingle,
peter, pecker, pork-sword, pud,
wiener.

Inside, a swift kick to Denis's gut, and then out.

"That's no good," the loser said when Beth withdrew before the party could start.

"I touched it," Beth responded. "That was the deal."

The loser began walking the beer back to the cooler. Beth followed him, and Denis followed Beth.

"You can't. I did what I said."

"What are you gonna do, sue me?"

"Call the police."

"A consensual act." The loser sounded like a man who knew his way around the sexual assault laws. "Your little brother saw it."

Yes, he had. If he had died right then, which he was considering, the coroner would've found the exculpatory evidence burned into his retina.

"Completely," the loser licked his skinny purple lips, relishing "con-*sensual*."

"That doesn't matter," Denis heard himself say, "when she's only fifteen."

On their way out with the beer, Beth grinned at Denis and patted him on the head. "Good job, little brother!"

"I DON'T WANT TO TALK ABOUT IT," Denis said, back in the car.

Treece took him at his word, and spoke over him to Rich. "I saw you chatting with Señor Weidner."

"Yes, and?"

"I always thought he was a handbag."

"So why are you telling me?"

" 'Cuz you're right there."

"And anyway, why would you think Weidner's gay? He dresses terribly."

"He's always lisping." Treece demonstrated, substituting interdental fricatives for her usual sibilance: "*¿Donde estha la cothina?*"

"That's Castilian. That's the way they talk in . . . some place in Spain."

"Castile," said Denis, on automatic.

"*Cathstile.*"

"I guess that's why you don't see many *Cathstillians.*" Treece thought this was tremendously funny.

"You know," Rich spoke over the loud whinnying, "it's not right to assume someone's gay just because of the way they talk, or look, or act."

Treece stopped mid-whinny. She regarded Rich with fond pity. "Nobody cares if you're gay."

"I'm not."

"No one cares." She threw up her hands festively. "So be gay already."

Rich thought, *No one?*

> *You're legal*
> *Oh my oh my oh my*
> *You're legal so*
> *Bye-bye bye-bye bye-bye*

The Licks song went into an endless fade, perfectly soundtracking the swirling collapse of Denis's mental universe.

Beth Cooper was a nice, pretty girl who always returned the pencils she borrowed. She did not touch dicks for beer.

> *Bye-bye bye-bye bye-bye*

"She's not Beth Cooper," Denis said quietly.

Treece furrowed one brow then the other.

"I'm pretty sure she is."

12.

NIGHT MOOS

MARTY, DON'T BE SUCH A SQUARE.
EVERYBODY WHO'S ANYBODY DRINKS.

LORRAINE BAINES

FIVE TEENAGERS DRANK BEER on a dark country road covered with a pale green mist. It was midnight.

"Ever been out here before?" Beth asked.

"Seriously?" Denis evaded. "I mean, *Old Tobacco Road* . . ."

Old Tobacco Road wasn't called that anymore. In the eighties, antismoking advocates insisted on changing it, but split between the heart-disease faction, which wanted Camino Corazon, and the cancer crowd, which wanted the more on-message Smoking Causes Cancer Road. In the end, the village board discovered the road was in an unincorporated area and that they had no authority to change it. Some time during the nineties, the county quietly changed the name to Gwendolyn Way, after somebody's mother. But all the teenagers who hung out there still called it Tobacco Road, or Old Tobacco Road, or recently, the OT.

"This place creeps me out," Beth said. She finished her tallboy and crumpled it in her fist. "I don't know why I keep coming out here."

"It's peaceful." Denis baby-sipped his Molson Dark.

"Except for the ghosts," Beth said.

DENIS HAD NEVER HUNG OUT on Old Tobacco Road, and had never been there after dark. He had only seen it once, one Saturday afternoon when he was ten, on a Tales of My Youth drive with his father. Denis's father had grown up in Buffalo Grove and never tired of showing his son his personal historical landmarks (the house on St. Mary's Parkway, the baseball field where he hit a grand slam, the water treatment plant where he saw a dead kid). Many of the elder Cooverman touchstones were not there anymore, or ruined somehow. Tobacco Road was exactly the same.

The narrow, barely paved road ran fairly straight but swooped up and down wildly, over hill and dale and steeper hill and deeper dale. Running along the eastern edge of the road was the Old Maguire Farm, the only major parcel of land in the area that had not been converted into a subdivision named for the English countryside. This was because Old Man Maguire had killed dozens of teenagers and fed them to his pigs, burying their bones in the corn, and therefore was reluctant to sell. Either that or he had killed his wife and nine kids one night by burning down his farmhouse, which reappeared every full moon, disappearing in the morning along with anybody foolhardy enough to have gone inside.

On the other side of the road was a three-story turn-of-the-century building that had once been a home for the criminally insane, or an orphanage, or a home for children who killed their parents, or a whorehouse, or an insane asylum-cum-whorehouse. Next to it was a small cemetery, haunted by the restless souls of insane whores, and next to that was a bog, which had monsters.

Denis's father had told Denis these tales (minus the whores) that afternoon, emphasizing they were just "silly stories" teenagers liked to tell each other. Denis's mother slept in the boy's room for the next three months, mostly to punish his father.

THE MOON WAS FULL. Beth's convertible was parked at the highest point of Old Tobacco Road, overlooking a soupy pea fog that was either slightly radioactive or ghost children at play. This was the ideal vantage point to see the reappearance of Old Maguire's farmhouse. It was behind schedule.

"How's that microbrew treating you?" Beth asked Denis.

The brew was treating him very well. His fifteen sips, approximately half a bottle, was six ounces more beer than Denis had ever consumed, and the dose was

having the psychopharmacological effects he anticipated: slight euphoria, tension reduction, loss of concentration. As a result, while Denis still knew Beth
Cooper was no longer Beth Cooper, he was having difficulty maintaining his distress, his mind wandering
over to Rich's point of view, that Beth Cooper's sexual
generosity with the physically less gifted could work
in the favor of a Denis Cooverman.

"It's good." Denis said. "Very . . . brewed."

He sat in the front passenger seat next to Beth, at
her invitation. Rich and Treece sat atop the backseats
and Cammy was out of the car, sulking over being
made to surrender shotgun to Denis. Why did she even
cede authority to Beth Cooper? Cammy was smarter
and had better technicals in all the beauty categories.
Was it simply that Beth was head cheerleader? Was
Cammy that much of a sheep?

"Nik-nik-nik-f-f-f-Indians!" Rich hollered as he drained
his first Molson Dark.

Cammy eyed him with appalled disinterest.

"Jack Nicholson in *Easy Rider*, 1969, Dennis Hop-
per."

"There's something wrong with you," Cammy said.

Beth popped open her second PBR, sucking off the
foam. For a moment she had a thick, gorgeous beer
mustache.

"You do know," Denis advised, "open liquor in the
car, you could lose your license?"

"Too late!" Beth tipped her can in toast, and then
chugged.

Denis had no idea that a woman guzzling cheap
beer could be so sexy, the way she kissed the rim and
her throat undulated as the golden domestic nectar
flowed through it. The *gulugulugugug* was less sexy
but could be filtered out.

Denis bit a swig off his Molson. That went so well
he took another, and another. Soon enough his lips

ceased parsing and the beer freely drained down his gullet.

Beth crushed her beer can and tossed it. Denis reflexively squeezed his beer bottle and it slipped out of his hand, spilling in his lap. He waved off nonexistent help, pinched the bottle by the lip and flung it into the dark. He immediately reconsidered. "We should probably pick those up," he said, leaning out of the car.

Beth prodded him with another Molson. Denis forgot everything his mother had ever taught him about caretaking this delicate planet and took the bottle from Beth. He twisted the top effortlessly, producing no effect. He applied more pressure and his hand slid off the cap. His palm was sweaty. Of course it was. Everything was. He could hear the sweat beading inside his ears. *Goddammit.* Before long he would need to explain he had not wet his pants, or, *oh, god, she wouldn't think that, would she?*

"You're having bottle trouble tonight." Beth took the bottle, gave it a quick twist, and to Denis's everlasting relief did not open it. Undeterred, she brought the bottle to her mouth, wedged it between her back molars and

she bit the fucking cap off!

"I know." She took a quick slug before returning the bottle. "I'm going to *ruin my beautiful teeth.*"

Denis's whole mouth throbbed.

Beth popped her third PBR, sucked it off. "So," she grinned, "ever come up here with Patty Keck?"

Denis glared at Rich.

"Girls talk," Beth corrected him.

Denis gulped his beer and winced. Beth Cooper talked to Patty Keck, his secret shame? This could not lead anywhere good. He searched his brain for a change of subject. What a mess it was in there. It was as if somebody had broken into his cerebrum and dumped all the neurons on the floor. They flopped around unhelpfully.

And then Denis heard, coming over the radio, driving eighties synthpop and a topic:

> *Will you recognize me*
> *Call my name or walk on by* . . .

"This song." Denis directed everybody's attention to the radio. "What if," he said, "our parents, on their graduation night, what if . . . ?" His ex tempore skills were below his tournament best. "They could have been sitting right here, on Old Tobacco Road, in their vehicles, cars that were available at the time, and they could have been parked in this exact spot, listening to this *exact same song*.

"Which *means*," Denis built to what seemed a profound cosmological observation, "we were here, too . . . *in cell form*."

There was a silence, which Denis took to signify amazement.

"I don't remember getting high," Cammy deadpanned.

"We're high?" Treece asked.

"I just thought it was interesting." Denis backpedaled from profundity. "How we all go through this. The same songs. The same rituals . . ."

"Intriguing, professor," Cammy said.

"I mean, we all . . ." Denis struggled for a common and yet precisely right word. ". . . *graduate*."

"My parent's didn't graduate to this song," Treece said. "They're forty-something. Plus."

"This song is at least that old," Denis said.

"They didn't have cool music back then," Treece argued. "That was, like, the *past*."

" 'Don't You (Forget About Me),' Simple Minds," cited

Rich, "from the sound track of *Breakfast Club*, 1984, John Hughes."

"Are you going to do that all night?" Beth asked.

"I can't help it. I'm like Dustin Hoffman in *Rain Man*." He did a slightly more nasal version of his Pacino.

I'm an excellent driver. Qantas.

The girls all turned away from him. He finished, involuntarily, "1988, Barry Levinson."

"If we want to get high, I could get us some," Treece offered, adding for the boys' benefit, "My dad's a lawyer."

Denis, incredulous: "Your *father* gives you pot?"

"Uh. *No.*" Treece huffed. "His *clients.*"

The prehistoric but cool song faded as a pretty pianissimo crossfaded up. *That* pretty pianissimo. All of the blood that hadn't coagulated in Denis's face drained out.

"I don't know how that song got in there," Denis dissembled. "Into that mix. I don't even know how I got it, must have been a compilation or something. Bonus track. Must be."

Beth was merciful. She signaled to Cammy, making walking fingers. Cammy shook off the sign. Beth gave a more adamant thumb jerk. Cammy sheepishly grabbed Treece's wrist and pulled her from the car. Rich joined them, glad to not be around when the first line of the song struck.

Beth, I hear you calling . . .

In the distance, Denis heard a chortle and a whinny.

THREE TEENAGERS WALKED after midnight down an isolated road known for its dungareed maniacs and zombie hookers. Rich, recognizing the sudden genre switch from raucous teen comedy to teen slasher pic, was a little jumpy. He reassured himself that either Cammy or Treece, probably Treece, would go first, and that as the comic relief he had a better than fifty percent chance of ending up being the killer, who might die, but only temporarily.

"Why are we walking?" Treece complained. "When I get my own car I'm never walking anywhere again. My dad was going to give me his old car but then Bitchtricia crashed hers."

"That's what you get for splitting up your parents."

"Mean, *mean.*" Treece turned to Rich. "Never admit your innermost fears to Cammy."

Rich didn't respond. He was preoccupied, toeing the middle of the road, eyes darting right to watch for plunging bloody pitchforks, darting left for oncoming bosomy corpses.

"I don't see what's so spooky," he said, affecting an air of unspookedness.

"They say the succubus Gwendolyn wanders in a white teddy," Cammy related a recent addition to the Tobacco Road canon, "looking for virgins to deflower and devour."

"Not *my* problemo," Rich lied. "Anyway, it's not like we're trapped in a house or on a boat or in the woods miles from civilization. There's all sorts of ways to run."

"Oh my god!" Treece gasped. *"Look!"*

Rich's feet left the ground. They made a jerky paddling motion as if trying to tread air. He landed off-kilter, and his "What?" came off less curious than craven.

Cammy indicated: "Cow."

Through the mist Rich could make out the silhouette of some creature, possibly a cow or a Hellbeast. It was about fifty feet off the road, standing in a meadow, increasing its cow chances.

"Let's tip it!" Treece was delighted with her own suggestion.

Rich tried to think if succubi could take cow form. Not in *Flesh for the Beast* (2003), or *Sorority Succubus Sisters* (1987), or *Necronomicon* (1968). There really weren't very many great succubus movies, Rich decided. He felt a sharp pain in his side.

It was Treece's elbow. "*Tip* it!" She pushed him toward the cow.

"Me? It was *your* idea."

"You're the guy."

"More or less," said Cammy.

"You know, these challenges to my sexuality are just *wrong*," Rich said, marching toward the cow.

DENIS WAS GETTING A GOOD LOOK at his lap.

Oh, Beth what can I do?

"Here," he told his crotch, "let me change it."

He fumbled in his pocket for his iPod. A hand pressed against his chest. He looked up. Beth was smiling at him.

"I was named after this song."

"You were named after a *Kiss* song?"

Beth fell back in her seat. "My parents were, you know, headbangers." She half-laughed. "Still are, kinda."

Denis's parents were normal kids who became normal adults with normal jobs. His father was an information systems analyst and his mother did freelance graphic design for progressive causes and products. So normal Denis had never given them much thought. But now Denis wondered what his life would be like with head-banging parents, being named for a song by a band who dressed in black-and-white face, spat blood, and whose other hits included "Lick It Up" and "Love Gun."

Beth was gazing through the windshield.

"I'm sorry," Denis said.

Beth sipped her beer. "Why?"

RICH HAD NOT NOTICED the barbed wire fence at first and this had caused a slight delay. He was now in the field, approaching the west face of the cow, not nearly fast enough.

"Go, go," Treece insisted. "Go!"

Rich turned around, tamping his hands as he stepped backward, "Don't . . . wake . . . the . . ."

PLORP.

Rich felt his shoe sinking into a thick mud that was not mud. It made a wet sucking sound, pulling his foot in deeper. He had stepped in quickshit.

He jerked his leg up. Balancing on one foot, he inspected the befouled area. It was bright yellow, the exact color of his socks. In horror, he looked down. The cow plop had swallowed the toe of his shoe and was methodically oozing up the tongue, threatening to breach the rim. He reached down to rescue it, lost footing, hopped and

SQUITT.

THERE SHE WAS, feet on the seat, arms around her knees, rocking back and forth, not at all in time to the music. Denis had something to say but decided to wait until the song was over in about twenty seconds.

"Beth," he said anyway. "I lied before. About this song. I mean, I wasn't expecting to be listening to it with anyone, you especially . . ."

Beth opened another beer. "Life's full of surprises."

"Not mine," Denis said. "Usually."

Beth turned off the car; the radio went silent. She swiveled toward Denis. She swigged her beer and perched the can on a kneecap.

She was staring into Denis's eyes, not saying

anything, but asking something. Denis didn't know what, and didn't care. He couldn't get enough of this eye-to-eye stuff.

And yet, just below Beth's eyes, her knees were ten inches apart.

It took all the willpower Denis possessed to not look up her skirt. *You've seen everything there is to see down there,* he told his visual cortex, *there's no need to—*

Hello.

spoke the panties.

Beth closed her knees without calling attention to Denis's pubic snooping. She smiled at him in a tentative way.

"So . . . why me?"

Denis had never considered this question, putting it on a very short list of unquestioned aspects of his universe. Beth Cooper was an axiom, an irreducible truth, like the sky being blue (though the latter is a more complex phenomenon, involving the differential scattering of electromagnetic radiation by particles with dimensions smaller than the wavelength of the radiation, as Denis exhaustively lectured Mrs. Anclade in the third grade). The choice of Beth Cooper was simple, and pure, and for Denis's purposes here, completely inexplicable.

"You?" he said after much too long a pause.

"Why not Claudia Confer? She's prettier than me, and a *lot* nicer."

"I don't think she's . . ." Denis began compiling a Beth Cooper vs. Claudia Confer Benchmark Comparison, but lacking sufficient data, he said the only thing that came to mind.

"I didn't sit behind Claudia Confer."

Beth laughed, dribbling beer onto her chin. She

wiped it off and licked her fingers. Denis decided that if reincarnation was real, through some heretofore undiscovered nonquantum mechanism, he would like to come back as one or more of Beth Cooper's fingers.

"You never even *talked* to me," Beth said.

"You didn't seem too interested." He stated a truth he had successfully repressed until now. "I'm surprised you even know who I am."

"I know who you are!"

Beth had two distinct memories of Denis Cooverman:

Denis, at a blackboard, finishing an equation. He turns around, his fly open, stars on his underpants; and

looking up Denis's nose as he says, "I love you, Beth Cooper."

Beth took a long slurp of beer. "How could I *not* know Denis Cooverman?"

RICH SCRAPED THE SIDES OF HIS SHOES along the grass as he approached the cow in anger. Earlier he had no beef with this specific cow, was merely going through the motions of tipping it. But now it had attacked him, indirectly, and it was going down.

The cow stood there, eyes closed, legs locked. This was the secret to tipping cows: they were fast asleep yet completely rigid. One push and they were sideways cows.

Rich positioned himself at mid-cow and placed his hands on its side about two feet apart. He pushed. The cow's belly gave slightly but its hooves remained firmly in the meadow. He shoved. The cow remained upright.

"Use your physics!" Treece advised from the sideline.

Rich repositioned his hands closer together, bent his head down, and put his back into it. He switched his feet back and forth, marching in place to gain a hold, and then running, his shoes spinning on the shit-slick grass.

He went down.

"Little help, ladies?"

CAMMY AND TREECE WERE LAUGHING at Denis again; he could hear their merriment in the wind. It was quiet in the car. Beth had stopped talking, the music wasn't playing, and Denis didn't know what to do. Before tonight, he had never spoken to Beth without her speaking to him first. He had had plenty to say, much of it well-rehearsed, but when the opportunity arose to say it, he had always *pussed out*, in Rich's helpful analysis. The lone exception had been graduation, and even then he had been careful not to look in her eyes, knowing that if she had seemed the slightest bit upset or saddened or repulsed by his declaration, his heart would have arrested and his face would have bounced off the lectern as he crumpled to the podium, dead. Or thrown up at the very least.

There were her eyes now, two delicious dog's breakfasts, watching him from behind a sixteen-ounce can of Pabst Blue Ribbon.

What was she thinking?

"What are you thinking?" Denis asked, cheating.

"Nothing."

Goddammit. That was all he had.

How could that be? Denis spoke nine languages, three of them real, had countless debate trophies (16), had won the Optimist Club's Oratorical Contest with a speech the judges had called the most pessimistic they had ever heard. Was there no romantic line, no conversation starter, no charming anecdote, no bon mot, no riddle or limerick he could pull out of his ass right now?

He swallowed some beer. And it came to him. Alcohol was amazing.

"We *did* talk," Denis said, arguing with something Beth had said nearly seven minutes earlier. "You borrowed a pencil once. You signed my yearbook."

Beth allowed the pencil, but "When did I sign your yearbook?"

Alcohol was a bastard, Denis realized. "Seventh grade."

"What'd I write?"

"I don't—"

"You remember."

He remembered:

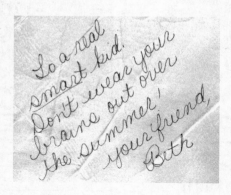

To a real smart kid.
Don't wear your brains out over the summer!
your friend,
Beth

Denis cringed as he recited it, and left off *your friend, Beth*, because it was already sufficiently pathetic.

Beth put down her beer. She reached out and touched Denis's shoulder. "I'm sorry I led you on."

Denis almost thanked her for the apology, but read her eyes, and laughed. So did she.

EIGHT MONTHS EARLIER...

SNNIFFFFF

SNAP!

This was going incredibly well. Denis was determined to keep it going until he figured out a way to destroy it.

"So, we can talk *now*. Here, how about: what are you doing after graduation? I'm going to, it's this six-year combined pre-med/med-school thing. After that I'm not sure if I want to practice or maybe do research . . ."

Beth retrieved her beer. "Hey, good luck with that."

"So, where are *you* going?"

"I dunno." She finished the can. "Maybe Harper's."
Offering credit courses in:
Applied Porcelain Sanitation;
Certified Dining Assistance;
Apparel Folding Science . . .

"Oh," Denis said. And: *"Yeah?"*

"Maybe. If I can afford it."

There, that wasn't so hard. It only took him thirty seconds. Not a record, but a solid effort. Denis couldn't determine what was worst, his dweebish braggadocio, Beth's disturbing educational plans, or that his condescending horror at them was so obvious.

"I have to pee." Beth got out, walked behind the car and squatted out of view.

Denis sat in the car, not sure of anything, only that he hated himself, and listened to her urinate.

TWO GIRLS AND A BOY lined up along the cow.

Treece sniffed. "Don't these things ever take a shower?"

"Sh," Rich hushed. "Okay, on four."

"Four?"

"You want to supervise this project?"

Cammy demurred.

"Then, on *four*."

Cammy was almost as bad as Denis, Rich thought. Almost. Denis was a real killjoy. He could construct a timeline between any idea and fatality. This had

prevented Rich from pursuing many intriguing no-
tions, such as sticking Alka-Seltzer up his butt (at
seven, Rich had never heard of an embolism, but Denis
made a convincing case against wanting one). Rich
chafed at Denis's brain ruining all their fun, and by
mutual agreement went to amusement parks without
him, but the doom-modeling had saved Rich's life on at
least five occasions:

the "Super Juice" made from Orange Powerade,
Batman Returns cereal, crushed Superman vitamins
and topped with Mr. Muscle oven cleaner (age 5);

the reenactment of the mining car chase from *Indiana Jones and the Temple of Doom* (age 9);

the *Harold and Maude* fake suicide reenactment
and sympathy ploy (age 14);

the bulk-up and get-revenge plan predicated on taking "steroids" supplied by Henry Giroux (age 16);

the April Fool's Day Columbine "gag" reenactment
(age 17).

Tipping a cow was less potentially deadly than any
of the above, but Denis's joy-killing might have proven
useful here.

"Uno, dos, tres, catorce!"

On *catorce*, they all began pushing and Cammy
muttered *quatro*. Had Denis been there, he would have
pointed out it was nearly impossible to tip a cow, for
the same reason Treece could not sleep on her stomach: ballast.

"This is stupid," Cammy grunted.

Denis would have agreed. Because, in addition to
the mechanical difficulties of overturning an under-
slung half-ton object, cows can't lock their legs and
they don't sleep standing up. This cow was just resting her eyes, and though she was laid-back, even for a
cow, she had come to the conclusion that these people
weren't going to go away by themselves. Her head
turned with remarkable swiftness, her muzzle close

enough to Rich's face that her whiskers tickled his lips when she screamed, *"Moo!"*

A HIDEOUS SOUND followed by a shriek disrupted absolutely nothing in the Cabriolet.

"What was *that?!*"

"Sounded like a cow," Beth said.

"A *cow?* That was no . . . ordinary cow."

Beth was deep into her fourth beer. "You're not afraid of cows, are you, Denis Cooverman?"

"Vaccaphobic?" Denis shook his head. "Of course not."

"Jesus fuck!" Rich sprinted out of the mist and hurdled into the backseat, winded. Cammy and Treece, falling over each other with throaty and nasal laughters, staggered up a few seconds later. Treece had to lean against the trunk with both hands to keep from passing out with amusement.

"What's wrong?" Denis asked.

"What's so funny?" Beth asked.

"Nothing's funny," Rich wailed. "A cow bit me!"

"Cows can't bite," Denis said. "They lack upper incisors."

Rich jabbed viciously at a fantastically large hickey on his neck. "Well, *this one fucking could*, Tiny Einstein!" He had never called Denis that in front of anyone else before.

Cammy traced a nail along Rich's throat. "It's just a love bite." She puckered her lips next to Rich's ear. *"Moo moo moo moo moo,"* she cooed.

"Hey," Rich said, "what if it was a mad cow?"

"She was pretty mad," Treece agreed.

Cammy gasped dramatically. "You're going to turn into a werecow." She glanced up and gasped again. "And it's a full moooooooon."

Rich turned to Denis, with need and regret.

"Now you want my expertise?"

"Yes. Please."

"There hasn't been a confirmed case of bovine spongiform encephalopathy in the United States for four years," Denis uploaded. "And even if this one did have mad cow disease, it can't be transmitted by biting, which cows can't do."

"You're useful," Treece said.

Beth's cute nostrils flared in an unpretty way. "What's that smell?"

Rich said nothing.

Cammy directed Beth's attention to the backseat. "He pooped his shoes."

Beth did not allow poop in her car. "Lose the shoes."

"These are my best shoes!"

"Well, now they're shit."

"I *paid* for these shoes!"

"They go," Beth said, "with *you* in them, or not."

Rich got out of the car. He shuffled to the side of the road, slipped off his shoes, and got back in the car. Treece and Cammy settled in around him.

"So!" bubbled Cammy, rubbing her palms together with camp perkiness. "And what have our head cheerleader and Tiny Einstein been up to?"

That didn't take her long, Denis noted. He didn't know she was saving *Dick Muncher and The Penis* for later. *What had they been up to?*

Were they connecting, opening up, sharing, in preparation for making out, or were they merely dancing around one another with Denis doing the herky-jerkoff?

"We were just—"

"Storytime!" Beth announced.

13.

SUBURBAN LEGENDS

HOW COME YOU DON'T HAVE ANY STORIES?
I'VE GOT LOTS OF THEM,
AND YOU DON'T HAVE ANY.

MICHELLE FLAHERTY

TREECE CLAPPED. She loved Storytime. Cammy smiled, too, in a slightly sinister way, Denis thought. Beth nestled her beer between crossed legs. She raised her hands, a call for silence. Her eyes widened. Her voice was soft but urgent.

"It was thirty-three years ago tonight . . ."

Treece began to sing,

Sweeeeeeet emohhhhhhtion

Cammy backed her on drums,

Dit-dit dah-dah dit-dit dah-dah

This was quite a production. Denis felt privileged they would go through all this trouble for him.

". . . on this very road," Beth continued. "A VW bus was parked in this exact spot."

Denis could see the bus. It bore a remarkable resemblance to the *Scooby Doo* Mystery Machine.

"It's a moonless night."

Denis killed the moon.

"Inside, this hippie and his chick . . ."

Denis had always identified with Velma, but took on the Shaggy role. He cast Beth as the hippie chick who stuck flowers in rifles in his Anti-American History class (its official name was "The History of Patriotic Dissent: Boston Tea Party to Kent State" and was taught by Ms. Calumet-Hobey, who probably should have worn a brassiere in the seventies).

". . . were smoking this humongous bong."

His seventies bong knowledge being limited, Denis improvised something psychedelic with a bright yellow smiley face on the bowl.

"The chick starts to tell this story . . ."

Hippie Beth spoke but Treece's voice came out.

"So, it was, like, the fifties, man."

Treece was the perfect hippie chick, but Denis was disconcerted at the sudden change in narrator.

Cammy and Beth sang,

One o'clock, two o'clock,
three o'clock rock . . .

This wasn't the first time the girls had told this story. Denis felt a little less special.

"And like, this, '57 T-Bird comes to a stop in this exact spot, dig?"

Denis questioned the use of *dig* but re-dressed his mental set. Big-finned coupe, sock-hop rock, and for some reason, the fifties were in black and white.

"And this dude, like, tells his lady he's out of gas . . ."

The biker jacket and ducktail looked good on Denis. Beth wore Chantilly lace and a ponytail all hanging down, with a light pink sweater and magenta poodle skirt. An ice cream soda with two straws sat between them in a historically inaccurate cup holder.

". . . and then he tries to get groovy."

Groovy was entirely the wrong word; at any rate, Denis was way ahead of her. His greaser doppelgän-ger took bobbysoxer Beth into his distressed leather arms and—

"She's not copacetic with that, and, like, bags him and tells him to go get gas . . ."

"Wait," Denis protested, "is this 'Hook Man' or 'Trippin' Hippies'? You're mixing up your urban leg-ends."

"Shut up," Beth said sweetly.

Denis shut up. In the backseat, Cammy and Treece quietly secured their seat belts. Rich didn't notice; he was mesmerized. It was like drama club, only the girls were popular and didn't cry all the time.

"So the chick is totally alone in the car . . ."

Totally an anachronism.

". . . and she, like, turns on the radio to keep her company."

Out of the radio came Cammy. "Hey all you cats and kitties," she growled in a truly remarkable impression that large-print readers will recognize as Wolfman Jack. "News flash, baby: a deranged killer with a hook for a hand has escaped from the local mental hospital!"

This was awfully elaborate, Denis thought; it must be a skit they did at cheerleading camp or something. Rich, meanwhile, was upgrading his opinion of Cammy.

"Now here's the Surfaris, y'all!"

Treece mimicked the deranged falsetto perfectly:

Yihahahaha hahahaha . . . Wipeout!

Okay, now it was just weird. Never mind the Surfaris didn't come along until the sixties . . .

Denis looked over at Beth. She was sitting forward, her hands on the wheel; the engine idled quietly.

"Just then," Beth picked up the narration, breaking the story-within-a-story structure, "there's a scratching at the door!"

Cammy did the scratching, quite effectively.

Didn't Beth turn off the car a few minutes before?

"The girl is so freaked out, she . . ."

Beth stepped on the gas.

THE CABRIOLET HAD EXCELLENT PICKUP. It helped that they were going downhill at a fifty-degree angle. The car plunged into the toxic haunted fog.

And then Beth shut off the headlights.

Denis heard himself scream. His teeth were clenched so tightly the scream was reverberating in his sinus cavity and coming out his nostrils, he hypothesized, and then realized the scream was coming from the radio.

We don't need no education . . .

There had been a family argument over whether to include this song in Denis's Commencement Mix. His mother felt it was bleak and arbitrarily antiauthoritarian; his father argued that Pink Floyd kicked major ass. A stupid dispute, Denis thought; this was the perfect song to die to.

We don't need no thought control . . .

The girls all shrieked as the convertible swooped through the dale of the hill and began rocketing up the next one. Rich shrieked, too, but clutched the broken seat-belt strap to his chest as if, well, his life did depend on it.

Denis had automatically fastened his seat belt when he climbed into the front seat and had never unfastened it. He was now trying to remember whether this Cabriolet came equipped with passenger-side airbags.

"BETH!" Denis shouted. "WHAT . . . *MODEL YEAR . . . IS THIS CAR?*"

She turned, hair in her face, lashing her eyes and nose.

"TO THE FUTURE!" she screamed.

Denis looked to the immediate future. Fog crashed against the windshield, scrambling in skittish rivulets to the corners. Visibility was zero. They were going to crash into whatever might be in front of them; for example, another car full of idiots. They were on a Highway to Hell, or Heaven, or the Endless Abyss that Denis's head and heart kept arguing about.

As if in answer to his ambivalent prayer, the mist swept away as the car climbed out of the ground cloud, and Denis saw they were headed straight for the moon. It loomed huge and yellow at the top of the hill, casting a cold shadowless light on the road before them. It was a small comfort that he would now be able to see what killed him.

All in all, it's just
another brick in the wall

Unlike most people his age, Denis did not feel the least bit immortal, and so did not enjoy impending death as much as the average teenager. Nor could he understand the appeal. He looked over at Beth. She had stopped singing. Her hair floated behind her. Her expression was neither happy nor sad. She blinked. A tear streamed sideways across her cheek. It was just the wind, Denis thought. After all, there were tears in his eyes, too.

All in all, you're just
another brick in the wall

BETH SWITCHED the headlights back on as the Cabriolet crested the hill, conveniently illuminating the car parked directly in their path.

She swerved.

The front of the convertible sailed clear but the end fishtailed. It careered into the parked car, screeching along its side. Beth slammed the wheel right and the Cabriolet whipsawed completely around. It skidded backward for about a hundred feet before coming to a stop.

We don't need no—

Beth killed the ignition. A high-pitched sound permeated the car. Denis's mouth was open slightly. He swallowed.

"Sorry. I was unaware I was . . . emitting that."

Beth pressed a finger into her eyebrow. "Denis Cooverman, please stop apologizing for being you." She turned to the backseat. "Anyone dead?"

Cammy was straightening her clothes and Treece was reapplying her lipstick. "Not yet," Cammy reported.

Rich clung to the belt. "Never been more alive." He tried to let go of the strap but could not.

Denis was palpating his abdomen for signs of internal bleeding when it occurred to him, "The airbags didn't go off."

"I sold those years ago."

"Isn't that illegal?"

"If it isn't, I got ripped off."

A metallic groan redirected Denis's attention through the windshield. It came from the car they had just hit, a late-model black Prius.

The crumpled rear door of the Prius whined open and a man backed out. He staggered, not because he was injured, but because his pants were around his ankles.

"Dad," Denis winced.

His mother emerged next, scooting into her slacks just slowly enough to reveal that while she could not abide her son socializing with a few small holes in his underpants, she had no problem, personally, going out in undergarments riven from stem to stern, and also that her insistence on naturalness in foods and fabrics did not extend to her pussy.

"Mom," Denis cringed.

"It could be worse," Treece said. "It could be *not* your mom."

Denis exhaled deeply. "I had a lovely time this evening," he addressed his friends, old and new. "But now I must die."

He started to unbuckle his seat belt. "You do not," Beth said, restarting the car, "want to talk to your dad when he's not wearing pants." She shifted into reverse and peeled out. The car's headlights disappeared into the mist as a thousand English schoolboys sang,

Hey, Teacher! Leave those kids alone!

"KIDS!"

Mr. C zipped his pants. "Goddamn kids!"

Mrs. C rubbed the back of his neck. "Still wish our son was more 'normal'?"

"Not if *that's* normal."

Mr. C got in the driver's seat and pressed the POWER button. The car made a long unfriendly beep.

"How could we be *out of gas?*"

14.

WHO'S SOIREE NOW?

MONEY REALLY MEANS NOTHING TO ME.
DO YOU THINK I'D TREAT MY PARENTS'
HOUSE THIS WAY IF IT DID?

STEFF MCKEE

VALLI WOOLLY LIVED in Duxbury Woods, an un-
wooded area that used to be part of Berkley Square
before a developer tore down a bunch of $300,000
homes and put up a bunch of $1.4 million mini-
estates in their place. Duxbury Woods out-fauxed all
the other local English countrysides—Devonshire,
Amberleigh, Manchester Green and even Canterbury
Fields—with an authentic British duck pond that had
to be constantly restocked with rare Aylesburys, on
account of their being quite loud and delicious. The
"private community" also adopted somebody's idea of
Her Majesty's address system; Valli Woolly's house
was located on Croydon-on-Duxbury, with no number,
just a name: Heathbriar. Thus, a letter addressed to:

VALERIE WOOLLY
"HEATHBRIAR" AT CROYDON-ON-DUXBURY
ARLINGTON HEIGHTS, IL 60004

got thrown in the undeliverable bin with the rest of
the irritating mail.

Beth circumnavigated the main Duxbury loop three
times, prompting two 911 calls, before locating the
Croydon tributary, marked only by a hand-painted
rock. Heathbriar was easy to find from there, being the
only tract mansion with all its lights on at 1 a.m. and
a valet parking kiosk in front.

Heathbriar was neo-Georgian, meaning it had red
brick on the front. It was otherwise a 6,000-square-foot
conglomeration of awful architectural ideas throughout
history executed in twenty-first-century Vulgarian;
chief among the offenses was a wall-to-wall, floor-to-
ceiling bay window that cantilevered out like a body-
builder who spent way too much time on his abs. The
steroidal terrarium was presently overpopulated with
high school students.

"Shit my panties," said Beth, dropping her keys close to the hand of a valet. She had never been to Valli's house, nor had anyone else in the car, nor had pretty much everybody already at the party. Valli was not much liked. This party wasn't designed to change that. It was designed to make all those people feel like poor morons.

"Weird," Rich said. "In the movies, the rich bitch is always the popular one."

"We're not in the movies," Cammy informed him.

"*I'm* popular, and *my* dad's rich," Treece said. "I mean, he has to hide it. From my mom. And Bitch-tricia. But he *has* to be rich. Some of his clients are *kingpins*. And *I'm* popular."

No one said anything, making Treece suspicious. "What are you trying to say, Cammy?"

"I didn't say anything."

"What are you trying to *not* say? That I'm not popular, or I'm not rich?"

DENIS STARED at Valli Woolly's house with a Denis look on his face.

"Maybe I should just wait out here," he said.

Cammy patted his head. "If she attacks, go for her throat. She'll be protecting the nose."

"*Cammy,*" Beth reprimanded. Her expression was hard to read. Her brow knitted and her lips curled up on one side and down of the other. "Denis Cooverman."

Denis figured out what it was: *affectionate frustration*. The kind a girl might have for a piddling puppy or a goofy boyfriend, annoying but still lovable.

Beth's head drifted in and out; she placed the heel of her palm against Denis's shoulder blade and put some weight on it. "Would you like me to take you home, Denis Cooverman?"

Oh, Denis refigured it out, *she's drunk.*

"I can walk. It's only a mile."

Beth jerked her hand away with a *whatever* flip. She pointed at Cammy and Treece, then pointed at Valli Woolly's house. "You know," she said over her shoulder, "she's probably pulling a train by now. She won't even know you're there." With that, she strutted up the walk, Cammy and Treece beside but also behind her. Her hips swayed in a wide irregular pattern. She stumbled, and Cammy caught her by the elbow. "Fucking bricks," Beth said, and went inside.

Denis watched through the bay window as the crowd greeted the appearance of the Trinity with cowering and hushed exchanges. A pack of guys swarmed over the girls, absorbed them into the partying mass, and they were gone.

Rich put an arm around Denis's shoulder. "We walking?"

"As long as we're here. What the F—"

They approached the party.

"So," Denis said, "Valli Woolly pulls trains."

"If you believe her blog."

Denis opened the door and was almost knocked down by the fun: the sound, light, heat of collapsing adolescence, boys and girls gone supernova, their last blast before sinking into the black hole of reality.

"Has it always been like this?" Denis wondered.

"Dude," Rich said, "we went to the wrong high school."

IT WAS LOUD. The entertainment for the evening was a black MacBook operated by Zooey Bananafish, an exotic-looking sophomore who claimed to be half Thai and half Cherokee (She was half Thai and half something, at any rate). Zooey charged $300 to bring her laptop to parties and press ▶. She was charging Valli an additional $300 because she didn't like her, and because Valli was insisting on a playlist that perversely only included songs with *friend* in the title. Right now Mr. Woolly's $45,000 MAXX Series 2 speakers wept as they faithfully reproduced the microdynamics of a wirelessly streamed crappy pirated mp3 of every twelve-year-old girl's favorite Queen song,

> *You're my best friend.*

This would be followed by Mariah Carey's "Anytime You Need a Friend," the Kelly Clarkson and Justin Guarini version of "That's What Friends Are For," the Rembrandts' "I'll Be There for You (Theme from *Friends*)," that Vitamin C song that wouldn't go away, several other dollops of sugar pop, and then finally, before she kicked everybody out, Fall Out Boy's "Champagne for My Real Friends, Real Pain for My Sham Friends."

Zooey wore softball-sized headphones, through which she was listening to Thelonious Monk.

IT WAS CROWDED. Of the 513 graduates in the class of 2007, 509 of them were in this house. (Luke and Matthew Andreesen were both in prison, on unrelated charges; Heather Lally was in labor; and Josh Bernstein thought he was at Valli Woolly's but was still at home, toasted.) In addition, there were a hundred or so graduating seniors from Adlai Stevenson and John Hersey High Schools, a few dozen BGHS juniors and underclassmen, and a handful of female eighth-graders who, unfortunately for Mike Bogar, did not look like eighth-graders. All of them were yelling to be heard over the music, which Zooey had started at 90 dBs and was increasing by one decibel every ten minutes. In about an hour, the people nearest the MAXX 2s would start falling down.

AND EVERYBODY WAS TOUCHING. Denis traced an epidemiological path from the foyer where he was, up the double-curved staircase teeming with intertwined limbs, and across the mammoth, two-story front room that held a writhing, sweaty beast with two hundred heads.

"This is a good way to get impetigo," Denis yelled to Rich.

"She invited *band* people," Rich shouted back. "She invited *mathletes—but not us!*"

Valli Woolly invited no one. She had disinvited just enough people ("I have to keep it small") for word to get around. She wanted everybody to be crashing, so that they would all feel unworthy and she could eject anyone at any time. She was that much of a bitch.

"Look," Rich yelled, "an ice bison."

From his disadvantage point, Denis could see only backs, shoulders and the occasional female head. He toed his way up the crowded staircase to get a better view. He wasn't interested in the ice bison.

The Woollys had spared no expense in lording their wealth over a bunch of teenagers. In front of the bay window was laid out a gratuitous buffet, offering top-dollar antipasti and crudités, chip, crackers and ethnic breads, along with dips, salsas and rémoulades that disconcertingly only came in BGHS school colors, orange and blue. Next to it was that ice bison, decorating a champagne fountain that had been spiked with green-apple-flavored vodka earlier in the evening by Scott Nigh. And adjacent to that was a pony keg, which was getting all the traffic.

"Your party was better," Rich yelled, and disappeared into the crowd.

BETH WAS EASY TO SPOT. Everybody in the room was oriented toward her, sort of orbiting her, radiating out in circles of diminishing popularity. Denis estimated he was in the Kuiper Belt, out there with Pluto, not even a planet anymore.

The innermost circle consisted of Treece and Cammy and seven guys Denis recognized from various locker-room towel-snappings. In most direct competition for Beth appeared to be Dave Bastable, all-state tight end and nerd tripper, and Seth Johansson, soccer star and deer killer. Beth had apparently forgiven Seth his vehicular Bambicide, judging from the way she was laughing at every goddamn stupid face he made. Dave would not be so easily cockblocked, however; as Beth finished one glass of fortified champagne, Dave was ready with another. Seth said something pithy or at least short, punctuating it with a simian grin, and Beth laughed and laughed. Dave left to get more alcohol.

Reality had returned to its usual programming.

DENIS SIGHED slowly and continuously until he was completely deflated. He felt not defeat, but release. He was philosophical: he had gotten more than he expected and, frankly, deserved. He had been straddled by Beth Cooper. He had spoken to her panties. He had been kissed on the cheek, patted on the head, talked to and laughed with. He had also been beaten with human bones, choked to near death, and crashed into his parents.

Denis had had two hours with Beth Cooper, and he should be simply grateful he had survived it.

With that epiphany all of Denis's systems went off high alert, his adrenals dropped to normal, and he at once felt exhausted, hungry and with a tremendous need to urinate.

He would pee, eat and sleep, in that order.

"Whup," a body said as it fell on him from above, escorting him through the air the four feet to the floor.

Denis was on his back, probably broken, and the body was on top of him. It was a big body and it smelled like beer, but also cherry and flowers and wintergreen. "Sor-ree," the body said and reared its head, redistributing its significant weight to Denis's bloated groin. "You 'kay?"

The body belonged to a big girl who Denis recognized as someone from the murky middle of his class, not smart or dumb, popular or pariah, or any category he could use to recall her name. He had seen her in the library. *Jane? Emily? Charlotte?*

"Hey," the Big Girl said, "you're that dork who gave that creepy speech!"

"I'd like you to get off of me."

"Please."

"Please."

"Woof!" the Big Girl barked and licked Denis's nose with a thick yeasty tongue, twirling the tip in one of his nostrils. She lumbered off him, pushing one hand, and the other, into his bladder to steady herself. By the time she was upright she had forgotten he was there and kicked him slightly in the kidney as she stumbled over him on her way to the pony keg.

Denis decided not to wait until the ambulance came and got up himself.

THE LAST BIG PARTY Denis attended had a bouncy house, in which Debbie Bauman had given him a bloody nose that lasted for three days. He stopped going to parties after that, around the same time he stopped being invited to them.

And yet, as he poked and prodded his way through this party, he felt oddly at home. More precisely, he felt like he was back in the halls of BGHS during passing period; he was in a hurry and nobody else was going anywhere. Life after high school was identical to high school, evidently; the people were the same, if slightly better dressed, arranged in the identical dyads, triads and quartets, all holding red cups. That was different. Yet for all their legendary powers, the red cups had done nothing to loosen the brackets of the teen taxonomy they had all lived inside since the sixth grade. No jock had his arm around any stoner, sharing a heretofore unknown common appreciation of *Hong Kong Fooey;* no hot chick was making over any mousy fat girl; no brainy nerd was heavily petting any popular cheerleader who had been won over by the depth and everlastingness of his love.

Denis chuckled at how naive he had been, up until three minutes ago, and was keenly reminded that laughter was not recommended on a full bladder. Feeling greater urinary urgency than he thought biologically possible, Denis staggered through his graduating class, more in his way than ever before, negotiating body obstacles and ignoring snippets of inanity begging rebuttal.

"When I get to college, I'm totally going off my meds." —Mike Barnathan

He squeezed by Eric Gallagan and Brett Pister, two future business administrators arguing over whether Valli's father made his money in commodities or derivatives (he owned fourteen KFCs) . . .

"Haven't decided. Either Electrical Engineering or Dance." —Jenny Blum

. . . sidestepped Eric's twin sister Julia, who was talking to Alicia Mitchell about the relative merits of Alicia's ninety-two-year-old Nana just dying already . . .

"I feel so old." —Chris Lamb

. . . frantically wriggled around an intransigent Goth brood, all of whom were mutely glowering and mentally dismembering every body at the party including each others' . . .

"Jesus. Stop talking about high school!" —Abigail Holstein

Denis finally saw an open door and, knowing he would pee in there whether it was a bathroom or not, dashed inside.

There was a toilet, which was nice if not strictly necessary. There was also, staring right at him, Valli Woolly.

SHE WAS EVERYWHERE. There were photos of Valli Woolly on the walls, small cameos of her cluttering the sink, and, above the toilet tank, a large oil painting done by Nelson Shanks, who did Princess Diana's official portrait, according to the *Philadelphia* magazine article that was framed just below it.

Denis stood before the painting and tried to urinate. He couldn't. Valli Woolly's eyes seemed to be following his penis. The pain, slightly past excruciating, only exacerbated the problem. His entire urogenital system was experiencing a fatal error; he would have to reboot. He closed his eyes and wiped away the image of Valli Woolly watching him pee. It was replaced by the image of Lady Di watching him pee. *This is just like that "Don't think about Pink Elephants" paradox,* Denis thought. And soon enough he was thinking of pink elephants and whizzing like one. It felt tremendous. It didn't sound right, though.

Denis opened his eyes and redirected the stream into the bowl. Fortunately, he hadn't hit any of the Valli Woollys. He would mop up later. He looked around the room, musing on whether turning your downstairs guest bathroom into a shrine to your daughter was an act of love or depraved parenting. Maybe both. The photodocumentation was unpleasantly complete:

Infant Valli sitting on a cloud dressed as an angel, nothing being cuter than a dead baby;

Toddler Valli, plump and happy right before being put on her first diet;

six-year-old Valli faking her first smile, commemo-
rating her tooth-losing debut, the missing chiclet en-
tombed in a separate mat;

assorted girl Vallis seemingly photographed to ac-
centuate her childhood nose, which mysteriously fell
off at summer camp when she was fourteen;

Sweet-and-Sour Sixteen Valli, shortly after breasts
miraculously appeared on her over Christmas break;

Malibu Valli, Paxil Valli, Hair-Extensions Valli, Cel-
exa Valli, Liposucked Valli, Stairmaster-Abusing Valli,
Ears-Pinned Valli;

Equestrian Valli, standing next to Spencer, her personal horse, his gigantic black schlong snaking up the
back of her jodhpurs . . .

That couldn't be right. Denis finished his business
and took the photograph down. The schlong was ana-
tomically incorrect and a recent addition, judging from
the stu𝒳 carefully inked into the corner of the frame.
Denis tried to rub the offending appendage off with
his thumb. Stuart Kramer only worked in permanent
marker, it seemed. Denis spat on Valli Woolly and
pressed harder. Imagining he was getting somewhere,
he placed the frame on the counter, spat twice, and
rubbed as hard as he could with the heel of his palm.
The glass cracked.

"Fine," Denis said aloud, "if that's the way you
want it." He wrapped a towel around his hand and
smashed the glass. He picked out the schlong shards
and tinkled them into the toilet. He then placed the
frame on the ground, as if it had fallen off the
wall.

Denis found it supremely ironic that he was doing
all this to protect Valli Woolly, after that vicious
whispering campaign she financed against him when
they both ran for student council vice president. He
uncovered the dirty trick when one of the hired lips

came up to him in the hall and said, "You know that Cooverman kid? My uncle's his doctor. Says he's got that disease where you don't have any pubes. That's why he doesn't go to gym." That her own henchmen didn't know who Denis was suggested Valli was wasting her money. Nevertheless, Denis assured his own defeat, over Rich's strenuous and colorful objections, by writing a letter to the *BG Charger* denying he had Kallmann's syndrome but arguing it shouldn't matter if he did as the presence or absence of pubic hair had no bearing on the duties of student council vice president, and that his gym attendance was not significantly below average. *Charger* editor Dana Musgrave illustrated Denis's impassioned defense with a photograph of a hairless micropenis she had found on the Internet. Dr. Henneman confiscated all copies of the paper, except for a dozen or so, which were enough. Denis and Valli subsequently lost by spectacular margins to Steph Wu, who handed out fortune cookies reading VOTE WU VP FOR STUDENT PROSPERITY.

DENIS WAS ON HIS KNEES, carefully arranging unmarked shards in a statistically likely scatter pattern on the floor, when he heard the door open behind him, then shut.

The smell of lunch meat and salad dressing permeated the bathroom.

"Good evening, Greg," Denis said without looking. He rose to his feet, his back still to the door. He sighed, and turned.

Greg Saloga's face was as large and red as it had ever been.

"Go ahead," Denis said. "If somebody's going to kill me tonight, it should be you. You've earned it."

Greg Saloga's lip spasmed with rage. His hands

reached for Denis's throat. They went past it. He dropped his big tomato head on Denis's shoulder and began to cry.

Denis's relationship with Greg Saloga was complicated. It had begun in the fifth grade, with threats and extortions, and had gotten physical in middle school. The usual bully-pantywaist dynamic. Then came high school. While other young thugs left behind the childish pleasures of brute violence and graduated to the more sophisticated sociopathologies of torment, terror and pain as theater (wedgies, swirlies, et al.), Greg Saloga did not have the mental toolbox for psychological abuse and could not understand the appeal of physical assaults designed to deliver more humiliation than pain. So he kept doing what he had been doing to Denis, figuring it was either him or small animals, and that led someplace bad. Denis wasn't happy with the stunted arrangement, but convinced himself that being Greg Saloga's punching bitch protected him from the state-of-the-art degradations that were visited upon Rich nearly every day. It didn't, but that's enabling for you.

And now Greg Saloga was bawling all over him, taking their relationship in a whole new sick direction.

"How did you know?" Greg Saloga wailed.

Denis reviewed the inner monologue he had attributed to this sorry mess on his shoulder:

"I am cruel and violent because I was unloved as a baby, or I was sexually abused or something."

Denis hoped it was the *something*. He wasn't prepared for either of the other conversations. What he didn't know was that Greg had already had those conversations with Becky Reese, his very special date for the evening. Over the past eleven hours Becky and Greg had shared ice cream and tears; Greg had admitted dark terrible things and Becky had assured him that he was still a good person and that he was loved. She would spring Jesus on him tomorrow.

And so, Greg Saloga was not looking to Denis for answers. He wanted forgiveness.

The blubbering went on for some time. Denis stood still, soaking up Greg Saloga's pain, a little afraid of what might happen if he tried to wrap it up. In the meantime, he concluded that Valli Woolly looked better with her old nose. It was very British royal family, a shame she lopped it off. Her new nose was too small for the available space, floating like a tiny sailboat in a sea of cheek.

After what in real time was less than two minutes, Greg Saloga lifted his head. He looked stricken. "Did I do that?" He reached tentatively for Denis's face, and pulled back, repulsed.

"No," Denis said. "An accident. Series of."

"Sometimes I don't remember doing it," Greg Saloga said.

"I'd have that looked at," Denis advised.

"Yeah," nodded Greg Saloga. "Can I call you? To talk about it?"

"Sure. Or maybe a trained professional would be better."

"Hug," Greg Saloga said. He hugged. "Hugging's good," he snuffled. Then he blew his nose on Denis's shirt.

Outside the bathroom, Greg Saloga checked to see if anyone had noticed them exit together. Satisfied no one had, he viciously twisted Denis's tit.

"Ahgg!" responded Denis.

"You're lucky I'm in a generous mood!" Greg Saloga yelled for the benefit of everyone, swaggering away.

Denis was ready to go home now. He would leave through the back, so as not to disturb the gang bacchanal Beth was no doubt hosting in the front room. *Wow,* Denis thought, he had gone from smitten to bitter in less than an hour; he was healing remarkably well.

THE KITCHEN was unnecessarily immense, as no one in the Woolly family ate anything with the exception of Mr. Woolly, and all he ate was scotch. It was done in Country Quaint, with lots of milk green and white cream slopped onto fresh-cut wood cabinets and floors that had been given "a story" by a guy named Tommy with a motorcycle chain. The endless counter space was covered with the asses of thirty party girls, dangling their legs like bait for the school of party boys who were rotating through the selection counterclockwise. It was less deafening back there, meaning the girls could understand the inane things the boys were saying to them. They didn't seem to care.

Denis wandered into a sales pitch Henry Giroux was giving two sophomore boys who were not yet onto Henry Giroux.

"You got any X?"

"What you wants is *f*-X," Henry Giroux said. "The *Effexor* be inhibitin' the reuptake *fo'real.*"

"How about acid? You got any acid?"

"The Ritz been known to cause some serious hallucinatin'."

"If you're into imagining insects and snakes crawling on you," Denis kibitzed.

"Whoa," the first sophomore said.

"How much?" inquired the second one.

GLANCING AROUND THE KITCHEN, not looking for Beth at all, Denis's eyes stumbled upon huge brown boob tops that to his amazement belonged to Divya

Gupta, his debating partner. She was across the room, wearing a party sari that was missing some essential drapings, accentuating her zaftigitty in a way that wool pants and white Oxford shirts never did. Her black hair was unbound from her skull and fell nearly to her waist. She was attended by two males, neither of them dweebs, who were obviously from another school and did not know her alter ego as Denis's studious but loose-lipped sidekick. So *this* was what those leibfrau-milching New Trier guys wanted, and not her negative constructive. Denis considered the proposition that while he had been off chasing an angel, the real woman for him was right in his own intermural backyard.

Their eyes met from across the room.

She gave him the finger.

"Let us vow to never again choose indulgence over excellence, whether it be getting sloppy drunk, revealing secrets and betraying our partner, or something else."

The wounds were still too fresh. He would try her again at Mr. Peterson's Declaration of Independence and Rebuttal barbecue in July. Denis continued toward the back door, pausing briefly to step on Angelika Steinke, who was on the floor playing a Sullen Girl original:

> *Sad Paper Mouse*
> *with Build-a-Bear Dreams*

"Sorry," Denis said.

"No, you aren't," Angelika whispered without missing a strum. She changed into a more depressing key and sang, apparently from the same song,

> *Our Vampire Feast*
> *Suck Me Suck You*

Denis didn't know how to argue with that, so he stepped over her.

DENIS WAS ALMOST TO THE DOOR when he noticed the phone. He should call, he thought, to spare
his parents the additional twenty minutes of anguish
it would take him to walk home, or better yet, get
them to come pick him up.

It went straight to message. (There were already several messages from neighbors wanting to know what
the hell was going on over there; and three from Denis's
mother, saying they were stranded on some old road on
account of his father always having to relive his glory
days, and where was her son, at which hospital?) "I
guess you're asleep," Denis said, *or still publicly forni-
cating and flashing vage,* he shuddered, "but I just
wanted you to know I'm on my way home, and . . . I
have an explanation and . . . I love you. See you soon, or
in the morning. Love you."

"*Le Coove!*"

Rich ambled across the kitchen, carrying two plates
heaped with nosh.

"Check it out," Rich yelled. "Pedophilia!"

Denis was still holding the phone. "There's no pedophilia here," he said quickly into the receiver and
hung up. "Where?"

In the pantry a compact balding man in pink polo
shirt and black warm-up pants had cornered Anna-
belle Leigh, technically now a sophomore. He was acting sophisticated and older-mannish, tossing a five-
pound bag of sugar from hand to hand.

"I always thought he was gay," Rich said.

"*Coach Raupp?*"

"The way he always watched to make sure we took
showers. Which just goes to show, my gaydar sucks
donkey dick."

Rich handed Denis one of his plates. It was filled
with all of Denis's favorite party foods, carefully ar-

rayed in the approximate order Denis would eat them.
It was like they were married.

"Thanks."

"Hey, did you know they call us 'Dick Muncher and
The Penis'?"

"I can't say I'm surprised."

"So, hey, ¿Dónde está Elizabeta?"

"Wherever." Denis folded some blue hummus into
his mouth to underline his ennui.

Rich swirled a bluish chicken wing in some orangey
honey mustard. "Told you that speech was a good
idea."

"What are you talking about? What that's happened tonight could possibly be construed as
'good'?"

"Closure, dude. If you hadn't given that speech,
you would've never found out what a scary whackjob
Beth Cooper was, so no other girl would ever measure
up to her mythic proportions, and the one you ended
up marrying because she got pregnant or your mom
was dying, she'd be haunted and tormented until she
had such low self-esteem she'd be willing to put on a
cheerleading outfit and a Beth Cooper mask just to get
some conjugal pipe."

"Do you write these things out or do they just *flow*
out of your ass?"

"Improvisation *is* writing."

"Well. She's not a scary whackjob." Then: "She's not
a whackjob."

"Don't backpedal, dude. Onward. ¡Vamanos! In fact,
your new unrequited obsession might be at this very
party. And speaking of, did you see Gupta?"

"She has lady parts, evidently."

"Talk about your hot and spicy curry coconuts!"

"Coconut curry is Thai, Rich, not Indian."

"I'll remember that the next time I have to write a
term paper about international boobs."

"Oh, no," Denis said.

Rich saw it, too, but his reaction was less dread than uncontainable glee.

"*Your secret shame!*"

PATTY KECK just happened to wander up, unconvincingly. She was with Victoria Smeltzer, or as she was known in the girls' locker room, Skeletori. Patty was wearing hip huggers and a belly shirt, neither of which was a good idea. Victoria had on a black shift and so much foundation it was disconcerting to see her upright.

"I didn't expect to find *you* here."

"Patty."

"I *loved* your speech, Denis," Victoria said. "You said some *very perceptive things.*"

Patty redirected her friend at Rich. "Richard, you know Victoria?"

"*Certanamente*," Rich said. "You've lost weight, Vick."

Victoria bared her see-through teeth. She bowed her head shyly, and noticed Rich's stocking feet. "You're not wearing shoes."

"Nobody wears shoes anymore," Rich said.

Victoria swooned, though it may have been her blood sugar.

"Denny," Patty said, using the special name Denis hated. "What happened to your poor face?"

Denis did not immediately answer. Patty, he knew from experience, did not require responses in order to keep a conversation going. Instead, he was thinking, *This is my rung.* This was where he was going to spend the rest of his life, in regrettable grapplings with women he was ashamed to be seen with, women who were his social and physical equals. Denis had dared to court the sun, and for this hubris he was hurtled back into the muck. He was the Icarus of love.

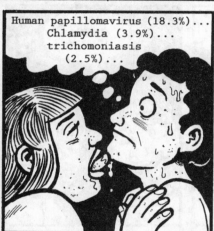

"—all purply and icky yellow," Patty was yammering. "Greg Saloga beat you up, I'll bet. Did you see him here with that wheelchair girl? What disease does she have again?"

Denis had a horrible thought: What if Patty Keck was it? What if hers was the only tongue ever to enter his mouth, rooting around like a dog with his head in a bucket of chicken? Or, what if Patty got that stomach stapling she always talked about, and it turned out she really would be cute if she lost forty pounds? That would be the end of him, most likely. Patty would move up to average-looking guys, and with Rich spending all his time with Skeletori over there, Denis would be alone.

"Valli Woolly *paid* someone to beat you up! Is that what happened?"

Patty paused, meaning Denis could speak now.

"Uh, no," Denis said, mentally sorting his accumulated wounds in correct chronological order. "First—"

"The Coove had a little dustup with Beth Cooper's boyfriend," Rich interjected.

Patty Keck's eyes slat. *"Beth Cooper."*

"Yeah," Rich casually falsified, "her ex-boyfriend, army, dark ops, couldn't stand the idea of Beth and the Coove together. So it came to blows. You think this is bad, you should see him."

Denis liked this scenario much better than the truth. "I feel terrible about it," he went along, shaking his head sadly. "He's at the hospital. I hope he makes it."

"Actually," Victoria said, "he's upstairs."

15.

THE DEAD KID

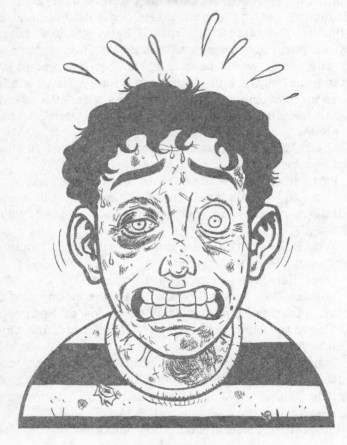

I THOUGHT THIS WAS
A PARTY! LET'S DANCE!

REN MCCORMICK

"WHOA, THE TIME!" Rich said, glancing at his bare wrist. "My female fiancée is getting off her shift, at Hooters, and we promised to meet her."

Denis was struggling with the back door. It was locked, dead-bolted, to prevent any of Valli's so-called friends from messing in her father's authentic English garden with its valuable antique gnomes.

Rich grabbed the back of Denis's shirt and yanked him in the other direction. Denis waved noncommittally as he was dragged away. "Nice seeing you."

"Me, too," Patty called after him.

THE FRONT DOOR TANTALIZED DENIS, three cliques ahead. He just needed to get past the French Clubettes, slurring the best French of their lives, some gearheads, not so surreptitiously casing the alarm system, and the mathletes who had made it just inside the door and stayed there. Denis could almost smell the safety of his home, of his bed, where he intended to spend the next ten weeks before leaving for Northwestern, where even the football players were his size.

Two large hands clamped his shoulders from behind, and spun him around.

"Will you remember me?"

It was the Big Girl, only she seemed bigger.

"I will remember *you*," she said, and then sang it,

I will remember you . . .

Then she remembered him, "Hey, you're that creepy dork who gave that creepy dork speech!"

Despite or perhaps because of this, the Big Girl cupped the back of Denis's head and mashed his face into hers, prying his mouth open with her strong, sinewy tongue. She pillaged his teeth and tonsils with a voracity that made Patty Keck's frenching seem coy.

Plus, there was suction. Denis once had a dream like this, involving Gardulla the Hutt, which did not end well. He tried to tear himself loose, but found that every move sucked him deeper inside her.

"Hwuwuw," Denis said.

Rich interceded, wedging a forearm between their necks and jimmying them apart. The Big Girl undocked with a wet pop, shook it off, and then fastened onto Rich. Rich grabbed her by the ears, and through a series of tugs and twists dislodged her. He steered her groping maw away and tossed it into the French Clubettes, where it lip-locked onto Elizabeth Nagle, who protested only momentarily.

ALL THAT STOOD between Denis and reaching adulthood was Ian Packer. Packer still had a wild hair up his butt about Denis's refusal to join in the mathletics program, which he felt had deprived him of a divisional championship. Denis declined participation because Packer made team members wear YEAH, I'M A MATHLETE T-shirts and even Denis had some status consciousness (named Rich). Packer contended the real reason was that Denis didn't have the r^3s to see who was the true Euclid of the class, Denis's barely more perfect SATs notwithstanding. So whenever the occasion arose, as it did now, he liked to hurl a fiery equation Denis's way.

"Riddle me this, Cooverman," Ian Packer said, blocking the front door. "If x is an integer—"

"Not now, Packer."

"Oh, come on, this should be easy, for the *valedictorian*."

"*Seven*, okay?"

Tragically for Ian Packer, the answer *was* seven. He stood aside.

Through the open door, Denis saw the rest of life. It

was dark, and getting chilly, but there was Rich, waiting for him on the porch.

A SCREAMING CAME ACROSS THE ROOM. It sounded inhuman, a car alarm or air raid siren, but very clear in its meaning.

"*Asshole!*"

The shriek was piercing enough to be heard throughout the house, even within the killzone of the MAXX 2s, even under the ear cups of Zooey Bananafish, who, sensing this party was finally happening, pushed ‖. The sudden loss of sound pressure popped ears across the room and created an aural vacuum; all anyone could hear was the persistent ringing they would be hearing for the next two or three weeks, if they were lucky.

Everybody looked to the staircase, the source of the scream. Valli Woolly stood about halfway down, in a stylish but easily accessible black tube dress. Lined up behind her on the steps were Kevin, Sean and the third Army Man.

Across the room, Cammy said what Beth was thinking.

"Choo choo."

Three and a half seconds later, Treece realized: "That bitch did our dates!"

DENIS COULD HAVE RUN AWAY. He could have crazy-legged it out of there, escaping under cover of ducks, humiliating himself in front of his entire class and for many classes to come. He could have done that. And he would have been happy to, but that bastard Ian Packer slammed the door on him.

Rich reopened the door just as Kevin's cavalry arrived, placing both him and Denis in elaborate and internationally unacceptable chokeholds.

Kevin took his time coming down the stairs. His fury had dissipated, having unleashed a good portion of it on a thirty-four-year-old male nurse who would not tell him where Beth was or explain why he had her cell phone. Nurse Angell had also begrudgingly supplied Kevin and his troops with a deluxe assortment of pills he'd been skimming off invalids and the elderly. Accordingly, Kevin moseyed up to Denis with his pain killed, mood elevated, and erectile function greatly enhanced.

"So . . ." Kevin grinned, his vocal molasses thickened into a treacly drawl, "we meet again."

Rich could not have been more delighted. "Blofeld in just about every Bond movie! Lon Chaney Jr. to Bela Lugosi in *Abbott and Costello meet Fr—*"

With a minor adjustment of his left index finger, Sean paralyzed Rich's windpipe. As if to further punish him, Kevin's next line was:

"Shall we dance?"

Using the reserve air left in his upper throat, Rich got out, "Jack Nicholson to Michael Keaton in—" before passing out. Annoyed, Sean disengaged his kill finger and shook the boy back into consciousness. Rich mumbled something incoherent, something like *urton.*

Denis had just thought of the perfect thing to say to Kevin, the thing that would keep everybody out of jail and the hospital, when Beth stepped between them. She had the saucy smirk and sloppy swagger of a person who thinks she has total command of a situation but really, really does not.

"Kevin. Stop this now." She raised a finger, but couldn't keep it stationary. "Let's just get you out of here"—she eyed Valli—"and get you tested for gonorrhea—"

Kevin took Beth's whole face in his hand. "Lisbee," he said, still quite friendly sounding, his thumb and forefinger digging into her temporomandibular joints. *"This isn't about you anymore."*

"Do you speak in *nothing* but clichés?" Denis blurted. (This wasn't the perfect thing he had been thinking of saying earlier.)

Kevin chuckled and roundhoused Denis in the abdomen, never letting go of Beth's face. Denis's arms were pinned back, preventing him from doubling over in pain but not the pain part, a sucking, searing, intensely special feeling that made Denis realize that he had never truly been punched in the stomach before, and that all the emotional setbacks he had previously compared to being-punched-in-the-stomach weren't all that bad.

"Oh, Denis," Beth said. This was the first time she had not used the affectionate yet trivializing *Denis Cooverman* construction, which Denis noted but did not dwell on, given more pressing matters.

"Promise," he said, "if he kills me, you'll break up with him."

Kevin placed a valet ticket in Beth's palm and squeezed her fingers around it. "Now why don't you get that pretty little drunken butt of yours in my vehicle," he gallantly ordered her. "And *sit* there."

Kevin moseyed off, signaling his soldiers to follow. They frog-marched Denis and Rich with them. Beth hung her head as Valli Woolly wiggled past.

"Gonorrhea?" Valli sniffed. "You *wish*."

ACTING ON PRIMAL INSTINCT, the partygoers pulled back to open a killing floor. Denis was dragged to the far end; Kevin assumed the lion position on the opposite side. Everyone politely awaited the bloodletting.

"Are you just gonna let this guy murder me?" Denis asked his classmates.

They were.

"Wait."

Valli Woolly wiggled over to Denis. She pushed into him, her breasts poking his chest, her nose stabbing at his face. Adenoids quivering, she hissy-whispered, "I am *not* worthless. Look at this party. Look at all my friends."

She smelled like masturbation.

Wiggling away, she waved regally and decreed, "Cause brain damage."

It was official. Denis was to be executed and no one would save him. Beth was gone, doing what she was told. Rich was seriously indisposed, and would be lucky to survive himself. Cammy and Treece were off to his right, Cammy with an expression that said, *This certainly is an awkward social situation,* and Treece mouthing, *Good luck.* Across the room, Patty Keck watched with worry and potato chips. Skeletori, beside her, snacked on no-fat fingernails. The Big Girl was holding hands with Elizabeth Nagle, wondering who the dead kid was. Ian Packer and his fellow mathletes lined the staircase, at a safe distance should the proceedings devolve into a wider geek beatdown. To Denis's left, a few rows back, Divya Gupta sat on the shoulders of two Stevenson gymnasts. Denis had never seen her smile before.

Valli Woolly's party had accomplished something. She wasn't the least popular person in the class anymore. Her parents would be so prou—

Valli Woolly's parents! Surely Mrs. Woolly wouldn't want Denis's common blood all over her Ethan Allen furnishings; Mr. Woolly wouldn't want Denis's skull smashed repeatedly into his thirteen-inch woofers and titanium dome tweeters.

"Help!" Denis yelled. *"Adults!"*

He'd have to yell louder than that. Mr. and Mrs. Woolly were at their condo in Cabo. Adult supervision had been left to Valli's twenty-three-year-old

brother, Willie, who had taken his heroin for the evening and was in his bed passively participating in a
threesome with Ryan Petrovic and Lucy Amo, who
only discovered Willie after they were already deep
into the proceedings, and were using him mostly for
leverage.

Denis's call for adult help broke the tension. Everybody had a good laugh, especially Kevin, who kept
laughing as he started toward Denis.

Denis's military escort shoved him into the killing
zone.

"YO!"

DENIS KNEW THAT YO! He hated that *Yo!* He was so
happy to hear that *Yo!*

Coach Raupp muscled his way onto the killing
floor, man-walked up between the predator and his
prey and placed a smallish hand on each of their
chests.

"Okay, ladies, some ground rules . . ."

"Wait," Denis said. "You're not going to *stop* it?"

"All I want is a fair fight."

"Fair? He's a *trained killer!*"

"You should've thought of that before you raided
his cabbage patch." Coach Raupp pistol-pointed as he
said it. "Don't worry, Cooverman. Just remember what
I taught you in boxing."

"I opted out of that unit!" Denis protested. "*I had a
note!*"

Coach Raupp addressed to the crowd: "Let that be
a lesson to you juniors." Then to the combatants: "No
biting, scratching, hair-pulling, any other sissy business . . ."

"Head butting?" inquired Kevin.

"Go crazy. But once your opponent loses consciousness, the beating is over."

Coach Raupp stepped back, raising a hand.

"Aaaannnnd . . . *fight!*"

Kevin presented his fists, knuckles out. He hopped up and down, scissoring his legs back and forth, thrusting out his lower lip.

"Shall we dance?" he repeated for the benefit of those who had not heard him the first time.

The crowd loved it, at Denis's expense, as usual.

Kevin didn't seem very serious about killing Denis, not as much as he wanted to make the slaying fun to watch. Denis, unaware of the change in Kevin's pharmaceutical status, found this chipper villainy oddly disturbing, though not nearly as disconcerting as his opponent's rather noticeable hard-on.

"*Yo!*" Coach Raupp snapped his fingers in Denis's agog eyes. "Dukes up, Cooverman!"

Denis kept his dukes down.

"I'm not going to fight."

"Are you shitting me?!" Coach Raupp screamed, his nipples like cleats.

"Violence isn't going to solve this."

"That's pussy talk, Cooverman!" the Coach explained. He puckered his lips and made a series of wet sucking sounds. "The call of the *PUH-say!*"

Denis knew he was a pussy. A pussy with a *plan.*

"Look, Kevin," he began, with the studied reasonability that had won him many worthless debate trophies. "You've won. You got the girl. I've been humiliated in front of all of my peers. I apologize and surrender unconditionally. Is that satisfactory?"

Kevin punched Denis in the mouth.

HE DIDN'T RECALL FALLING, but warm liquid had collected in the back of his throat, leading Denis to conclude he was supine. He swallowed and was slightly surprised to taste blood. He ran his tongue along the inner rims of his teeth. None was outright missing but two incisors on the upper left were loose. That side of his face burned and stung and ached and felt wet and sticky.

Denis opened his eyes. Zooey Bananafish was staring upside down at him.

"Any last requests?"

" 'Here She Comes' by Very Sad Boy."

Zooey's head exited and was replaced with a right-side-up Kevin face.

"Upsie," Kevin's face said.

"I'm bleeding. Happy *now?*"

In answer, Kevin reached down, took Denis by the shirt, and lifted him to his feet and two inches farther, dangling him on tiptoes. Adding insult to impending injury, Zooey Bananafish had overruled his last song request, replacing the downbeat dirge with some uptempo sino-blaxploitation. Kevin seemed to approve, pursing his lips with white-boy negritude and bopping Denis up and down to the beat.

" 'Battle Without Honor or Humanity,' Tomoyasu Hotei," Rich explained to Sean, "originally used in *Shin Jingi Naki Tatakai*, 2000, Junji Sakamoto, recycled in the chop-socky pastiche *Kill Bill, Volume One*, 2003, Mister Quentin Tarantino."

"Fuckin' A," Sean agreed.

Kevin continued to shake Denis like a maraca, apparently waiting to pummel him at the upcoming horn break. This was beyond embarrassing. It was sorry enough to be beaten to the delight of your peers; to be made to perform meat puppetry as your own premurder entertainment was at the very least unsporting.

"I am not your plaything!" Denis said, all pissy insistence. "Hit me or put me down!"

"Glad to oblige." Kevin cocked his fist.

Then, as is often the case with carefully planned military operations, something huge jumped on Kevin's back.

"Leave my friend alone!" Greg Saloga yelled, latching on to Kevin's eyebrow ridges and yanking hard. Kevin let go of Denis and staggered backward, spinning and stumbling as the big red boy clawed his face and throat. The third Army Man stepped in, and in a flurry of expert hand combat mixed liberally with playground flailing, disengaged Greg Saloga and secured his arms. This annoyed Greg Saloga. He screamed and threw his head back, butting his captor's eyes. The soldier fell to the carpet.

Sean released Rich and grabbed a crystal ladle from the champagne fountain. He swung it at Greg Saloga, who allowed the leaded glass cudgel to shatter harmlessly on his temple. Greg Saloga then harmfully kicked Sean in the testicles. Sean went down.

Coach Raupp stormed over to Greg Saloga.

"Yo, *time out,* Saloga—"

Greg Saloga punched Coach Raupp in the throat. He went down.

Kevin, in villain tradition, had stood back and watched his henchmen vanquished like henchmice. With the seething hulk of Greg Saloga now facing him directly, Kevin had the option of fighting this obviously less skilled and now exhausted boy, or honoring the other villain tradition and running away. Kevin began to edge back toward the door. There was no need. Greg Saloga glanced at the inert and writhing bodies around him and fell to his knees, letting out the most primal wail anyone had heard in a couple hundred thousand years. He covered his face and screamed into his hands, "Why must I . . . *hurt?*"

An electric whirr preceded Becky Reese as she maneuvered her wheelchair through the crowd and motored over to Greg Saloga. He grasped both wheels and dropped his terrible head into her withered lap. He sobbed, and she stroked his greasy hair, for wasn't he also one of God's creatures after all? And the only boy in the entire class who had ever voluntarily talked to her?

Everyone had forgotten about the execution of Denis Cooverman, and were caught up in the heartrending saga of borderline retarded Greg Saloga and his repulsive love for the genetically defective Becky Something, until Greg Saloga looked up and screamed, *"Stop looking at us!"*

Everybody stopped looking at them, and turned back to . . . *Denis?*

Kevin himself was surveilling the perimeter for his missing plaything:

Rich was at the champagne fountain, rubbing his raw neck on the ice bison . . .

some kid . . .

Cammy staring back with light contempt . . .

Treece with vacant evasiveness . . .

another kid . . .

nice tits . . .

Valli with a needy grin . . .

"Yeeuh! Stop breathing up my skirt!"

Kevin ratcheted back to Treece. She stepped sideways, swatting behind her, revealing Denis crouched there, breathing up her skirt.

Denis reflexively went back into debate mode. "Kevin, let's assess." The swollen lower lip and blood dripping off his chin undermined his rhetorical authority to some extent. "It appears as if I'm gonna require major dental work, which I think we can agree was your *ultimate* goal . . ."

Kevin did not agree. He started coming for Denis, and he wasn't laughing anymore.

Another huge something jumped on his back. This time it was the Big Girl. She was not trying to save Denis. She just thought it was a party game.

"Wooo!" she whooped, riding Kevin. "Wooooooo!"

From there it degenerated quickly. Assorted skirmishes, some four years coming, broke out. Eric Gallagan and Brett Pister mixed it up over their junior year Young Trump project, which failed because Gallagan used too much peanut butter or because Pister couldn't market fresh assholes at a homo convention. Jon Eggert had always wanted to punch someone and thought this the ideal cover; unfortunately he chose Aaron Farrington, who had just completed his black belt in Kuen-Do and had been looking for an ethically acceptable situation in which to use it. The gearheads started peeling the Mathletes off the stairs, one at a time.

"Yeeee-ha!" the Big Girl yelled in response to Kevin hurling himself backward into a wall in an attempt to dislodge her.

Stuart Kramer tried to get a food fight going, first by chanting "Food fight! Food fight!" and then by flinging a couple of fistfuls of corn relish around, but nobody took up the challenge, perhaps because once a class clown graduates, he loses all his power to amuse. Valli Woolly emerged from the bathroom, shrieking, "Which one of you degenerates pissed all over the floor in there?!"

In the midst of all this, Denis made his escape. He skirted along the buffet table toward the door, dodging assorted scuffles and avoiding anybody he might have referenced in his valediction. He had gone as far as antipasti, just flatbreads from the door, when he heard a monstrous bellow that seemed to be directed at him.

It was Kevin, of course. He lumbered under the Big Girl, lurching toward Denis, lunging with arms outstretched in the manner of classic monsters and zombies. Denis responded with a classic silent scream.

And that's when the front of Valli Woolly's house exploded.

THE INITIAL BLAST CAME from behind the buffet table, which upended in rather dramatic fashion, sending chip shrapnel across the room and spraying dips and salsas in less dynamic but more devastating arcs. Denis took a platter in the chest. The two-story bay window blew out at ground level, with the upper panes raining down in a cascading shatter of glass. All this was accompanied by the requisite screaming, shrieking, and religious conversion.

Everyone thought: terrorists. Because, really, what else was there to worry about? Valli Woolly immediately suspected those animal rights losers who wore bloody chicken suits in front of her father's restaurants, and, being Valli Woolly, was annoyed they would firebomb her party and not one of her father's boring business dinners.

It was a few moments before anyone noticed the large repurposed military vehicle sitting halfway in the living room.

"Go go *go* go go," Beth Cooper called urgently from the Hummer.

Kevin stopped bucking the Big Girl and simply gaped. The Big Girl swayed. "I wanna get down," she said, and threw up on Kevin's head.

Denis couldn't see what was going on, because his face had been blown off. Cold chunks of cheek or forehead flaps hung over his eyes, assuming there were still eyes under there. Denis thought about changing his specialization from neurosurgery to facial reconstruction, though it just occurred to him that the wet stuff on his hair might be brains.

"DENIS COOVERMAN."

It was a female voice, but booming, echoing from on high. An angel. *Shit.*

As Denis turned toward his celestial escort, the pieces of his face fell away and into his hands: roasted red pepper and hot *sopressata.* That would explain the smell.

"Final boarding call for Denis Cooverman," Beth announced through the Hummer's external speakers.

Denis shook off his imagined injuries and started toward the Hummer, picking his way through the party carnage.

Something grabbed his ankle.

It was Coach Raupp, lying on the floor, holding his throat.

"Don't get in the car with her," he rasped.

This was excellent advice. However, Denis noticed some movement at his back, which he correctly suspected was Kevin. He yanked his ankle away and ran to the vehicle, its front wheels already spinning in reverse, spitting orange and blue hummus on everyone and everything. Denis only had one foot inside when the Hummer lurched out of the living room and onto the lawn with Denis suspended between the front seat and the swinging door. Treece and Rich pulled him inside as the Hummer crashed through the valet stand, killing no valets, and then roared through Duxbury Woods, upsetting the expensive ducks.

CELL PHONES FLIPPED OPEN throughout Valli Woolly's house. "Can you come get me?" a sophomore asked her mother. "Party ended early."

Kevin, covered in puke and defeat, couldn't believe it: that little shit had his girl *and* his car. Until that moment Kevin had been just playing, in his fashion. He was merely pretending to kill Denis, and was only going to continue killing him until Denis became convinced he was genuinely being killed, and then stop. This was Kevin's idea of a funny joke.

He wasn't in a joking mood anymore.

Kevin didn't even feel Valli Woolly beating him on the back, and he couldn't hear her screaming, "You ruined it! You ruined everything! I can't believe I gave you a blumpkin!"

Jacob Beber, bystanding, looked confused.

"Oh," Valli Woolly shrieked at him, "go Google it!"

16.

HOT NOSTALGIA

ALL I'M SAYING IS THAT IF I EVER START
REFERRING TO THESE AS THE BEST YEARS
OF MY LIFE—REMIND ME TO KILL MYSELF.

RANDALL "PINK" FLOYD

THE MOOD INSIDE THE HUMMER was mixed.

Beth was pumped up, drumming the steering wheel to some song playing only in her head. *"Wow!"* she kept repeating, with increasing insistence. *"WOW!"*

"Yeah," Cammy said flatly. "Wow."

"Was that not the coolest thing you ever saw?"

"It was very realistic," Treece said.

Rich was ambivalent. While the practical side of him recognized that driving a car into somebody's living room was going to attract a bunch of negative attention, his artistic side felt the movie of his life finally had the kind of action sequence that would make for a kick-ass trailer. "Great production value," he said.

Denis was pumped, too, but not up. *"Do you know how many laws you just broke?"*

By Denis's count:

Grand Theft Auto;

Criminal Destruction of Property;

Assault with a Deadly Weapon;

Aggravated Battery;

Leaving the Scene of an Accident;

Speeding; and, just now,

Failure to Signal.

"Seven—*at least!*"

"A new record!" Beth declared.

"I don't think that's a record," Treece said.

Denis took a closer look at Beth. Her eyes were bloodshot, rheumy. The tip of her nose was cute, and pink.

"Are you intoxicated?"

"Eight!"

Beth took her hands off the steering wheel.

"What are you doing?"

Beth crossed her arms. "I'm too drunk to drive."

The Hummer went through a red light.

"Nine!"

Denis took the wheel and successfully kept them from crashing into oncoming traffic, had there been any at two a.m., but in his zeal to survive he pulled too far to the right and started riding the curb. Beth grabbed the wheel back, swung the Hummer off the curb and into the relative safety of the left side of the road. "Where did *you* learn to drive?" she mocked.

"You're on the wrong side of the road."

"How do you know we're not in Europe?"

"*Please* drive on the other side," Denis pleaded.

"Beth, stop being a twat," Cammy added from the back.

Beth harrumphed and swerved the Hummer back into its lane, where it *baWHUMPed* over something large.

"*Good call*, Denis Cooverman."

Treece glanced out the rear window, and delivered the good news: "It wasn't wearing clothing."

"Beth." Denis tried to sound calm and authoritative. "I think it would best if you pulled over."

"Fuck you." Beth didn't respond well to calm authority figures. "How about, *Thank you, Beth. For saving my life . . . again?*"

Denis had imagined that he and Beth would be one of those couples who never quarreled, that when they weren't kissing they would be laughing or lying in each other's arms, serenely, deliriously happy. He could never have imagined that she would make him so crazy angry he would scream at her in front of their friends. But in that instant, he learned a little about love.

"Saving my life?!" Denis screamed at Beth in front of their friends. "*Saving my—?* You almost ran me over with a military vehicle, owned by that homicidal rage ape you call a boyfriend who has thus far this evening attempted my murder with: 1) a hurtled microwave, 2) playground strangulation and 3) well, a beating . . . a *to-the-death* beating!"

Denis's cathartic breakthrough left Beth miffed. "You're spitting blood on me."

"You're supposed to keep your bodily fluids to your-self!" Treece admonished.

Denis dutifully covered his mouth but continued venting. "You know what? This is not fun anymore!"

Beth, so calmly: "Who said it was supposed to be fun?"

Denis shrunk back to himself.

"You forgot the skeleton attack," Rich pointed out.

"We missed that," Cammy said.

"It was pretty cool. Like *Karate Kid* meets *Pirates of the Caribbean*."

"So," Treece addressed Rich, "you were making out with E. J."

"Who?"

"E. J. Charlotte? The best girls' basketball player in the country maybe? Big girl?"

"Her," Rich said. "I wasn't making out with her."

"It sure looked like you were making out. Denis, too."

"What are you, like a blogger now?"

"I just thought it was interesting. I mean, it was like, *almost* heterosexual."

"Yeah, that's right," Rich said, overdoing the sar-casm. "I'm trying to work my way back. When I'm ready for a real woman, I'll let you know."

"Okay," Treece said.

"MUSIC!" BETH DECIDED.

She turned on the radio, predictably tuned to US 99.5, America's Country Station, this month heavily rotating Sgt. Dirk Dugan's post-*Idol* debut:

> *Can't come home*
> *Until we're done*

'Cuz, baby, you know me
I don't cut and run

Beth fiddled with the dial. "87.1, yeah?"
"Yeah," Denis mumbled, resenting Beth for ignoring his outburst and rebuking himself for not following through on it, and for outbursting in the first place.
Beth caught the tail end of Cheyenne Kimball's cover of Chrissie Hynde's version of an old Rod Stewart hit, based on a song by Jakob Dylan's dad:

May you stay
forever young . . .

Beth liked the first three chords of the next song, or felt the need for noise, and cranked the Hummer with the petulant guitars and angsty beat of Happy Talk and their hot new power bummer, "Passing Through."

All these years and I'm alive
This town does her killing slow

Amid the emo cacophony, it got very quiet. They were driving down Dundee Road, which for the want of an actual downtown served as the main drag, a strip of malls, of chains and franchises, that collectively constituted what they conceptualized as their *town,* or to be municipally correct, *village.**

Takes you to her drying breast,
suckle sucks and won't let go,

Everything was closed but all the lights were on. The music and the hour and the drink made for a melancholy parade through their adolescence.
There was the Jewel-Osco where checker Cammy staved off workplace rage by mentally totaling the items she swiped endlessly across useless scanners,

*Incorporated 1958.

where Beth bought the family groceries, where Rich shoplifted his first *Premiere* magazine.

There was the José O'Foodle's Rich got fired from, where Beth, Cammy and Treece went after basketball games and thirty-year-old guys with mustaches bought them ice-cream drinks, where Denis begged his mother not to picket the Szechuan Veal Stickers.

There was the AMC Loews Six where Denis and Rich saw *Star Wars I, II* and *III* at crowded midnight previews, where they saw *The League of Extraordinary Gentlemen* by themselves, where Cammy saw *Bring It On* in the sixth grade and inexplicably decided to become a cheerleader, where Treece was caught sharing a seat with a patron and got fired.

There was the old Starbucks, where they all acquired their first addiction.

That Curves used to be Comics & Comix, where Denis bought his comics and everybody else bought their paraphernalia. Next to Curves was a Baskin-Robbins where Mrs. Rama fired you if you gained more than ten pounds and where Rich worked the summer between eighth grade and high school after Mrs. Rama ran out of thirteen-year-old girls.

> *I was born here,*
> *I won't die here too*

On the left was the PJ Fingerlings Rich got fired from, and where Treece lost her virginity, out back. Next to it was the Blockbuster where Rich still worked, at least until the next time he talked a divorced father into watching *Sin City* with his twelve-year-old son. In the same strip was Payless Shoes, where Beth worked thirty-five hours a week, where Rich had bought his best shoes, currently composting at the side of Old Tobacco Road, and where Denis went shoe shopping more than necessary.

And just up the road was the White Hen Pantry where only three BGHS students were allowed in at a time, supposedly, and where Beth Cooper touched that guy's dick.

I'm not stayin',
I'm just passin' through

Denis had included this song based on its popularity and adherence to theme, but he didn't like it—*drying breast? suckle sucks?*—and moreover didn't understand it, couldn't grasp the desperate desire to escape your upbringing, to kick off the dust of crummy towns that rip the bones off your back.

Why would you want to leave, and if you did, what's stopping you?

Beth turned off the music.

"WE ARE THE BISON!"

They were passing the high school, and Beth was cheering, and clapping, and not holding the steering wheel again.

Mighty, Mighty Bison
Say hey-hey, hey-hey . . .

Maybe she really is a scary psychobitch, Denis thought, as he found himself screaming again.

"*Put your hands on the steering wheel!*"

Beth stopped cheering. She stared ahead sullenly and put her hands in her lap.

"Never take your hands off the steering wheel!" Denis screamed. "You *never* take your hands off the steering wheel! You keep your hands at ten and two! *Ten and two!*"

Denis took Beth's hands from her lap and applied them to the wheel in the proper configuration.

"*Ten* . . . and *two*," he said in a tone that even he recognized as patronizing.

Beth gripped the wheel tightly, elevating her dainty wrists, and turned to Denis with a wide, iced smile.

"Better?"

"Eyes on the road."

Still looking at Denis, Beth executed an acute left, using proper hand-over-hand technique, at a speed that would have rolled over anything short of a tank, which was more or less what she was driving. As fortune would further have it, where she turned there was also an exit.

The Hummer pulled into Buffalo Grove High School's parking lot. Beth accelerated straight toward the school, all the while maintaining approved driving form. A few seconds before they would vault the curb and crash into the gymnasium, making the national news, Beth applied the brake aggressively, stopping with a satisfying skid, an inch from the sidewalk.

Denis was gripping the door handle with one hand and the chest strap of his seat belt with the other, a fairly typical pose for someone riding shotgun with Beth Cooper.

Beth, cordial: "You requested that I pull over?"

"Thank you," Denis said.

Beth opened her door and dismounted the vehicle. She began running toward the back entrance to the school. Cammy and Treece got out on their respective sides, and ran after her.

"What are they doing?"

"Something," Rich said, and jumped out to join them.

Denis did not like not knowing what he was doing, which he had already had quite enough of this evening. But, the alternative was staying in a stolen vehicle owned by a drug-addled maniac who had thrice attempted his murder. He arrived at the door just as Beth reached into her purse and produced a large brass master, the kind usually only found on janitors.

"You have a key?"

Treece answered for Beth. "Head cheerleader is a position of trust and responsibility."

"Fools," Cammy added.

DENIS WAS IN THAT DREAM, the one he would continue to have for the next thirty years: wandering through Buffalo Grove High School at night, everything the same and oddly off, comforting and disconcerting, a feeling that he needed to be here and didn't belong, that he had forgotten to prepare for *something*. At least, in the present version, he was wearing pants.

"Could I ask what we're doing here?" he asked Beth.

"Homecoming."

"At the risk of repeating myself and continuing to aggravate you, which is not my intention at all, you do know this is pretty illegal."

Perhaps it was his tone, polite and petrified, that softened her, or perhaps she had slipped into a more mellow state of inebriation, but Beth gave him those *poor puppy* eyes again. "Denis Cooverman. This is the *least* illegal thing we've done all night. Relax. You're going to enjoy it."

She winked at him.

While he processed that massive emotional data dump, Beth and the others disappeared into the gymnasium.

THE GYM WAS HALF LIT, dusky and cool. The chairs from graduation were stacked on rolling carts, a few orange tassels scattered on the floor. The podium was still up. Denis wondered, if he had it all to do over again, knowing all the injuries and indignities that would befall him, would he still give that speech?

"Ready?"

Beth stood at center court, legs apart, arms akimbo.

Yes, he would, *yes*.

"Hit it!"

Beth, Cammy and Treece began to cheer.

> *Are you ready?*
> *Ready for the best?*
> *B-G Number One!*
> *Oh yeah, nothing less!*

Rich joined the girls. His moves were suspiciously perfect.

> *Going to the top*
> *We can't be stopped*
> *Let's go girls,*
> *Yell orange . . .*

They all stopped and looked to Denis. He was the crowd, apparently. He played along: "Orange."

> *Yell blue!*

He yelled: "Blue!"

> *Mighty Bisons (oh yeah)*
> *Let's fight!*

Denis wasn't especially spirited or overly true to his school, but he choked up, a little. He would miss those basketball games, with those players whoever they were, winning or losing or whatever they did, and with Beth, there on the court and on the sidelines, smiling and jumping and, yes, bouncing. And he would never forget tonight, when she cheered one last time, just for him. That last part wasn't true, and he sort of knew it, but if you can't lie to yourself, who can you lie to?

The cheer, for whoever it was, wasn't finished.

"And now," Beth said, *"real slow."*

Cammy and Treece decelerated sensuously. It was as if the imaginary marching band accompanying them had vanished and been replaced by a seedy jazz quartet.

"Can you feel it?" Beth cooed.

"What?" co-cooed Cammy and Treece.

"Feel the *heat.*"

The girls bumped and ground in a not-for-game-day version of the cheer, the one they did at camp, or sometimes for a small audience of generous dates. Rich was thrown at first, but quickly got with the saucy program.

"Orange and Blue," Beth moaned.

"How sweet," Cammy and Treece and Rich rejoined.

Together they throatily chanted,

> *With spirit and spark*
> *We steal the show*
> *We're Mighty Bison*

"Kiss Kiss," Beth meowed.

"Gotta go," the girls and Rich purred.

Treece, Cammy and Rich hopped up and down, clapping gleefully. Beth just stopped. Her shoulders dropped and her hands fell to her sides. She caught Denis noticing this and curtseyed.

Rich puffed out his chest in a halfway decent impression of Coach Raupp. "Good game, ladies!" With two crisp claps, he woofed, "Hit the showers!"

To Rich's surprise and Denis's astonishment, Beth shouted "Showers!" and trotted off the court. Treece giggled and pranced behind her; Cammy cocked her head in a *what-the-hell* and joined them.

Rich double, triple and quadruple took, mugging between the girls and Denis. "They're *hitting the showers!*"

Rich ran all the way out of the gym before having to run back in to get Denis.

17.

SKINNY DRIP

SAY "WHAT THE FUCK" . . .
IF YOU CAN'T SAY IT, YOU CAN'T DO IT.

MILES DALBY

"COME ON."

"What are you doing?"

"Come on."

"What are you *doing!?*"

"Come *on!*"

Rich was dragging Denis down the double staircase that led to the girls' locker room. From inside could be heard the giggly echo of girls taking off their clothes.

"We weren't invited."

"I'm pretty sure we were." Rich tugged.

"Rich, you don't have to prove anything."

Rich released Denis's wrist and went into the locker room by himself.

Denis watched the door close. He rubbed his wrist, contemplating the three-dimensional nude model of Beth Cooper he had rigorously constructed in his brain. Many data points were mere speculation, placeholders lifted from magazines and the Web, and it would be interesting to compare his hypothetically nude Beth Cooper with live field observations. It was what any true scientist would do.

"*Muy chiquitas!*" Denis heard through the door, followed by assorted girlish sounds.

DENIS STUCK HIS HEAD IN. Spinning blades did not decapitate him. He stepped all the way inside.

The girls' locker room smelled different than the boys', but less different than he thought it would; it was the same sour milk and lemon bleach mélange, overlaid with stale perfumes playing on a dozen piquancies simultaneously. The place smelled exactly like his Great-Aunt Peg.

Denis moved toward the giggling. The locker room was laid out, as he suspected, as a mirror image of the boys'. That meant, he calculated as he crept, the showers were just off the very next row of lock—

Beth Cooper's butt.

He saw it for only a moment.

At 2:32 a.m. on June 4th, in the two-thousand-and-seventh year of Christ (Our Lord).

A Monday.

It was more than perfection: more round, more buoyant, more everything you could want in an ass. It had a single, perfect flaw: a birthmark, on the right cheek, exactly where it would be if Cindy Crawford's face were a butt.

And then it was gone, with the rest of her, into the showers.

Denis had been so enraptured he only now noticed Treece at the end of the aisle, facing him stark naked as well as totally nude in addition to fully, frontally, *au naturel.*

"Come get wet," Treece said, and ran to join her two nakedly nude female friends.

Denis considered the possibility that he had fallen asleep watching Showtime Extreme.

"That invitation good enough for you?"

Denis also hadn't noticed Rich, on the floor at his feet, struggling to get his pants off without taking the time to undo his belt and unzip his fly.

"I don't know about this, Rich."

Rich was up, trying to undo all the buttons of his shirt at once.

"What's to know? Stop thinking with your brain, dude!"

The girls were laughing, shrieking and, apparently, slapping wet parts of one another.

"They're drunk."

"I know! We are *so lucky!*"

"I just don't want to ruin anything."

Rich was down to a pair of slightly irregular Tommy Hilfiger boxer briefs.

"Dude, first of all, there's nothing left to ruin, I regret to inform you. Except *this.* And this, my friend, is a rare occasion. Chances like this don't come along every day! In fact, they *never* come along! *This does not happen.*"

From the showers Treece singsang, "You guys *coming?*"

Rich pointed both hands in the direction of the moist female pulchritude. "*Carpe diem! Seize the day, boys; make your lives extraordinary!* —Robin Williams, *The Dead Poets Society. Eat, drink and be merry, for tomorrow we die* —William Powell, *The Thin Man. You only go around once in life!* —Some beer commercial!"

"Tonight I'd be happy just to stay alive," Denis said.

Rich shook his head as he shoveled off his underwear. "You're not alive unless you're living."

"Who said that?"

Rich looked up, surprised.

"I think I did."

He ran to the showers, where he whipped out his Nicholson:

Heeeeeeeeeere's Johnny!

The girls whooped.

Denis stared down the aisle. Draped across the bench that ran lengthwise between the locker banks was a predictable progression of shoes, blouses, brassieres and skirts. And there, at the end, was a swath of white cotton with tiny pink lettering.

Hello.

it called to him from afar, welcoming him to the party.

The panties talked him into it. "*Carpe fucking diem!*" he shouted, well aware of the misplaced modifier. He didn't care. He was going to go for the gusto, *carpe* the *diem.* He was going to shower naked with three beautiful girls and his gay best friend. He was going to live. He certainly was!

Denis sat on the bench and unlaced his shoes. He removed his right shoe, then his left, and placed them next to one another on the bench next to him. He removed his right sock, then the left, and stuffed them into his right and left shoes, respectively. He stood up, unhooked his belt, and began carefully snaking it out of his pants.

"Hey," he heard Rich giggle. "I can do that myself!"

Denis pulled the belt from his pants like a ripcord. He dropped his trousers, quickly folded them over his arm, and opened the locker, looking for a hanger. A hand reached over and took the pants from his arm. Denis closed the locker door and there was Kevin, holding Denis's pants with one hand and punching him with the other.

Denis stumbled into the bench and fell onto it, landing on his back with his legs on either side. Blood poured from both nostrils in symmetric streams down his cheeks. Kevin swung one foot over the bench and stood astride Denis, looming above him.

Denis was confused. "How did you find us?"

"LoJack, dipshit."

"But *I'm* the geek," said Denis, truly aggrieved. "*I'm* supposed to use technology against *you!*"

Kevin smiled. It was an insane, Cheshire smile, floating above Denis like a scythe.

"You are so very smart," Kevin almost whispered, "and yet you did not figure out that all this could have been avoided, simply by according the proper respect. And perhaps pissing yourself a little."

Denis groaned. "I went at the party!"

"Alas, it is too late. Whereas I was previously only trying to—the word is 'persuade'?—*persuade* you that I was going to kill you, subsequent actions have *convinced* me that I must now actually kill you."

Kevin wound up to deliver a face-changing blow, targeting the strike with cruel precision.

"Stop punching me!" Denis insisted.

Denis scooted on his back, in modified crab walk, sliding twenty feet until there wasn't any more bench. He launched off the end and *oofed* onto the concrete.

Still straddling the bench, Kevin speed-waddled down the aisle until he was once again on top of Denis. He reached down and

SWHACK!

"Jah!" Kevin fell back, grabbing his eye.

SEVENTY-FIVE INCHES of dripping freckles, packing two twisted white gym towels, thrust out a sunken chest.

"Taste my wet blade!" Rich cried.

Kevin came at him. Rich coolly snapped once, striking Adam's apple; he advanced, snapping both wet towels with synchronous precision, driving Kevin back down the aisle.

The girls rushed in behind him, gathering up clothing.

"Doyle, Klepacki!" Kevin screamed.

"Klepacki?" Treece vaguely recalled. "Oh, right. *Dustin.*"

Sean Doyle and Dustin Klepacki stormed in, hoping to see the female flesh Kevin had forbidden them (he was an abusive lout of a boyfriend, but a gentleman). To their disappointment, the only flesh on display was pale, red and male. The girls were wrapped in tiny towels that nevertheless left far too much to their meager imaginations.

Kevin pointed angrily at Rich.

"Aren't you going to say, '*Get them!*'?" cracked Denis, back on his feet. "Or, '*Bring them to me!*'?"

Kevin chose, "Kill them both!"

"Oh, boy!" Rich said. "Gollum in *LOTR: The Two Towers*—"

Sean and Dustin advanced. Rich killed them both, snapping their outermost nipples.

". . . 2002, Peter Jackson."

They came again. Rich overhanded them in the mouth and ear, respectively.

"Also Vladislaus Dracula in *Van Helsing*, 2004, Stephen Sommers." Rich tossed a wet towel back to Denis, who caught it with unexpected élan. As Rich tactically retreated, Denis moved forward until they presented a united defense. "Go," Denis called over his shoulder. "We can handle these three. We've been preparing for this all our lives."

Without even looking, Denis snapped Kevin in the belly button, which he knew from experience was exquisitely vulnerable.

THEIR FRESHMAN YEAR, Rich was on the receiving end of a mass towel-snapping that briefly landed him in the hospital. He feigned unconsciousness to halt the assault; the school nurse, who once sent a headachy kid back to class with meningitis, called an ambulance. The MRI, which his father was certainly not going to pay for, showed nothing, and Rich was sent home with a doctor's note that kept him out of gym for the rest of the year.

Rich vowed he would never again be the victim of this specific sort of attack, and dragooned Denis as his sparring partner. Together they developed the perfect *rat tail*, experimenting with rolling patterns and moisture levels; they discovered the most devastating towel was rolled wet, so tightly as to wring it nearly dry, and then resoaked just before use. They practiced on each other, first using Indiana Jones, the Skywalkers and the Bride Who Killed Bill as battle models, moving on to bullwhip fetish videos that weren't terribly useful, eventually graduating to enthusiast Web sites and barely legal books such as *Filipino Fighting Whip* (Tom Meadows, Paladin Press, $20), which taught Advanced Training Methods and Combat Applications based on the ancient martial art of Kali. They got quite good.

Denis was not the towel master Rich was, but could hold his own, as evidenced by the double snap he had just applied to both of Kevin's cheeks, very nearly simultaneously. They were backing up the staircase, casting long shadows on the wall like some black-and-white guy from some old movie, with Rich supplying the matinee sound track.

"Dah dah *dah*-dah, dah dah-*dah*," he *Indiana* a cappellaed. "Dah dah-dah, dah dah dah-dah-*dah!*"

The army men, despite their combat experience, couldn't seem to outflank these two boys and their John Williams score.

"Dah *dah*-dah! dah *dah*-dah! Dah *dah*-dah! Dah dah-dah dah dah!"

Near the top, Kevin perceived an advantage and led a charge.

"Yaaaaaaaa—*ach!*"

Rich tagged him right on the tongue.

Kevin recoiled onto his compatriots and they all tumbled down the stairs together, landing in a hopefully broken heap.

"Classic!" Rich yelled.

"Great. Let's get out of here."

"You go." Rich assumed the heroic persona. "I can hold them off."

"They'll kill you."

"They don't want me. They want you. And I can run twice as fast as you can."

That was debatable, but with the forces below rapidly regrouping, Denis decided to accept the gesture as best as one teenage boy could accept the love of another.

He handed Rich his towel.

"I'd hug you, but you're naked."

"Understood."

18.

THE PUNCHLINE

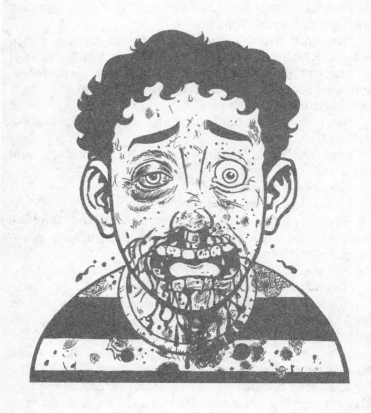

THAT WAS WAY HARSH, TAI.

CHER HOROWITZ

THE GIRLS WERE AT THE BACK ENTRANCE, discussing something, when Denis arrived. He was pinching his ruptured nose, to little stanching effect.

"What's ub?"

"We're fucked," Cammy said, summing it up nicely.

Flashing lights directed Denis's attention outside, where a police car was parked next to the Hummer. A Buffalo Grove peace officer had a clipboard wedged against her belly and was writing down license plate information.

Denis was about to be arrested. He was trespassing in his high school, and he wasn't wearing pants.

"It's like that dream," Denis said.

"Shush," Beth said. She pointed. Fifty feet from the Hummer, its wheels half up on the curb, was her Cabriolet. Kevin had taken it from the party, after Sean and Dustin had persuaded a valet that he didn't need a ticket. Denis had never seen it with the top up; it was a crummy little car.

"Come on."

"Come *what* on?" Denis asked.

Beth and the girls had slipped out the door and were darting between clumps of bushes en route to the convertible. Denis briefly balanced the positives and negatives of eluding the police with the positives and negatives of surrendering to the police multiplied by the exclusively negatives of the infantry men behind him, and followed.

BETH CRAWLED to the passenger side, the one facing away from the crime scene. She discreetly opened the door and climbed in. The others bunny-hopped and monkey-walked into the car. The stealth was unnecessary; the police officer was on the phone with her husband, telling him where the goddamn diaper wipes were for the five-hundredth goddamn time.

"Fuck," Beth whispered, finding no key in the ignition. She reached into the sun visor. "*Fuckety fuck*," she said, "fucker took the fucking *spare*."

Denis had never heard a complete sentence that was more than fifty percent *fuck* before.

"Listen," Denis suggested. "Maybe we should just—"

"Shut the fuck up, Denis!"

Beth reached under the steering column and popped a panel out of the dashboard. She fiddled with some wires. Nothing could surprise Denis at this point, and yet this did.

"*You also hotwire cars?*"

"I'm a talented girl."

The car started. Still hunched below windshield level, Beth put the Cabriolet into drive.

"Wait," Denis said, "Rich!"

"Forget him," said Cammy. "He's already dead."

"I can't leave without my friend." Denis reached for the door.

Beth grabbed his thigh in such a way as to not cause an erection. This was remarkable; Denis sometimes got erections from grabbing his own thigh. Beth was gritting her teeth and Denis saw something in her face he had never, ever seen before. She was desperate.

"Denis," she said. "I could go to jail."

You're going to jail anyway, Denis thought, *and you'll probably go to less jail if you turn yourself in.* But he knew a little about Beth now, and a lot about desperation, and so he determined this advice would likely not be received in the spirit it was given. He also knew he wasn't leaving Rich behind, which meant letting Beth go. Rich wouldn't approve.

Nevertheless.

Denis tried to think of an appropriate exit line, something romantic and yet manly, like *See ya in the funny papers, Funny Face,* except it would have to make some sense in this context and not use the same adjective twice. Ironically, if Rich were here he'd have the perfect line, only then it wouldn't be necessary. That was ironic, wasn't it? It was so hard to tell anymore.

Beth's desperation was beginning to take on exasperated and peevish undertones.

"I won't give you up," Denis said finally, too late to have any iconic impact, even if it hadn't come out as *I woe gib oo ub.*

Denis reached for the door again but the handle fell away. A long speckled creature clamored across his lap and into the backseat.

"We should probably go," Rich said.

HAD THE POLICE OFFICER been paying attention, she would have noticed the driverless convertible drop off the curb and slowly roll away. She was, however, dealing with a domestic disturbance. "Oh, well, *here's* an idea: you get a job that pays for more than your *goddamn beer* and then I'd be goddamn *delighted* to stay home and take care of *our child!*"

Through the rearview mirror, Beth could see the officer waving her arms and screaming into her cell.

"What's she doing?"

"She's calling for backup," stated Denis.

"HEY!"

The yell came not from the police officer but from the entrance to the building, where Kevin, Sean and the one called Dustin had just emerged.

"Shit," Beth said, and floored it. The police officer noticed this, sighed, "I gotta go, sweetie," and hung up the phone. She did not leap into her patrol car, light the cherries and peel out while shouting into the radio about being in pursuit of suspects traveling west on Dundee Road, because this was Buffalo Grove. There were no high speed chases in Buffalo Grove, especially of teenagers, because in Buffalo Grove, the teenagers, no matter what they had done, eventually went home.

She pulled out her clipboard and added a line to her report.

BETH HAD THE REMARKABLE ABILITY to dress herself under a towel without revealing anything, while at the same time driving recklessly at high speed.

Clothing flurried about the backseat as two girls and a guy sorted out their wardrobes.

"That's my top," Cammy accused Treece.

"I'm borrowing it."

"You're going to boob it all out."

Treece threw the top, hitting Rich on the face. He caught it in his teeth, and offered it up to Cammy, doggy-style.

"Drop it," Cammy commanded.

Denis wasn't getting dressed. He was squeezing his nose and estimating his rate of blood loss.

"Where's your pants?" Beth asked.

"Your boyfriend has them."

"Well, they're not going to fit *him*." She glanced at Denis, frowned, reached behind him, and extracted something from inside his collar.

"Oh, those," Denis explained. "They must've gotten there when I slid—"

"I don't care, Denis," Beth said, pulling on her panties as she cut off an eighteen-wheeler and veered onto the on-ramp for I-53 North.

"Where are we going?"

"We broke ten laws. We've got to get out of town."

"Let's go to my dad's cabin!" Treece suggested. "He lets me go there any time I want, as long as I don't tell Mom where it is."

Denis shook his head vigorously, reopening the nasal bloodgates. "I can't 'get out of town'!"

Beth angrily shook the splatter off her hand.

"Enough, Denis. *Enough*, okay?! *You* started this!"

"*Me?*"

"Yeah, *you*. You're the geek who stood up in front of our entire school, and all our family and friends, and declared your 'love' for someone you don't know a *thing* about!"

"He knows a *lot* about you," Rich defended Denis. "Quiz him!"

"He didn't know about Kevin," Treece pointed out.

"There were lapses in the intelligence," Rich acknowledged, then remembered: "He can do your signature!"

"You said it was sweet," Denis murmured.

Beth snorted. It wasn't a nice snort.

"*And* you came to my house!" he countered her snort. "If you didn't think it was sweet, why'd you come to my house?!"

Beth didn't answer.

Cammy answered.

"What do you think, super genius? We thought it would be *funny*."

"Oh," Denis said.

Rich went for the face save: "Us, too. I mean, the head cheerleader and captain of the debate team? That's *always* hilarious . . ."

DENIS'S BRAIN PLAYED it all back for him another hilarious episode of:

LEAVE IT TO PENIS

"THE GRAND DELUSION"

FADE IN:

INT. BUFFALO GROVE HIGH SCHOOL -- CAFETERIA

STANDING AGAINST THE CINDER BLOCK IS DENIS "THE PENIS" COOVERMAN. HIS GRADUATION GOWN DRAGS ON THE GROUND AND HIS MORTAR IS TOO SMALL FOR HIS HUMONGOUS HEAD. HE FIDGETS AND TWITCHES AS HE TRIES TO ASSUME

A "COOL" POSE AGAINST THE WALL. HE DOES A DOUBLETAKE AS HE NOTICES...

BETH COOPER, HEAD CHEERLEADER AND PROM QUEEN, IS WALKING TOWARD HIM.

DENIS GYRATES AND CONTORTS IN AN EFFORT TO LOOK LIKE HE DOESN'T NOTICE. HE LOOKS LIKE A SPAZ.

SFX: LAUGHTER

BETH STOPS A FEW FEET FROM DENIS. SHE IS SLIGHTLY TALLER THAN HE IS.

> BETH
> You embarrassed me.

DENIS'S MOUTH HANGS OPEN. A BEAT. ANOTHER BEAT.

SFX: LAUGHTER

> BETH (CONT'D)
> (BEGRUDGING) But it was so "sweet",
> I'll have to let you live.

> DENIS
> (VOICE SQUEAKING) Great. That's great.

SFX: LAUGHTER

BETH, UNCOMFORTABLE, LOOKS BEHIND HER. HER TWO FRIENDS, CAMMY AND TREECE, ARE LAUGHING. THEY URGE HER TO CONTINUE.

> BETH
> So... Henneman must've given you major
> junk.

> DENIS
> (ACTING "COOL") Some junk. Little junk.
> A modicum of debris.

BETH ROLLS HER EYES.

SFX: LAUGHTER

> BETH
> (CHANGING SUBJECT) Was it like 800
> degrees in there? Like boiling?

DENIS SNORTS POMPOUSLY.

> DENIS
> ("PROFESSOR KNOW-IT-ALL") Actually, the boiling point

-- of water -- is 212 degrees. Fahrenheit.

HE SWITCHES TO HIS "COOL" GUY.

> DENIS (CONT'D)
> (COCKS FINGER) One-hundred Celcius.

SFX: LAUGHTER, CONTINUING, AT HIS EXPENSE

DENIS FELT LIKE he had been punched in the heart.

He let go of his nose. The blood poured forth like tears, only red and disgusting.

Beth expressed some concern.

"Are you going to keep bleeding?"

"For about three days."

"Tip your head back."

Denis tipped his head back. He made a face.

"Now it's running down my throat."

Treece's hand appeared next to his head, holding two tiny white cylindrical objects.

"Here, stick these up there. They're super absorbent."

"Gah!" Denis said.

"They'll fit," Treece assured him. "They're comfort minis."

Denis batted her kind offer away. She dropped them in his lap.

"Fine," she said. "Bleed to death."

Denis quietly bled to death.

It was all a joke.

Or, more accurately, *he* was all a joke. A beaten, bleeding, pantless joke.

Denis picked up the tampons.

Perfect, he chuckled, choked on some blood, and cacked it onto his lap.

19.

LOVE MEANS

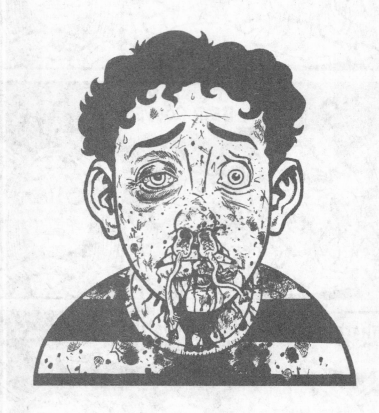

LOVE MAKES ROOM FOR FAULT.

GIDGET LAWRENCE

THE ROAD WAS DARK, lit only by fireflies.

They were headed north through Lake County, which was known for its lakes. Fox, Griswold, Nipersink and Pistakee Lakes. Lakes Catherine, Louise and Marie. There were a few hundred thousand others, according to the brochures.

Denis had never been to any of them, though he had snorkled in three oceans and four seas. His parents had wanted him to be cosmopolitan, rather than a child.

It was almost 4 a.m. In the backseat, Treece was asleep on Rich's shoulder, her mouth wide open. Rich, in turn, was leaning on Cammy, dreaming in widescreen. Cammy considered shoving him off her. Instead she closed her eyes.

The radio kept playing DJ C's Slamming Graduation Mix. They had been through:

"Graduation," by Third Eye Blind, "The Graduation Song" by Dave Matthews, and that Vitamin C song that wouldn't go away;

"Graduation Day"s by Head Automatica, Kanye West, Chris Isaak and Gym Class Heroes;

The Goo Goo Dolls' "Better Days" and 10,000 Maniacs' "These are Days";

"Bittersweet Symphony" by the Verve or Semisonic or one of those;

"Blackbird" by the Beatles and "Free Bird" by Lynyrd Skynyrd and "Fly Like an Eagle" by Steve Miller and "I Believe I Can Fly" by R. Kelly and "Fly Away" by Lenny Kravitz, and Dropline's "Fly Away from Here (Graduation Day)".

Now playing was the Calling's "Our Lives," or the Ataris's "In This Diary"; Denis had trouble telling them apart.

These are the days worth living . . .

DENIS AND BETH HAD NOT SPOKEN to each other through any of it. It was possible that they would never speak again. Denis would never figure out if Beth was nice, crazy, sad or mean, or some combination and in what proportions. Beth would never learn that beneath Denis's geek exterior there was a far more complicated Denis, roiling with neurosis, obsession and fear, and if that wasn't enticing enough, beneath that lay a sea of undifferentiated rage, the kind women like. Beth and Denis would be like two ships, two ships that sideswiped, causing ugly but not irreparable hull damage, and then passed in the night.

What kind of fool was Denis to ever imagine it could have been any different? There was no fool like a high-IQ fool. He could calculate π two different ways, the Wallis method and the Leibniz Series, but he could not see what any idiot could see, what everyone saw, many of them idiots: Beth was beautiful, popular and had a peerless derriere, and he was just another dweeb with two bloody tampons hanging out of his nostrils.

Let's make the best out of our lives

"HEY," BETH SAID. She turned down the radio. She did not look at him, which was for the best.

"I wanted to say," Beth said, "about what Cammy said. *She* thought it would be funny. I mean, we all thought it would be like a fun thing, and . . . I guess I did think it would be kind of funny. I'm sorry."

Denis said nothing.

"But I—" Beth went silent for several seconds.

Then she said:

"Guys tell me they love me all the time. But that's usually when . . . they want something."

Denis had not wanted *that,* not specifically, not right away.

"So I just . . . I don't know."

She seemed finished.

"Well," Denis said, "it *was* kind of funny."

He took the ends of the tampons and strung them out, making a superabsorbent handlebar mustache.

Beth laughed, and gagged. "Is it possible that you could please take those out now?"

"Let's see." Denis comically yanked the strings.

It hurt so much.

His nostrils had stopped bleeding, but now they burned like he had huffed fluorine. Denis dangled the assailants in front of his face. There were tiny hairs stuck on the end. Denis blinked back tears so as not to undercut the humor of his amusing mutilation.

"Voilà," he said with brave insouciance. "Do you have, one of those, um . . . bags?"

Beth reached down next to her seat and pulled out a McDonald's bag. She looked away as she handed it to him.

"Thank you," Denis said, debonairly dropping the bloodied wads into the bag. "You know, it's funny. Or interesting. *Tampon* is the actual medical term for the cotton plug they use to treat epistaxis, or nosebleeds . . ."

"Fucking Kevin," Beth said, slamming the steering wheel with her palm.

Denis sensed the subject had changed. He didn't have a lot more on tampons anyway. "Yeah," he said in support of Beth's statement. "Fuck that Kevin."

"Have you ever been in love?" Beth asked Denis.

Denis didn't know how to answer that. He knew the answer, or thought he knew the answer, but this didn't seem like the appropriate time to bring it up.

"I mean, truly in love," Beth continued, as if responding to what he thought. "In *true love.*"

A couple of weeks before, Denis had gotten an e-mail from Rich.

From: RichMunsch@yahoo.com
Subject: True Love
Date: May 19, 2007 11:25:39 PM EDT
To: *DenisCooverman@yahoo.com*

"There's her poop. It just came out of her butt. I can feel it. I can feel the poop. It's warm. It just came from her butt. This was just inside of her. My girl. I'm touching it. It's her poop. It's Wendy's poop. I know it may seem weird that I touched her poop, but it was inside of her."

—*Timothy Treadwell*

It was a quote from a movie, like most of Rich's e-mails were, and while Denis never figured out which movie, he found himself agreeing with it. That was true love. By that definition, he had not quite made it to true love.

Beth had a different definition.

"You know, where you love someone, with your whole heart, you just *love* them, and they can be mean to you, and hurt you, not physically, but hurt you, you know, make you feel like shit or worthless, but you still love him? You know what I mean?"

"I'm beginning to," Denis said.

Beth smiled.

"It can really suck, huh?"

Denis could see what was happening here, what he was being repurposed as, but it was better than nothing, he figured.

"How long have you two been going out?" Beth's new friend who was a boy asked.

"Since Christmas. We met right after. And, you know, he's been away since then, but we kept in touch, and the whole thing sort of happened through e-mail."

"That's great."

"He's a really sweet guy," Beth said. "Online."

"Sweet," Denis repeated. So both he and an abusive whoremongering, child-killing cokehead were *sweet*.

"You don't want to talk about him," Beth said. "Let's talk about something else."

Too tired, perhaps, Denis spoke without even over-thinking.

"Can I ask you a personal question?"

"Is it about my boobs?"

"No, but I do have several queries in the arena, which I'll get to."

"They're Cs. Bs during basketball season. Ms. Levitt doesn't like us flopping all over the place. Except Treece. She can't help it. I'm sorry. What was your question?"

"Oh, I was just wondering about your brother."

"What about him?"

"I don't know. Like, what was his name?"

Denis had speculated that his name was Dennis.

"David."

"What was he like?"

"I have no idea," Beth said. "He was already sick when I was born. He died when I was two. He was twelve. I don't remember him at all. There's this picture of me visiting him in the hospital, but it's like he's just some sick kid."

WHEN DENIS WAS TEN, he told his parents he wanted a baby brother. Since he had never expressed any interest in a sibling, they asked him why. He said that he thought he might be coming down with leukemia, and that he would need a close blood relative for bone marrow transplants. He had read about the

bioethics of parents having a second child to provide
marrow for an ill sibling in an issue of the *Journal of
Juvenile Oncology* that he had been secretly subscrib-
ing to. He theorized there would be no ethical issue if
his parents had the child *before* he was diagnosed, as
a preventative measure. Only he used the word *pro-
phylactic.* That's when they knew he was going to be a
doctor.

Denis's parents said they would see what they could
do, but they didn't, not really.

"LEUKEMIA," DENIS SAID.

Beth was spooked. "How'd you know that?"

"What else do little kids die of?" Denis said.

"Oh, right," said Beth. "You're the doctor."

"I'm sorry. About David."

"It's kind of stupid. My big sad story. It's like the
dramatic tragedy of my life, and I wasn't even there.
And it's not even an interesting story. Excuse me."

Beth stopped the car, opened her door, and threw
up. She closed the door, and continued driving.

"You okay?"

"That was shitty champagne." She turned to Denis,
smiling through watery eyes and lips glazed with
vomitus. "Yours was much nicer."

The radio was now playing Ataris's "In This Diary," or the Calling's "Our Lives," whichever the other
one was.

These are the best days of our lives

"Um," Beth said, "Can *I* say something personal?"

Please do. "Uh. Yeah. Sure."

"You kind of . . . reek."

Denis sighed heavily. "It's the fear."

"I think it's your shirt."

Denis looked down. His rugby shirt was a goulash

of putrefying meats, molding cheeses, salmonelling creams and ptomaining tapenades.

"I kind of spilled some dip on it."

"Take it off."

Denis's pupils constricted involuntarily.

"I'm not going to *molest* you."

"I wasn't terribly concerned about that."

Denis removed his shirt in the manner of a girl at a strip poker game, maintaining maximum coverage until the last possible moment.

"Personally," Beth said. "I hate hairy chests." She put out her hand and snapped her fingers. "Hand it over." Denis handed it over.

"Let's give it a little air . . ."

Beth held the shirt out of the window and shook it. Smelly bits and rancid ooze took to the wind and the whole operation went swimmingly until the shirt flew out of her hand.

"Oh, shit!" Beth laughed.

She slammed on the brakes.

In the backseat, Cammy woke up to discover she was cradling Rich like a baby. She flung him off like he was a severed head that had landed on her in a horror movie.

Treece, who lay in Rich's lap, jostled half awake. "Okay," she mumbled. "Okey-dokey . . ." She started to unbuckle Rich's belt. Rich reached down and eased her automated mouth away from his fly. She happily went back to sleep.

Beth threw the vehicle into reverse and spun the wheel to execute a three-point turn in only two points.

"THERE IT IS." Denis spotted the shirt crumpled at the side of the road. Beth stopped.

Nobody said anything for a moment.

"I'll get it," Denis said.

The cold gravel on his feet and cool breeze on most of his skin reminded Denis: he was a man in underpants. He crouched as he entered the high-beamed proscenium, reflexively covering his ass, and was further reminded: he was a man in *lucky underpants*. Lucky, sagging, incomplete underpants.

Denis swiveled to remove his rear from direct view, sidling away from the headlights in nondominant primate fashion. He reached down for his shirt, intending to tie it around his waist like a big-assed girl, and discovered he was not alone.

He saw their eyes first. Four red circles, vibrating. Then he heard the high chittering sound. Two raccoons were inspecting his shirt, and finding it delicious. From inside the car, where Beth and the others were watching, they must have looked awfully cute. But from Denis's perspective, low to the ground and close enough to see their rabid little teeth and razor yellow claws, they appeared as what they were: fierce competitors for a valuable resource.

"No," Denis said. "That's not food, it's a polyblend."

The raccoons switched from nervous trill to robust snarl with stunning alacrity. Denis was back in the car almost as quickly.

They all watched as the raccoons clutched the shirt, nibbling, and then scampered with their catch into the woods.

Cammy and Rich found this rip-snorting.

"Oh, Denis," Beth said, utterly contrite. "I am *so* sorry." And then she cracked up.

Denis smiled, and grinned, and chuckled, and began to laugh, for the first time in a very long time. It possessed all of the therapeutic effects he had read about.

Beth was laughing, and gazing at Denis with amusement and what seemed genuine affection. "Look at you. You're naked. Cam, throw me my poncho."

A bright purple knit poncho flew into the front seat.

"It's okay. Really. I'm kind of hot, right now, actually."

"Put it on."

"I don't see any need, at the moment, to wear a purple poncho."

"It's fuchsia," Beth said, spreading it in front of her coquettishly. "And it's my favorite."

20.

FOOL MOON

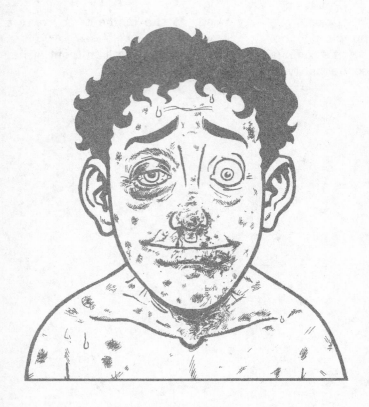

**IT'S REALLY HUMAN OF YOU
TO LISTEN TO ALL MY BULLSHIT.**

SAMANTHA BAKER

TREECE'S FATHER'S CABIN sat on Lake Hakaka, named by the Ho-Chunk after their word meaning "dead male bear," for reasons that were not immediately apparent. It was one of Lake County's lesser lakes, usually left off tourism materials and occasionally official maps; once the county argued, unsuccessfully, that it was in Wisconsin. The lake had water, though, and was private, being unpopular, and only smelled like a dead male bear from late July through early September.

Three girls, a boy, and a ponchoed figure of indeterminate sex approached the cabin by the light of the setting moon.

"Originally it was Al Capone's," Treece inaccurately related the cabin's history. "He used it as a hideout, because if the police raided, he could just run into Wisconsin. And then the guy who played Bozo the Clown, not the main guy but some local Bozo, had it for a bunch of years, and threw these really sick clown parties up here. There's supposedly a couple dead clowns buried in the woods over there. And then Sammy the Seal or Snake or some other S animal owned it, and that's how my dad got it."

Treece turned on the light. She yawned. Everybody else gasped.

Fowl and fauna lunged from the walls and coffee tables; animal skins draped all the woodsy furniture; the outside of a grizzly bear lay on the floor.

Rich dropped the bag of snacks.

"Feel the death," Cammy said.

Several of the animal cadavers came paired in death-throe tableaus: a glass-eyed owl with a flexiformed snake "writhing" in its talons; a former fox tearing apart an ex-squirrel; and, *holy crap*, a tanned hunting dog retrieving a stuffed pheasant. Denis was by no means an animal lover; he consumed animals, he dissected them, but he didn't *hate* them. This cabin felt like an act of revenge.

"I think maybe animals killed his parents," he said.

"Oh, my dad just bought all this stuff," Treece responded blithely, adding with a rare note of disdain, "He's never killed *anything*." She pointed to above the fireplace, where a hunting rifle was mounted between the heads of a mother deer and its fawn. "Aren't they cute?"

She opened the refrigerator, pulled out a bottle and frowned. "Weird beer." She opened the freezer, and brightened. "*Yodka!*" she bellowed in what she supposed was a Russian accent.

AN OLD BOOM BOX channeled Denis's iPod:

Here's to the nights we felt alive

The Eve 6 song, regarded as a graduation classic, was in reality from another venerable rock genre, the "Let's Spend the Night Together and Then I Must Be Ramblin' On" song.

Are you cool with just tonight

Nobody cared. The mood of the music combined with the crackling fire and the wilderness milieu to create an irresistibly maudlin setting. The five stood around a wicker Tiki bar, drunk and/or punch-drunk, as Treece poured generous *yodkas* into the only five available vessels:

a ceramic pineapple;

a pink coffee mug shaped like a breast;

a monkey head carved out of a coconut;

a *Playboy* toothbrush tumbler;

and a World's Greatest Dad Trophy.

"There," Treece said, and "*Yikes.*"

She was looking at Denis's face. And then everyone was looking at Denis's face, in the light for the first time in a couple of beatings.

"Pretty bad?" Denis asked.

The eye had coagulated into bold concentric circles of red, yellow and black. The bruises from the boning and scrapes from the bushes provided a muted backdrop for other dramatically battered facial features: the nose a magenta bloom with rusty crust around the nostrils; the lower lip a fat purple sausage split open on the right.

"Not that bad," Beth said.

"Better than dead," said Rich.

"Your lip looks great," Treece said. "Bitchtricia paid like two grand to have that done to her lips."

"Yes," said Cammy, softening her usual deadpan. "You look totally hot."

"A toast!" Treece said, lifting the World's Greatest Dad Trophy. "You know what's weird? I didn't give him this."

Everybody grabbed a drinking container; Denis, not fast enough, got the Titty Mug.

"To . . . ," Treece said, thinking. "I know: Here's to the nights we felt alive!"

Beth touched her pineapple to Denis's ceramic nipple.

"Ching."

She chugged her shot.

"I'm going out for a smoke."

With a tilt of her head, she bid Denis to follow. Denis, as always, followed, adding one last brushstroke to his chiaroscuro portrait of *Beth Cooper, Girl in My Head.*

"She smokes."

BETH DANGLED HER LEGS off the end of the dock, lighting a cigarette. Denis sat down next to her.

"No cancer statistics, please."

Every eight seconds, someone in the world dies from tobacco use.

Every minute, ten million cigarettes are sold.

There are 599 government-approved additives for

tobacco, including chocolate, vanilla, prune juice, di-
methyltetrahydrobenzofuranone and "smoke flavor."

Tobacco companies have also been adding ammo-
nia, arsenic, formaldehyde and mercury to their ciga-
rettes to help achieve that great taste.

A 1998 study showed that smoking significantly
reduces the size of the smoker's erect penis.

Or how about, Denis thought, *this harmless but fun*
conversation starter:

"Did you know that smokers fart more than non-
smokers? It's been proven."

"That's why *I* do it," Beth said.

She tilted to one side, lifting a buttock off the
dock.

If she farts, Denis vowed, *I will become a priest.*

Beth wriggled into a more comfortable position.

Denis sighed audibly, which Beth took to be more
criticism.

"Sorry." She waved the smoke away. "I just gotta
have something in my mouth right now."

"Okay," Denis said. He slapped a mosquito on his
forearm.

Beth blew out a stream of carbon monoxide, hydro-
gen cyanide and forty-three known carcinogens.

"I always think the full moon is so pretty."

The moon, hanging just above the water, was waning gibbous with 93 percent of its visible disk illuminated. The technical full moon had been Friday. But it
was, Denis agreed, pretty: golden.

"It's the Honey Moon," he said. "The first moon of
June is called that. It's where *honeymoon* comes
from, because people used to get married at the
summer solstice, which is June twenty-first this
year."

"It's huge," Beth said.

"That's an optical illusion. It only looks larger when
it's close to the horizon. The prevailing theory, used to

be, was that it's a Ponzo illusion, that we see it as bigger in context to the objects around it, but that's been discredited. There's a couple intriguing alternatives, but nothing proven."

"You know everything, Denis Cooverman."

Denis Cooverman was back.

"Not everything. No, no. There's things I don't know. Multiple things." He slapped his thigh.

"Here's something you don't know," Beth said, sucking in some early menopause. "If a girl tells you the moon is beautiful, or that it seems really big, you know what you say?"

"Not what I said, I assume."

She blew out secondhand smoke rings.

"You don't say anything. You put your arm around her."

Was Beth suggesting—

"Just something for future reference."

"Thanks," Denis said, pulling his arm back. "I'll remember that."

"SAY ALLO TO MY LEETLE FREN . . ."

Rich was using the rifle from the mantel as a prop for his one-night-only one-man show.

"Pacino, *Scarface*, '82, DePalma . . ." The attribution was hurried and sloppy, an indication that he did not chug vodka often. He repositioned the gun, switched the accent.

"*Hasta la vista, baby*—Schwarzenegro, *T2*, '91, Cameron Crowe."

Treece and Cammy sat on the leopard, calf and sheepskin couch, passing the bottle back and forth. Treece giggled maniacally; Cammy chortled unironically.

Rich held the gun straight up, bowed his legs and thrust back his shoulders. He placed a hand over one eye and swaggered his shoulders.

"*Fill your hands, you son of a bitch!* —John Wayne, *True Grit*, '69, directed by some guy."

Cammy guffawed.

Treece fell off the couch. "Uh-oh," she squealed, "I'm *peeing!*"

"It's not *that* funny," said Rich, clearly rattled by this level of positive feedback.

"It's funny," said Treece, presumably no longer peeing, "because you . . . *you—*"

"What?" Rich snapped. "Because I'm homo-ly sexual, or so you think? You think incorrectly."

Cammy smiled, almost kindly. "The lady doth protest too much, *me*thinks."

"Oh, like *you* know Shakespeare."

"Queen Gertrude to Hamlet, act three, scene two." Then, in perfect mimicry: "1602, William Shakespeare, or possibly Edward de Vere."

Rich fell a tiny bit in love.

"Just because we're beautiful, it doesn't mean we're stupid," Cammy said.

"Yeah," Treece added.

THE HONEY MOON MELTED into the lake. Beth smoked, and Denis swatted.

"Careful what you wish for, huh?"

"Huh?" Denis scratched his neck.

"So . . . still love me?"

"What?"

"Now that you know me. Am I everything you ever masturbated to?"

"No. I never . . . not to *you.*"

That was such a lie.

Beth took a long drag, leaving a silence for Denis to fill with a truthful answer to her question.

"You're different than I expected," he answered accurately. "I mean, you're not—"

"*Perfect.*"

Beth Cooper was like a Persian rug, her imperfections proof that God exists. Unfortunately, that last vodka shot had knocked out Denis's metaphor center, and he was on his own.

"Not perfect, but better. You're not . . ." He smacked his forehead. "You're still great, and it's . . . real. You're real. A real kind of real." Denis stared down at his knees, and the five mosquitoes feasting there. "I'm not good at talking . . . about things."

"*Denis Cooverman!* You're a debate state finalist!"

"How'd you know *that?*"

"We were going to go cheer for you. Well, we joked about it. But anyway, you were talking about how real I am."

"Well, one example: you're pretty, but not like a picture. And you have a . . . personality."

"*There's* a compliment."

"You're sweet."

"I don't get accused of that very often."

"You are. And you're interesting, and you're smart—"

Beth put her fist to her throat. "I am *not* smart, Denis," she hacked. "I'm kind of an idiot." She laughed, and coughed.

Denis was prepared to argue but had no contradictory facts at his disposal. Instead he itched. Beth puffed her cigarette, coughed a couple more times, and puffed again.

A few seconds passed like nothing.

"You're a lot of fun."

Beth laughed. "I thought you said this wasn't fun."

Denis looked at her, the unswollen parts of his face forming an expression of excruciating sincerity.

"All my memories from high school are from tonight."

Beth looked away.

"You need to get out more."

21.

THE SEX PART

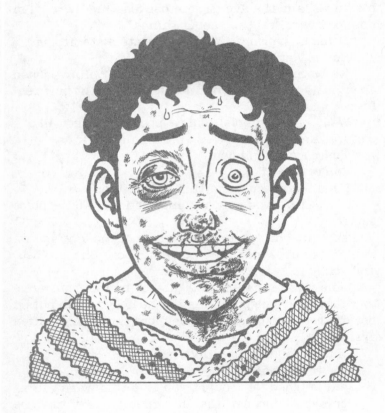

FUCK ME GENTLY WITH A CHAINSAW.

HEATHER CHANDLER

INSIDE THE CABIN, something was happening, and Rich suspected the worst. As if through telepathy or subtle hand signals, Cammy and Treece had agreed to play some game, and not only were they not telling him what it was, Rich sensed the game they were playing was him.

Cammy sashayed up, revealing for the first time that she had hips, took a long suck on the vodka bottle, and handed it to him.

"So, hetero-boy," she said with, if this is possible, sultry sarcasm, "if you're so not gay, why so unchubby in the shower?"

"I was just being cool." He took a big swig of vodka to underline this. "And it was uncool of *you* to notice."

"*And* you pushed Treece away when she tried to service you in the car . . ."

"I did?" Treece asked, simply curious. "That sounds like me." And then realizing the grievous insult to her reputation, "Yeah, what is *wrong* with you? I'm really good at that! I'm *known* for that!"

"You were *asleep*. So that was me being cool, once again."

"No seventeen-year-old boy is that cool," Cammy said.

"*I* am that cool," Rich disagreed, and then lost interest in that subject. He picked up the bag he had dropped earlier.

"*¿Quien quieres las snaquitas?*"

"You know, Rich," Cammy said. "The movie quotes, the bad Spanish. Not working. Too many shticks."

"It is kind of not ideal," Treece agreed, "from a branding point of view. Unless you only quoted movies in Spanish. And there's like, what, five of those."

Rich unwrapped a Suzy Q, considering the criticism. He sat between the girls on the couch.

"Which shtick do you like better?"

"Ooh, that's tough," Cammy said.

Rich shoved the Suzy Q in his mouth and bit it in half.

Cammy chuckled.

"You, Richard Munsch, have never been with a woman."

"Whuh?" Rich said, creamy lipped.

"I NEVER BOUGHT BEER BEFORE. I never went on a joyride, I mean, a reckless one; was never in a car accident; never, well, I've been beaten up, but never with that many spectators; never broke in anywhere; never skinny-dipped, and I almost did, I was going to; never eluded the authorities before . . ."

"Never sniffed a girl's panties before?"

"I *did not*."

"You were down there a long time."

"I closed my eyes and held my breath. That's how I lost consciousness." He scratched his cheek.

"Well," Beth said, lighting another cigarette, "sounds like I really popped your cherry tonight."

Denis did not want to talk about his cherry.

"You know, even if your grades and SATs aren't amazing, you could still go to a good college. You could get a cheerleading scholarship."

"A cheerleading scholarship?"

"They have cheerleading scholarships. Not at Northwestern. But there isn't anything to cheer at Northwestern anyway."

Beth exhaled. She sounded a little tired.

"Denis, it's nice you're watching out for me, but look: I'm not even that good of a cheerleader. You, you're going to go on and become a doctor and cure cancer or whatever new diseases there are, but this, this is about it for me."

Beth seemed so matter-of-fact, so resigned.

"I know high school wasn't that great for you."

"No," Denis said. "It was, some of it was . . . The last eight hours: pretty fantastic."

"I know about all the swirlies, and wedgies and all the nicknames . . ."

"What nicknames?" Denis asked. "I know about Penis."

Beth chewed her cigarette. "Here's the thing. High school was *really* great for me. I had a great, great time. But now that's over. Everything from here on out is going to be . . . ordinary."

Denis couldn't believe that, wouldn't accept that. "You're not ordinary. You're *beautiful.*"

"I may be pretty, but not enough to make a living at it. Except maybe in porn."

The mere thought of this gave Denis the creeps, and wood.

"I'm not doing porn, Denis."

"Oh. Good. It's a limited field."

"Besides, I'm going to get fat."

"You won't get fat."

"I'll have to introduce you to my mom."

Denis knew enough about obesity and genetics to argue against, and for, Beth's proposition. Instead, he sat there, slapping and scratching, and thinking about what she had said. He had never looked at his life the way Beth described it, as *promising.* It was obvious and true, but Denis had always been too caught up in immediate terrors and humiliations to look forward to anything; even his obsessive long-term planning was mired in worry over whether it was currently on schedule. And Denis had never given much thought to Beth's life—her real life as opposed to the one he had constructed for the two of them (and even this life was more a matter of moments and scenes than a fully articulated existence). What Beth said about her own life was pessimistic but not inaccurate. Her family, her finances—she was always at that shoe store—her academic credentials, none of it augured well for the kind of future that guidance counselors talk about. Beth would do fine, Denis had no doubt, but her life was unlikely to get *better* than it was right now. That Beth knew and accepted this broke Denis's heart, and impressed the hell out of him.

It occurred to him: *I'm the idiot.*

"You know, Beth," he said, "for someone who claims to not be smart—"

Beth tossed her cigarette in the lake. "You wanna mess around?"

"You and me?"

"I'm not gonna ask twice."

Denis was an idiot, but not that much of an idiot. He kissed her.

She kissed him, right on his swollen, ruptured lip.

"Ow," Denis said.

"Ooh," Beth said, kissing an unbruised patch of his cheek. "Sorry."

"It's a good *ow*," Denis said. "Please continue."

She did. And it was.

Sweetest memory
Sweetest memory

QAJE, THE GORGEOUS quadra-racial singer who had once been or still was a man, filled the cabin with the kind of sensuous jazz-inflected pop that grown-ups like to pork to.

Rich sat in the middle of the couch, gripping vodka and snack cake, with the quick rigidity of a rabbit surrounded by animals that eat rabbits.

Treece was curled up on one side of him, and Cammy was stretching her long legs, resting her toes on his knees. They were both holding up freshly peeled Suzy Qs, spokesmodel style.

"Watch," said Cammy.

"And learn," said Treece.

The two girls oriented their pastries vertically, and proceeded to lick the creme from their crevices in alternating short and long strokes.

Rich wondered what the MPAA Ratings Board would make of this.

Cammy pulled her face out of her Suzy Q; she had a white dollop on her nose. She put a foot in Rich's lap.

"You cool?"

"Long as everyone else is cool."

Treece leaned in and ran a creme-filled tongue up his cheek.

"See?" Rich said. "I'm liking that. I'm"—he pointed to his crotch—"*reacting* to that."

"How about *this?*" Treece gave Rich what he had previously known as a Wet Willie. Something about it being a girl's tongue in his ear and not some guy's licked finger altered the tenor.

"Oh, yeah." Rich swallowed. "That works."

Treece continued wet-working the left side of his face, and Cammy began to unbutton his shirt. Rich wondered, *How far do they plan on taking this joke?* Were there people waiting to jump out when he took off his pants? No, they could have done that back in the girls' locker room. Maybe this was a game of sex chicken. If that was the case, Rich thought, then *cluck cluck cluck cluck cluck.*

"Hey, this is all great and all, but, unfortunately, I left my latex sheaths back at the house—"

"Don't worry," Cammy said, twirling Rich out of his shirt. "Treece has got some. Don't you, Treece?"

Treece reached behind her back and her top sprang off. "Gobs."

DENIS COOVERMAN WAS MAKING OUT with Beth Cooper.

CAPTAIN OF DEBATE MAKES OUT WITH CHEERLEADER HEAD

SIGN OF 'END OF TIMES'

Perversion of Caste System
Cited as Dogs Mate with Cats,
Cities Plunge into Boiling Seas

The corporeal reality of making out with Beth Cooper was different than all the hypothetical times he had made out with her. It felt better, and hurt more. Also, even in his wildest dream scenarios, it was always just him and Beth, and not a carnal blood orgy of the two of them and nineteen thousand six-legged females with wings.

More troubling were the stylistic differences. Where Denis was a (mostly theoretical) adherent of soft kisses and slow caresses, Beth was apparently more of a rutter. She had pulled him on top of her within moments and had her hands under the poncho, grabbing and scratching his back. That was much appreciated. Yet Denis did not know what to make of it when she wrapped her thighs around one of his legs and started humping him dryly and, he couldn't help but notice, fiercely.

She was making a lot of noise. Louder and more guttural than was warranted, Denis felt, but something else as well. Intermingled with sexual growls and bucking grunts was a high keening moan, one Denis knew from his reading could signify pleasure but which he sensed did not.

Denis sat up.

"Listen . . . I'm sorry." And he was truly, profoundly sorry, and would be much sorrier later, he suspected, and for a long time after that. But he had to ask: "Why me?"

Beth remained on her back on the deck. Her eyes glistened, too much.

"Because it's graduation night," she said. "And to not be with someone would just be too sad."

Don't be sad. I can't stand you sad.

"Okay," Denis said, and climbed back on.

> *I don't want to be*
> *just your sweetest memory*

CAMMY, TREECE AND RICH HUDDLED NAKED under leopard, calf and sheep skins, respectively. They all had the glazed expressions of people who had just shared a terribly intimate horrific mistake.

"That was," Cammy said, "expeditious."

Treece found the silver lining. "At least we know you're not gay."

"Tell that to my dad," Rich said.

"What's his number?"

Rich's father wouldn't have answered. Rich's mother was sitting by the phone, waiting to hear back from the Coovermans and the police. But Mr. Munsch was fast asleep, as he had been for much of Rich's life, because, as he liked to explain at parties or anytime his BAL went over .08, "After three daughters, I really wanted a boy."

What wasn't being discussed in the cabin was what had happened *after* Rich had proved he was not gay. That took only a few seconds, but then things . . . continued. Rich had originally thought no one had noticed his startling emission and continued to play along, but it gradually dawned on him that his participation was not strictly necessary. He was not having sex with two girls. They were having sex with each other on top of him. Rich withdrew to a neutral corner and watched, with distressing disinterest, as matters reached mutually agreed-upon ends.

"And you two can't be gay," Rich pointed out, "because my penis was in the mix."

"Right," Cammy said.

Treece frowned. "I just realized. My dad's juices are probably all over this couch!"

Even worse: "And *Bitchricia's.*"

Treece shuddered, then seemed absolutely fine. "This is why I'm so screwed up," she said matter-of-factly.

DENIS WAS TRYING to get into the spirit of things, servicing Beth while ignoring the sorrowful surroundings. As Beth bucked into him, he bucked back, until they had a satisfying rhythm going. On his own volition, he had put his hand into Beth's blouse and had managed, with some difficulty, to roll and fold her brassiere up around her neck.

He fondled her breasts, stroking and pinching and randomly manipulating them, not thinking the whole time, *Holy crap, I'm fondling Beth Cooper's breasts*, but praying, *Please, God, make this feel good.*

His other hand rested on her hip bone, occasionally squeezing it. Beth took the hand by surprise and slapped it on her panties. Denis's fingers twitched, then settled into the fabric. He felt a raised stitching, and giggled into Beth's mouth.

"What's so funny?"

"Hello."

"You *did* look!" She slapped him on the ass. Once there, her index finger found the second largest breach in his underpants.

"Woo," she said, wiggling her finger inside.

Denis reacted much like those foxes in that video Ariel Kaminer always played in the cafeteria during lunch, in other words, as if 240 volts of electricity had been pumped up his anus. It really fluffed out his fur.

To say he flew off her would be an exaggeration, but he was off before either of them knew it was happening. He sat up on the dock, trying to catch his breath. This was where he would ordinarily spiral into abject mortification, wishing he were dead or invisible, or vaporized, accomplishing both. Instead he found that between gasps he was laughing, at himself, and happily.

"That was . . . *ha,* I was taken by surprise there," he said. "It wasn't you. I'm sure you did it perfectly. I'm just . . . unaccustomed . . . Let's try that again, shall we?"

Beth was already sitting up, lighting a cigarette.

"It's okay." She left her brassiere dangling around her neck.

"No, really," Denis said. "I would very much like to."

"Maybe later."

Goddammit goddammit goddammit goddammit goddammit goddammit goddammit goddammit goddammit goddammit goddammit goddammit goddammit goddammit goddammit goddammit goddammit goddammit goddammit.

Denis tried to quickly retrace the steps that had taken him to this point, not *this* point but the one immediately preceding it, the one with him on top of Beth. He couldn't find a way back on top. Events and actions stretched into the past in an unbreakable chain of cause and effect, to the talk they just had, to all the talking, back through each of his injuries, each a new intimacy between them, to Rich answering the door when she arrived, to the moment in his speech in which he said *I love you, Beth Cooper,* to the week before, when Rich talked him into saying it, to the first time he sat behind her and smelled her hair. There were so many things he would do differently, but any of them done differently would have arrived at a different moment, and the odds of any of those other moments involving Denis Cooverman on top of Beth Cooper were incomprehensibly high.

And so, he decided to take another tack. It was a time-honored one, and one that showed our Little Denis was becoming a man, unfortunately.

"Beth," he said, putting his arm around her. "I really do lo—"

"Oh, *fuck me!*"

Only she didn't mean that. She meant that Denis's face frightened and repulsed her. Given that only a few minutes before she had found it kissable, that was saying something. Now, by the light of the submerging moon, Beth could see that Denis's face, in addition to its previously catalogued irregularities, was a swarming mass of mosquito bites. So much blood coagulated and contused up there it was rather remarkable that he had been able to maintain an erection all this time.

Beth reached out and touched Denis's cheek gently.

"That must itch."

"I was distracted before, but now it does, yeah." Denis scratched, leaving four red streaks down his cheek.

"Don't do that," Beth said.

Bloody mosquito bites were a turnoff with no turn back on, Denis realized. "So," he asked for posterity, "am I the most hideous creature you ever kissed?"

"God no," Beth said without hesitation, making Denis feel both good and bad.

Beth stood.

Yes, Denis realized, it was time to go.

He turned to get up and that's when he saw the two headlights, very far apart, coming very fast.

THE HUMMER RUMBLED ONTO THE DOCK at a speed inadvisably high for a rotting, waterlogged structure built by a drunk handyman. The vehicle didn't indicate any intention of stopping. When it did finally do so, five inches from the end, Denis was in Lake Hakaka. Beth stood at the edge of the dock, her knees touching the bumper.

22.

DEATH IN DENIS

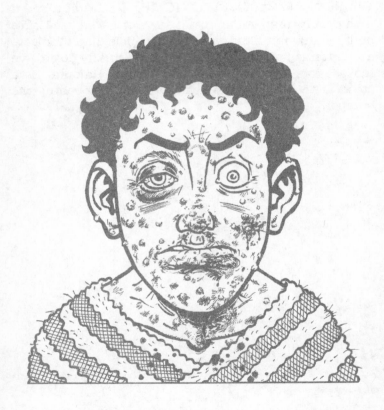

MAKE UP YOUR MIND, DUDE, IS HE
GONNA SHIT OR IS HE GONNA KILL US?

JEFF SPICOLI

SEX WAS A TERRIFIC ICEBREAKER.
"Really?" Rich asked Cammy. "You're studying acting at U of I? *¡Yo tambien!* I mean: Me, too. And directing. I'm in business but I'm transferring as soon as my dad's not paying attention."
"Your dad sounds like a real prize."
"Oh, you know, he doesn't hit me."
They were all huddled together under the bearskin rug, nude but aggressively oblivious to their recent sexual interactivity.
Rich rolled over, facing Cammy.
"Wait, if you want to be an actress, why weren't you in drama club?"
"Survival."
"Good call."
Rich laughed, stroking Cammy's shoulder. "Good call."
Treece pulled a furry paw to her neck. "Hello?" she pouted. "It was a *three*some."
The ensuing silence was awkward for only a moment, because of all the screaming.

THREE NAKED TEENAGERS shuffled to the window under cover of bear.
"What the Christ?" Rich said.
Sean was dragging Denis out from under the dock as the one called Dustin struggled to maintain control of Beth, whose kicking and shrieking showed a lot of stamina after the night she had had. Kevin was in the Hummer, trying to back up off the narrow dock and swearing quite a bit.
"How'd they find us?"
"Oopsie," Treece said.
Cammy's right eyebrow requested elaboration.
"I kind of invited Sean up here before," Treece explained, before getting defensive. "Well, he should've known he wasn't invited anymore!"

Rich had a strange feeling, a sort of déjà vu, that he had been here before, only he had been Kevin Bacon. And then he remembered where he had seen this: *"Come on, I love you." —Kevin Bacon to Jeannine Taylor, shortly before they fornicated on a bunk bed and he was impaled by an arrow through the throat, in* Friday the 13th, *1980, Sean Cunningham.* And then he remembered the countless other times he had seen the same setup, always ending the same basic way, with sometimes clever variations.

It fairly freaked him out.

"Don't you *get* it?" He rattled the bearskin to get their attention. "We're stupid teenagers who just had sex in a cabin by a lake! We're dead! We are *so very dead.*"

Cammy was unfazed. "I'd hardly call that sex."

Treece, meanwhile, was getting excited. She grabbed them both by the shoulders and momentously announced, "I have an idea!"

She was disappointed in their reaction.

"I have ideas!" she pouted.

"SEE THAT?" Kevin jabbed at the front grille of the Hummer, which looked remarkably intact, considering. "My dad is gonna shit," he whined, mostly to himself.

"That's your *father's* car?" Denis was bewildered. "I thought you were from Texas, or a swamp."

"He's from Glenview," Beth spat, still flailing against her restraint. "He went to Maine North. He only talks that way to be cool."

"Talking like a hillbilly is cool?"

Kevin sauntered over to Denis. "We'll see how cool you talk when I'm through with y'all."

"I'm pretty sure that's a misuse of *y'all.*"

Kevin whispered in Denis's ear: "By the time I am through with *y'all,* y'all will be *begging* me to kill *y'all.*"

Denis smiled.

Kevin took umbrage.

"Is that a *cliché?*" He pronounced it with excessive southern elongation. "Is *this* a cliché?"

Kevin punched Denis in the left eye, the only unaltered portion of his facial topology.

"*Stop punching me!*" Kevin's Denis was a fluttery, effeminate clown. "Talk about your clichés."

As he passed Beth, Kevin noticed her brassiere necklace. He registered this with feigned disinterest. He flicked her hard on the nipple.

"Dick," she said.

"Whore," he replied, both syllables.

"As matter of fact, it is," mumbled Denis, returning to full consciousness a few beats behind the conversation. With his less recently pummeled eye, Denis watched Kevin return from the back of the Hummer with jumper cables.

"Gentlemen," Kevin addressed his military colleagues, "remember all those excellent techniques the CIA taught us, which we were subsequently forbidden to employ?"

The troops nodded approvingly.

SUDDENLY, A FEROCIOUS WILDCAT leapt out of the bushes!

"*Ya!*" Sean said, throwing Beth at it.

Further suddenly, a huge owl flew at the Dustin guy! He dropped Denis and batted about his head frantically.

"Run!" Treece yelled, holding the owl.

Cammy thrust the wildcat at Sean again, and he reflexively cowered.

Denis and Beth ran past Kevin, who, though disappointed in the performance of his troops, was amused by the outcome and not terribly concerned.

"Now just *what* did y'all hope to accomplish with that?" Kevin mused, as he pivoted into the barrel of a gun.

"Create a temporary distraction," said Rich, "so they could escape and I could get the drop on you." He wore the bear as a cowl and cape, its claws draped across his chest. Unlike the girls, he had remained otherwise naked, excepting the condom, which added a certain tribal quality. "That was the general idea."

Cammy tipped her wildcat in Treece's direction.

Treece curtseyed with her owl.

"You don't know how to shoot that thing." Kevin took a step toward Rich.

Rich had never held a gun before, but had mimed one a million times. It was a showy, movie move, but the gun cocked just the same.

Kevin stopped. "It isn't even loaded."

This was Rich's best impression.

"You gotta ask yourself one question: Do I feel lucky? Well, do ya, punk?"

"Oh," Treece exclaimed, "I know that one!"

Kevin put up his hands. "Let's cool it, okay, guy?" He dropped the army accent, sounding much more like the teenager he still was. "We were just goofing on you. Maybe we went a little too far. But if you shoot us, what's that going to look like?"

"Self-defense," Cammy said.

"Enough." Denis shook his head. "Kevin, just get in your dad's car and drive away. Don't come back. Never bother Beth again . . ."

"Denis," Beth chided.

"Okay," Denis revised. "Never bother *me* again."

Rich gestured toward the Hummer with the rifle. "You heard the Coove."

Denis rolled his eyes.

Kevin, Sean and Dustin marched with Rich at their

backs. Rich, imitating a move he had seen in *Cool Hand Luke, Deliverance, et al.*, stuck the rifle butt in the crook of his arm and let the gun swing down at his side, casual-like.

The barrel fell off.

"Yee," Rich said in a tiny voice. He dropped to the ground, scrambling to stick the barrel back into the stock. He was quickly surrounded by three sets of black khakis.

RICH WAS ON HIS STOMACH, his wrists and ankles bound together with jumper cables, the ends of which were clamped to his ears. He rocked back and forth on the dock.

"Could someone turn me around, so I could see?"

Sean kicked Rich in the head, spinning him toward the lake, where the action was.

"Thanks, dude."

"Any time."

Beth, Cammy and Treece watched forlornly as the canoe paddled further into the lake.

"Cheer up, ladies," Sean said. "Once Michaels teaches mini-Romeo a lesson, we're going to party."

"I'm kind of partied out," Treece said.

"No," Dustin said, "you're not."

EARLY TWILIGHT gloomily illuminated the small canoe as it slid across the dead lake. Denis was paddling. Kevin played coxswain, smacking Denis every few seconds to keep him on task. It was more humiliating than painful at this point.

"Your error was not striking when you had tactical advantage back there."

Denis kept his head lowered and continued paddling.

"How long can you swim, Cooverman?"

Water was the only thing that had ever come close to

killing Denis. His mother had left the bathroom for only a moment, to get a cleaner towel. The toddler was face-down in the tub when she returned. He wasn't moving.

"I don't know."

Baby Denis's eyes were open, watching. He was fascinated by the no-slip fish and was unaware he was drowning.

"Well then," Kevin said, "let's you and me find out."

Denis could swim forever. His father had made sure of that. The boy had been snorkeling since he was five, diving since he was ten. He had a half dozen international scuba certificates, including one for diving in caves. Water had tried to kill Denis, and he had made water his bitch.

So Denis was certainly not afraid of getting thrown in some smelly puddle. He could sink to the bottom of the lake and swim underwater all the way to the shore without being seen. He could hide in the woods until morning, or until the authorities arrived to dredge the lake.

The only problem with that plan was that it once again required Denis to run away.

"I hope you fucked her," Kevin said, making conversation.

He wasn't afraid of Kevin anymore, Denis realized. These constant attempts on his life were getting annoying, as a matter of fact.

"It would be a shame for you to die without the privilege of fucking Beth Cooper," Kevin said. "No, *privilege* isn't right. More like, without getting *your turn*."

That inchoate rage deep inside Denis was beginning to differentiate itself.

"You did fuck her, didn't you?"

The rage had a face.

"Won't say? You're a *gentleman*? Well, that would be a first for her." Kevin peered into the water. "This is deep enough."

Kevin saw the paddle but wouldn't remember it.

FROM THE SHORE, it was difficult to tell who had gone into the water. Then Denis stood up in the canoe, legs apart, and thrust the paddle into the air. The poncho helped immeasurably in completing the cinematic silhouette.

Rich grinned. "*Star Wars* one-sheet, 1977."

Sean kicked him in the head again.

HIS MOMENT OF GLORY savored, Denis turned his attention to his victim. He scanned the water around him.

"Kevin?"

Kevin's face floated a few inches below the surface. The eyes were closed and a thin red ribbon wafted off the temple. The face grew darker as it sank.

A vision of Dr. Henneman, uncharacteristically dressed as Obi Wan Kenobi, appeared to Denis.

*Denis, with your SAT scores, you'd practically have to kill someone to not get into Northwestern.**

"Oh no," Denis whispered. "I've practically killed someone!"

Denis threw off the poncho and dove into the lake.

NO ONE ON SHORE wanted Kevin completely dead, and there was a general sense of relief when Denis resurfaced and started back with the soldier in tow.

Treece nudged Sean.

"Go! Get in there and help!"

Sean, insulted: "Do I look like a *fucking marine?*"

Denis did not need the help. Among his assorted international diving certificates was one for lifesaving; he had even worked a couple of summers lifeguarding at the Cambridge on the Lake condominium complex,

---

*His brain filled in the *Northwestern.*

where his main duty was finding out whose kid was pooping in the pool.

As he reached chest-high water, Denis shifted Kevin onto his shoulders in a fireman's carry. He emerged from the lake, clad only in wet tighty whiteys, and it became apparent to all assembled he was no 98-pound weakling. He was 105 pounds of sleek swimmer's physique, previously hidden by shy hunching and frightened cowering. His hair was wildly tousled and his wet hairless body shimmered in the first morning light.

Treece was awed. "It's like when Clark Kent turns into Batman."

"Check out the underpants," Cammy said approvingly.

"I have," said Beth.

DENIS DUMPED KEVIN onto the grass. "I'm going to need some help," he said, rolling the body over. He looked to Sean and Dustin. They looked back.

"Don't they teach you guys CPR in the army?"

"Yeah," Dustin shrugged. "I wasn't really paying attention."

"The job's not really about *saving* people," Sean said.

"I know CPR." Beth crouched next to Kevin.

"Okay," Denis said, "you do breaths and I'll do compressions."

"I'm not putting my mouth on his! We're broken up."

"You are?" Denis asked a little too transparently.

Beth was annoyed. "Why would I mess around with you if I was still with him? *What kind of person do you think I am?*"

The tiff would have to wait.

Kevin rolled to his side and vomited some water. After several seconds, he opened his eyes. He smiled.

"There you go, Cooverman," he said with a wet rattle, "giving up your tactical advantage again."

Kevin shoved Denis to the ground as he staggered to his feet. He cleared his throat and clasped his hands. "Okay!"

"It's getting real late," Dustin complained. "Can't we just beat the shit out of him and go?"

"Fine," Kevin said. He lifted his foot to stomp on Denis's kidneys. He was in this pose when the spotlight hit him.

"Step away from the boy," a loudspeaking voice said.

The squad car flashed its cherries and gave a short burst of siren for emphasis. The other Lake Hakaka police car pulled up behind it.

The army men seemed perplexed by this turn of events.

"Duh," Rich informed them. "We called the police."

"We're not like stupid teenagers," Treece added.

23.

THE MOST EXCELLENT AND LAMENTABLE TRAGEDY OF DENIS AND ELIZABETH

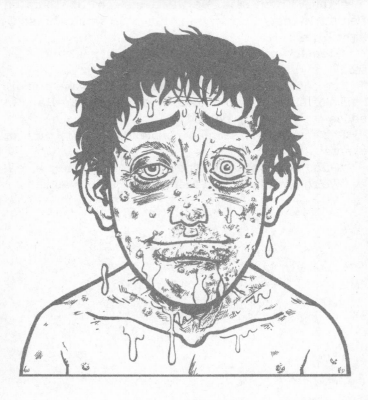

I'VE JUST HAD THE BEST SUMMER
OF MY LIFE, AND NOW I HAVE TO GO AWAY.
IT ISN'T FAIR.

SANDY OLSSON

IT WAS MORNING when the squad car pulled up to 22 Mary Lu Lane, a tiny ranch house only a block from where Denis's father grew up. This was what was known as Old Buffalo Grove, which local Realtors touted for its large selection of *starter homes*.

Denis, Rich and Beth were in the backseat, being delivered home by a Lake Hakaka police officer who, in all honesty, had nothing better to do. Cammy and Treece were escorted in the other patrol car, after sitting on Sean and Dustin's laps for the ride to the station.

Denis's anxious predictions to the contrary, it did not appear as if Beth was going to be charged with ten crimes. Kevin's father had quickly agreed to forgo larceny charges in exchange for Denis's statement that he didn't feel as if he was being murdered at any point in the evening. Treece's father dealt with the Woolly family, persuading them that seeking justice for the front of their house was not worth a class-action lawsuit over knowingly serving alcohol to minors at a party supervised by their drug-addicted son. Later it would turn out that none of the kids at the party had seen anything anyway.

On the ride home, Rich had entertained Officer Peasley with Pacino cops from *Serpico*, *Sea of Love*, *Heat* and *Cruising*, as well as Pacino robbers from *Dog Day Afternoon*, *Scarface*, *Donnie Brasco* and *Dick Tracy*, and some *Scent of a Woman* just because.

Denis and Beth fell asleep on each other, briefly, and at different times.

BETH GOT OUT OF THE CAR. She left the door open to say good-bye.

"Thank you for a *very* memorable evening."

"We'll have to do it again sometime."

"Sure," Beth said.

Denis said, "Sure."

"Good luck. With Northwestern, and everything."

"You too. With everything."

She extended her hand. Denis took it. Beth grinned, and bent down and kissed him. On the forehead.

Quite unlike him, Denis stood and kissed her, square on the mouth. She let it go on for a respectable interval.

"You're getting better at that."

"I was bad before?" he asked, still Denis.

She was already walking away.

Denis got out of the car. "Wait."

Beth turned around.

"See you at the reunion," Denis said.

"Yeah."

"If you're not too fat, I'll marry you."

"Thanks," Beth said. "That's a promise."

She fluttered her fingers in farewell, and started back toward the house. None of the lights were on. She took out her keys and let herself in.

Denis got back in the squad car.

"YOU'LL SEE HER AGAIN," Rich said as the car pulled away. "She's had a taste of the Coove."

"Please stop calling me that."

"You know, I think we might have more traction with 'The Penis' anyway. We just need to spin it, give it a legendary angle—"

"You said it would be better if I got over her."

Rich didn't answer right away.

"I just want what you want."

A minute or so later, Rich spoke again.

"Hey, guess what? I think I'm gay."

Denis's reaction was more pronounced than he thought it would be.

"Dude," Rich said. "I'm not gay *for you*."

"That's great." Denis recovered. "I mean, the first part."

"I may be bi. Cary Grant was bi."

Denis spoke next, but not for two minutes.

"So," he said, "what're you doing later?"

"I gotta go get my shoes."

"After that, want to come over?"

"What for?"

"I don't know."

"Sure."

THE PATROL CAR TURNED onto Hackberry Drive. Rich spoke again.

"Hey, the DVD for *Go, Mutants!* just came out," Rich said. "On the unrated disc, Shanley Harmer is 30 percent more nude."

"I thought you were gay."

"Celebrity nudity transcends sexual orientation. You want me to bring it over?"

"By all means."

Denis's parents were waiting for him on the front lawn. His mother gasped, swallowed that, put on her stern face, dropped it, and attempted a *c'est la vie* expression, which pulled something.

"I can't talk about this," she said finally. "I'm going to go make a frittata."

She hugged her little boy, whispering, "Or did *she* already make you breakfast?"

Mrs. C watered up, and ran into the house.

Denis and his father walked to the door.

"I hope you had fun," he said.

"I did. I had fun."

They stepped over the apple tree.

"You know we're going to have to punish you . . . somehow."

"I know."

"What do they do these days? Do they still ground you? I don't even know."

"Whatever it is, it was worth it."

Mr. C put his arm around his son.

"Let's not tell your mother that."

24.

THE CRAWL

ALL MY MEMORIES FROM HIGH SCHOOL
ARE FROM TONIGHT.

DENIS COOVERMAN

Denis grew seven inches that summer,
and gained nearly forty pounds. Growing
pains kept him in bed for most of July,
but he didn't mind.

Rich gave homosexuality a shot,
didn't like that either, and was holding out
to see what the other alternatives were.

Cammy and Treece decided they were just
good friends, who should not drink so much
around each other anymore.

Denis didn't see Beth Cooper again
until late August, a week before
he had intended to leave for school . . .

OBLIGATIONS

I've always thought that endless acknowledgments have no place in a novel, but then I wrote one, and found a place.

And so I must thank my book agent, Sarah Burnes, without whose hounding this book would never have been written. And all my other agents—Gregory McKnight, Matthew Snyder and Jeff Jacobs—who keep my children fed. And my old agent, Cara Stein, because I adore her.

I must also thank my editor, Lee Boudreaux, who I signed with because she was the only one to offer me a goddam Diet Coke, but then it turned out she is also magnificently underhanded and makes your book good without you even noticing it.

Thank you to my parents, whose loving upbringing meant I had to write a novel, rather than a much better-selling memoir. And thank you to my foxy wife, Becky, and I'm sorry for the long summer of not showering and acting more like a writer than usual.

For lending their real names to this book when I got tired of making up new ones, I thank: Jill Rosenbaum, Ariel Kaminer, Claudia Confer (who really was the nicest and prettiest cheerleader at BGHS) and my brother, Kevin, and his sons Sean and Dustin (who really aren't that villainous.)

Future obligations to Kurt Andersen, Dave Barry, David Schickler, and Tom Perrotta for reading the thing and risking their reputations by endorsing it.

And thank you, Beth Cooper, all of you.

ABOUT THE AUTHOR

ABOUT THE BOOK

READ ON

Insights,
Interviews
& More . . .

MEET LARRY DOYLE
HOW TO BECOME A SIMPSONS WRITER IN ONLY TWENTY-SIX YEARS: A MEMOIR

Courtesy of Larry Doyle

Buffalo Grove High School, Class of '76

HOW DID YOU get to be a writer on
The Simpsons?

I get asked this question a lot. I believe
the expected answer is:

*Go to this address, room 203. Knock
three times rapidly, then twice slowly. A
contract will slide under the door. Sign it
and slide it back. The door will open. It will
be Matt Groening. Smile, but do not touch
him. Congratulations! You are now a writer
for* The Simpsons.

My answer, unfortunately, is tedious and

only helpful as a contrary example. But here it is, with all of the boring parts included, because I think they're probably more instructive than the exciting parts.

I decided I wanted to write when I was about twelve years old, after rummaging through my father's closet for the *Playboys* he slipped between copies of *Golf* magazine. I came across two yellowing clips from an Irish newspaper. They were short stories. The byline read, "by Larry Doyle."

I remember writing my first humorous story for eighth grade English for Mrs. Bone. She was a skeletal, bluish lady, who had some sort of fungus on her elbow she was always scratching. If she talked to you for more than a minute, she always left a fine sprinkling of dust on your desk. The story I wrote had something to do with me dying and my mom wrapping me in tin foil because she didn't want to waste money on a coffin. Kids laughed.

At Buffalo Grove High School, I submitted a short story to the *BG Charger* newspaper contest, about a guy who is talking to his buddies about breaking up with his girlfriend, and then he walks over to her, and she breaks up with him. Very O. Henry. I won second prize, and got a check for five dollars. I have a Thermo-Fax of that check in my office.

On a visit to my future alma mater, the University of Illinois, I stopped at a Little Professor Bookstore and bought copies of Woody Allen's *Without Feathers* and *Getting Even*. Shortly thereafter, I wrote a story called "The Professor and the Case of the Unaccompanied Parakeet." My girlfriend typed up this twenty-page masterpiece (on onionskin to save on postage), and I sent it to *Playboy*. They rejected it. Seeing that many of Woody's pieces had been published in *The New Yorker* (which I had never read), I sent it there. Politely rejected. I then sent it to every magazine at the library, as well as *Hustler* magazine (which said the story "does not meet our needs at this time"). ▶

❝ I decided I wanted to write when I was about twelve years old, after rummaging through my father's closet for the *Playboys* he slipped between the copies of *Golf* magazine. ❞

WRITING LESSON: If at first you don't succeed, give up.

Instead of sending that terrible piece all over the place, I should have been writing my next terrible piece.

My freshman year at the U of I, I spent a huge amount of time in the undergraduate library, not studying but excavating ancient bound copies of *The New Yorker*, discovering the work of Benchley, Thurber, Parker and Salinger. On a bus trip to visit my high school girlfriend in Canada, I bought a copy of Donald Barthelme's *Unspeakable Practices, Unnatural Acts* and read the whole thing straight through. When I got back, I checked out every one of his books.

Anyway, I took a couple of fiction writing courses with Mark Costello, who told great stories, usually more than once. I wrote many Woody Allen and Donald Barthelme stories there. After the final course, Mark Costello told me that I was good with words and should pursue a career in writing, but that I obviously wasn't a fiction writer.

I also worked at the *Daily Illini*, where I did the Campus Scout humor column and wrote three different comic strips with three different artists. I read nearly every *Pogo* comic strip in the back issues.

I dropped out of psychology graduate school, and got a master's in journalism, mostly because it gave me the opportunity to edit the *Daily Illini*'s weekly magazine.

I graduated, and was unemployed for about a year.

Finally, a friend of mine, Beth Austin, told her boss at United Press International that my parents were going to throw me out of the house if I didn't find a job. So I became a Unipresser. There I learned to write whether I felt like it or not.

WRITING LESSON: Just write.

UPI was going under at the time and bouncing paychecks; anybody who could find

> ❝ WRITING LESSON: If at first you don't succeed, give up. ❞

another job found one, which left a lot of room for advancement. I became UPI's chief medical reporter and filed more than twelve hundred stories in one year. Meanwhile, some college friends and I formed a writing group in order to make us actually write. I wrote several Barthelme pieces, which I sent to *The New Yorker*, and which were politely and pro forma declined. Then one day, a personal note from Julia Just (now children's book editor at the *New York Times*) was added to the rejection, encouraging me to submit more. I probably submitted a dozen pieces, which received longer and more polite rejections.

Simultaneously, I had been trying to get *Escaped from the Zoo*, a college comic strip I did with Neal Sternecky, syndicated. No one bought it, but the Los Angeles Times Syndicate remembered us when Walt Kelly's family decided to bring back *Pogo*. After about two years of try outs, negotiations and delays, we were hired.

The strip was a failure. It started in more than three hundred papers, and we were on the *Today* show, but every time a newspaper did a poll, we came in last and were dropped. This was primarily because the writing wasn't very good.

WRITING LESSON: Do your own thing.

One of the pieces I had sent to *The New Yorker*, a non-Barthelme manqué inspired by the years I had spent pining for an old girlfriend, was not outright rejected. They asked me to make some changes. I was terrified. A year later, with *Pogo* going down the tubes, I decided that my non-rejected *New Yorker* piece was preventing me from a complete wallow, and I revised it. They accepted it.

It ran on January 15, 1990.

I was thirty-one years old. My life had changed, I thought.

I was a published *New Yorker* writer. I planned on spending the rest of my days ▶

> **" Then one day, a personal note from Julia Just (now children's book editor at the *New York Times*) was added to the rejection, encouraging me to submit more. I probably submitted a dozen pieces, which received longer and more polite rejections. "**

at a big white house in Connecticut. Adding to this delusion, only three months later, *The New Yorker* published another piece, a parody of Thomas Pynchon's new book, *Vineland*.

I didn't publish another piece in *The New Yorker* for almost four years.

However, Randy Cohen, then a writer for David Letterman (and now "The Ethicist" for the *New York Times Magazine*), read "Life Without Leann" and said I should submit material for *Late Night*. I did, and did not get the job. But Randy Cohen passed my material on to Susan Davis, a talent scout for HA!, a precursor of Comedy Central, and I got a job on *Afterdrive*, a comedy talk show starring Denis Leary and Billy Kimball.

WRITING LESSON: Make friends with talented people.

I moved to New York.

The show ended thirteen weeks later.

I was unemployed.

Randy recommended me to Cara Stein at William Morris. I was still unemployed, but had an agent.

I wrote a spec script for *The Simpsons* called "Bart Burns Down the House." This was 1991, the second year of the show. Randy sent it to George Meyer, a friend of his, who sent it back saying he couldn't read it because he had just written an episode in which Homer set the house on fire (the legendary "Homer the Heretic").

I answered a want ad, and landed a job on the *National Lampoon*, which was coming back as a monthly under George Barkin (Ellen's brother). He had this idea that America was ripe for a really smart, literary humor magazine. He was fired a few months later. Along with Chris Marcil, Sam Johnson, Danny O'Keefe and Ian Maxtone-Graham (who I had met on *Afterdrive*), we were allowed to put out a couple more issues before being fired.

66 WRITING LESSON: Make friends with talented people. 99

I was unemployed again. Then Ian Maxtone-Graham got a job writing an MTV game show pilot, and hired me. The pilot wasn't picked up.

This time I was unemployed for several months. Then Susan Davis suggested me to a producer that was doing a pilot for *Spy* magazine. That pilot went nowhere, but I met *Spy* founder Kurt Andersen, and later pitched him the cover story, "1,000 Reasons George Bush Should Not Be Re-Elected." (Little did I know that eight years later we would elect another George Bush who would make his predecessor seem like Lincoln.) I was hired at *Spy* by then–Deputy Editor Susan Morrison (who now edits "Shout and Murmurs" at *The New Yorker*, among other things), and worked there until a few months after Kurt left.

I worked for HBO for a while, developing shows nobody ever saw for Comedy Central. Chris Marcil and Sam Johnson had gotten jobs writing for a new cartoon, *Beavis and Butt-Head*, and recommended me. I wrote a bunch of episodes, as well as two books, one of which you can now buy used for a penny. I also got more pieces in *The New Yorker*, usually a few clumped together and separated by years. Ian Maxtone-Graham recommended me at *SNL*, and I managed a meeting with Jim Downey (who, in classic Jim Downey fashion, scheduled a 1:00 p.m. interview, emerged at 11:00 p.m. and invited me to dinner with the cast and writers), but did not get the job. I was almost hired at *Conan*, I think.

Kurt Andersen took over *New York* magazine, and hired me. I worked there for a few years, writing two go-nowhere (non-WGA-minimum-paying) movies on the side. Then in August 1996, when I was on my honeymoon, Kurt was fired. I resigned.

I was unemployed again.

Mike Judge recommended me to *Rolling Stone* to write a faux profile of Beavis and ▶

> " I worked for HBO for a while, developing shows nobody ever saw for Comedy Central. . . . I wrote a bunch of episodes [of *Beavis and Butt-Head*], as well as two books, one of which you can now buy used for a penny. "

Meet Larry Doyle *(continued)*

Butt-Head to coincide with the movie. While in L.A. that November (the idea was that I was following B&B around Hollywood), I visited Ian Maxtone-Graham, now working at *The Simpsons*. He introduced me to Mike Scully, the new executive producer. Both Ian, and Ron Hauge, with whom I had worked at *National Lampoon*, recommended me. I submitted "Bart Burns Down the House."

That's how I started writing for *The Simpsons*. But I'm sure there's a faster way. ⌒⌣

A RUDE INTERVIEW WITH THE AUTHOR, CONDUCTED BY THE AUTHOR

You write sitcoms and big dumb Hollywood movies. What made you think you could write a novel?

The same thing that made those Hollywood hacks Fitzgerald and Faulkner think they could do it, I guess. You know, if Balzac were alive today (he's not, right?), I'm sure he be writing unfunny French comedies and Dostoevsky would be cleaning up on *Law & Order*. At least that's how I sleep at night.

Folks seem surprised, and a little distressed, to discover I've written a novel. Why? I wrote for *The Simpsons*. I wrote movies starring Drew Barrymore and Ben Stiller and Steve Martin and Daffy Duck! What possible reason could I have for putting words on paper bound in cloth, sold by homeless people on the streets?

My mother naturally assumed it was because I could no longer find real work. She worried, as she did when I left the television show to write movies, about health insurance. My friends figured I had gone a little crazier, or had finally figured out how empty and soulless Hollywood was. What my mother did not know—and please don't tell her—is that I can never find real work, until I do. And what my friends forget is that I was always pretty crazy and that I despised Hollywood before I got there, and so have been mostly pleasantly surprised.

I've always wanted to write a novel, of course. Or to have written one. What prevented me from doing so until now is there was nothing stopping me from not writing it.

There were also significant barriers. Novels are long. My first novel also needed to be better than Thomas Pynchon's *V.,* ▶

A Rude Interview with the Author, Conducted by the Author

(continued)

and later at least as good as Don DeLillo's *White Noise*, and then as funny as Bruce Robinson's *The Peculiar Memories of Thomas Penman*. I'm a reasonably industrious guy, but not the kind you find awake at 4:00 a.m. scribbling on legal pads for a few hours before leaving for his advertising job. So it took a while.

In the end, why did you write this novel, rather than one of those good ones?

It was mostly an accident.

In the fall of 2005, I had a dream: I'm giving my high school graduation speech, but I veer off text and declare my love for a girl I had a crush on in the seventh grade.

That's an idea, I thought. But I didn't know for what.

I originally thought it might be a *New Yorker* piece, with the title "The Valedict," a thousand words of a valedictory address that goes off the rails. Then I began thinking of the consequences of such a speech, and I thought maybe it could be a movie. I worked up about a hundred pages of a script/outline and showed it to my movie agent, who showed it to a couple of producers I've worked with.

They all agreed:

it's "too small,"

Hollywood jargon explicitly meaning a character-driven story without a commercial hook, but can also mean they didn't like it;

and "execution dependent,"

a curious Hollywood concept that means that if it's not done well, it won't succeed. It's curious because it implies its opposite: that there are ideas that will sell well even if they're executed terribly. You've no doubt seen some of these movies, which is why they keep making them. Saying something is "execution dependent" can also mean they don't think *you* can execute it, or that they didn't like it;

and "not castable."

This means there's no part for Will Ferrell. Someone suggested that perhaps one of the characters who hangs out with the teenagers on graduation night could be a former graduate, with a nickname like "Wooderson" or "Tank" or something. I thought having a thirty-five-year-old in the backseat of a teen sex comedy might alter the tone somewhat.

Nobody thought they could sell it. *I Love You, Beth Cooper*, the movie, was dead.

Then I received an e-mail from Sarah Burnes, a literary agent at the Gernert Company. I had met her a couple months earlier, and had promised her I would write a novel. She wanted to know where it was. I sent her the *ILYBC* outline, saying that I had wasted my time on this instead. She called me a couple days later, and said, "This is a novel." And more importantly, "I can sell this."

I wrote a hundred sample pages, which took me only twenty pages into my outline. She sent it out, and folks were interested. I arrived in New York on a Monday in March 2006 to meet with book publishers, and got a call from my film agent. Everybody in Hollywood had the one hundred pages and wanted to talk about making it into a movie.

We sold the book to Ecco, and then I actually had to write the thing. As you might imagine, writing a novel is a bit harder that writing a screenplay. I have some experience writing prose, but the longest piece of fiction I had written to that point was about five thousand words, and awful. Fortunately, though, I had to meet a deadline, and I am much better at doing that.

My original outline changed in myriad ways as it unfolded on the page; the characters deepened, and their complicating relationships changed the course of the original story. The book also became a commentary on the very movie I was going to write, which I now realize would not have been great.

I never had as much fun writing something.

That fall the full manuscript was optioned by Chris Columbus (the director of *Home Alone* and the first two Harry Potter movies, among many others). Just as the hardcover was being released, we sold the project to Fox Atomic. I'm supposed to be writing the script right now instead of doing this interview (it's July 9, 2007), and by the time you read this, the movie should be available for your illegal downloading pleasure.

What's the difference between writing for the movies and writing novels, besides the coke and hookers?

Very little, in terms of the doing.

I sit in front the computer screen, desperately hoping something I'm writing will require internet research with which I can kill the rest of the day. There are differences in the form, of course, but these are fairly obvious and I'm saving them for "The 12 Top Secrets of Writing Hit Comedies," the book and Learning Annex course I'm planning once I can't find work anymore.

The real difference is after it's written. You may have heard the old joke:

Q. Did you hear about the Ethnicity-Reputed-to-Have-Low-Intelligence Actress?

A. She slept with the writer.

It's not really a joke. In the movie business, writers are tolerated as a necessary annoyance, whose utility is measured primarily by their ▶ willingness to do what they're told. Even then, they'll likely be

A Rude Interview with the Author, Conducted by the Author
(continued)

replaced. Because writers are to movie-making what turtles were to Yertle.

One story:

I wrote a screenplay that later became associated with a film called *Duplex,* starring Ben Stiller and Drew Barrymore. The script was developed for a year or so with the two stars and the original director, who left six weeks before shooting. Danny DeVito was brought in to replace him. I had one very pleasant conversation with Danny at his very nice house, and *then I never talked to him again.* I was invited to the set by one producer, called back and informed that, while I had a contractual right to visit the set, Mr. DeVito didn't want me there. He didn't acknowledge me at the press junket—where the junket reporters were also none too happy at having to talk to the writer instead of cute Drew or hunky Ben or fat Danny. I only glanced at him during the premiere, because he was sitting so many rows in front of me. I should add here that Ben and Drew and their producers Stuart Cornfeld and Nancy Juvonen were mostly delightful to deal with, as was the original director Greg Mottola. But Mr. DeVito's attitude about writers is pretty pervasive: once the script is written, the dream writer would turn into a pizza and six-pack, to steal another old joke.

Another story:

I wrote a book for Ecco, which you either own or are still reading in the store, and should purchase immediately. After handing in the manuscript, I received a long, thoughtful letter from my editor Lee Boudreaux, describing what she liked and what I could improve. This sentence at the end caught my eye.

"I really don't think you're going to have much trouble with any of my comments but, I hope it goes without saying, it's *your* book and these are *your* choices."

You couldn't get that sentence out of a movie executive or director with jumper cables.

I Love You, Beth Cooper *was clearly inspired by classic teen movie comedies. Was there one in particular that you stole from more than others?*

I tried to steal equally and fairly. The book's obviously a mash-up of teen comedy material—the geek, the homecoming queen, buying beer, sneaking into the girl's locker room—and on some level I was trying to both honor those tropes but also subvert them. The thought was to see if I could start out with these stereotypes and fill them out in unexpected ways, while also sending the reader on a wild ride. In that sense, it was an exercise similar to *The Breakfast Club*, which started out with all these high school stereotypes, mixed them up and revealed their different sides.

Also, since Denis was such a neophyte to teenage ways, I tried to get him to experience every traditional coming-of-age ritual in one night. Clearly the model there is *American Graffiti*.

Though, in truth, the book was constructed as a devilishly ingenious homage to Joyce's *Ulysses*, as well as a modern retelling of that epic Virgil poem. A lot of people miss that.

Is there a reason you chose to set the book in your own hometown, in your own high school alma mater, rather than taking the fifteen seconds to come up with something original?

I go through phases when I want to create my own Yoknapatawpha, and others when I decide that as a literary device, it's become an uninteresting affectation. So I was either in that latter phase when I decided to write this, or just lazy.

Originally I was also going to use the real name of the girl who inspired the story—I sat behind her in seventh-grade math, and had a crush on her that did not make it to high school, and otherwise had no idea who she was or what she was like—but my attorney wrestled me to the ground and convinced me otherwise. There's a stat of what she wrote in my seventh-grade yearbook—at Cooper Junior High—on page 131.

There really was an Old Tobacco Road that was renamed—though not to Gwendolynne Way—and that we used to race along without headlights, being immortal. But the spooky, foggy road was Quentin, which has a Piggly Wiggly now, which I believe is haunted.

In the legal matter at the front, though, you'll see I wrote: "The village of Buffalo Grove depicted herein is the product of a faulty memory and sloppy research, and should not be relied upon by anyone planning a vacation there."

Being old, how did you manage to capture what it was like being a teenager today? As the New York Times Book Review so cleverly quipped, "That a 48-year-old is so up-to-the-minute with teenage vernacular is either impressive or creepy."

I just wrote about what high school was like for me, and updated the props. And I have the advantage of being a man and, therefore, never growing up.

Seriously, I don't think being a teenager has changed much in the last fifty years. The cliques, the rituals, the anxieties, are all the same, with different names and levels of extremity.

Plus, there's more blowjobs. Or so I've heard. ▶

A Rude Interview with the Author, Conducted by the Author
(continued)

Speaking of creepy, you have a MySpace page.

They made me.

Upon selling my book, I was told, and then told again, that I needed to establish "an online presence" if the book was to have any chance of achieving nonfailure. And then I got a few dozen e-mails about it. Book publishers have embraced cybermarketing based on the belief that it is the best way to reach young readers, and also that it is largely free.

I was afraid of MySpace. I had become convinced that should I even visit the site, within moments the FBI would crash through the ceiling with evidence I had ogled underage blurbs. But I did what I was told. I set up an account, and put up some information about the book.

Not good enough. I needed to make my page more "personal" so that people would know it was operated by me and not some HarperCollins cybot. So I did that.

Now, I was told, I needed to "make friends."

This involves poking around and finding people who share similar interests and begging them to be your friend. I was leery of this, being old and odd looking, and also selling something. I had heard that MySpace had recently suffered cool depletion due to "commercialization" and here I was running around the place with a commercial. Anyway, I got over that.

And curiously, I've actually made some friends on MySpace. All of whom are over eighteen.

You use a lot of brand names in the book. How much were you paid?

I could probably have made more money in placement if the products were real rather than made up, and the references were positive rather than negative.

I was doing it to try to accurately convey the world in which teenagers live. And I do think that consumption is, and always has been, a signifier for teenagers.

Denis Cooverman is not exactly hero material. Was he autobiographical?

I do see Denis as a heroic figure. He does go on a journey, some of it on water, and learns to use his superpowers properly. In that sense, he wasn't autobiographical.

What's the deal with Beth, Treece, and Cammy? It seems like they have unnecessary dimensions added to them.

I wanted the girls to be interesting. I'll be sure to flatten them back for the movie.

Have any real Beth Coopers been in touch with you since you wrote the book? Their lawyers?

Three Beth Coopers e-mailed me when they heard about the book, and I got the idea to include a page of Beth Cooper pictures. It's on the Web site, www.iloveyoubethcooper.com. There are a few famous Beth Coopers up there, and one of them is actually the head cheerleader of her high school, just like the Beth Cooper in the book, only [please insert standard legal disclaimer here].

I've run out of interesting questions. So how about: What is your writing process like?

I used the little-taught disgorgement method, which is what I also use for writing screenplays.

I sit down and write anything I can. The next day I do that again.

Eventually I get to the end of the story, and I have something that is mostly outline, with some dialogue and scenes set. Then I go through the whole manuscript again, adding scenes and dialogue where I can, changing things along the way. And again, and again, and again, until I reach the point that I think that at least the story is in the right order—at this point the actual thing may only be a third "done." And then I write through the whole thing more methodically, usually starting the day by reading and revising what I've done so far and trying to get a little further through the piece. Once I get to the end, I may be about 80 percent there.

Then I do several polish passes.

This I call a first draft.

Um, okay. Biggest influences?

Writers I have stolen from: Charles Portis, Kurt Vonnegut, Donald Barthelme, and Thomas Pynchon.

Any kind of special pen? Or other kind of tool?

I wrote most of *ILYBC* on a G4 Macintosh Powerbook, using Starbucks coffee. I'll be writing my next book on an iPhone.

In terms of my other writing tools, I used to hoard reference books—I have a few thousand, including books on opera and calculus I have never used—but now I do almost all my research online. I have ▶

A Rude Interview with the Author, Conducted by the Author
(continued)

thousands of bookmarks in various categories, and I usually create a new category for each project and add links as I go along. For *I Love You, Beth Cooper*, I relied heavily on Google, Wikipedia, and IMDB. I also use the Social Security name database, http://www.ssa.gov/OACT/babynames/, when picking names, so I know that a name I choose was somewhat popular when the character was born.

Wrapping up, what's next for Larry Doyle?

My next book is called *Go, Mutants!* It will come out sometime in the next thirty years.

Excuse me. Sorry. It appears we are several lines short. Um. So. Read any good books lately?

The Summer of Naked Swim Parties by Jessica Anya Blau.

Great. Okay. Any other questions, anything I haven't asked?

I can think of a couple:

> You have superpowers, and yet you refuse to use them to help mankind. Why is that?
>
> What's that thing on your face?
>
> In this book, you mention snakes three times for no apparent reason. Is there some psychosexual childhood trauma you'd care to share with us?
>
> What was it like, dating Annette O'Toole?
>
> You did five years at Joliet. Why was that?
>
> What have you got against the Turks?
>
> As a writher, do you feel that all your bad behavior is a furtherance of your art, and therefore commendable?
>
> Are you crying?

Good questions. Let's start with the one about Annette O'Toole.

I would, but I'm afraid we're out of space. ᦇ

SELECTIONS FROM THE
I LOVE YOU, BETH COOPER
AGONY/ECSTASY CONTEST

Last summer, readers of I Love You, Beth Cooper *were asked to share "your best of days, your worst of nights, your most mind-blasting, soul-crushing, thrilling, terrorizing, delightful and humiliating memories of high school" in exchange for a chance to win some meager prizes. Surprisingly, they did. Below are some of the winners.*

ESCAPE FROM DOWNTOWN

I believe it was sophomore year. I know for sure it was at Brown Bill's[1] house (Brown was so named because of his love of brown corduroy pants). Brown's parents weren't home often. He had a grandmother who was hard of hearing and who lived upstairs, though no one ever saw her much. Anyway, Brown was throwing one of his usual Saturday night parties. One hundred kids congregated on Bob's one-plus acre, drinking heavily, smoking clove cigarettes, Marlboro Lights and pot (of course), and listening to Boston at painful volumes.

I headed inside Brown's four-bedroom split-level, because it was chilly out and I didn't have a jacket. I went into the basement and bumped into Matt Roberts—who was basically the George Clooney of high school. He was athletic, smart, and adorable. I sat next to him every day in homeroom and considered him a friend. But every girl worth her salt had done something with Matt, and seeing him there, all alone, made me think perhaps tonight was my turn. Anyway, I gave Matt my best come hither look, then I plunked myself down on the sofa.

Someone had thought ahead and lit the fireplace, which really did wonders in the ▶

---

1. With the exception of the authors, all names have been changed.

ambience department. Sure enough, five seconds later Matt joined me. Never one to waste time, he proceeded to kiss me. It was good. Matt was well versed in the art of making out. No drooling, no overbearing tongue action, just enough contact without venturing into noisy lip-smacking territory . . .

After a few minutes of this he said, "Let's go in Bill's room," which seemed reasonable enough. After all, it was hard to cuddle on the stiff mid-century modern sofa that adorned the rec room (and smelled of mold). However, apparently cuddling wasn't on Matt's mind as he had all his clothes off in about five seconds flat.

He hopped in the bed, leaving me standing there wondering why it was that he was fully naked. After all, wasn't this about cuddling? Or perhaps its lesser cousin, spooning? I decided that Matt was just suffering from the heat. He was Cuban and perhaps his blood ran a touch hotter than most. I strapped my naïve cap on and climbed into bed with him.

We got back to the making out, though now he was all naked which was disconcerting because really, we had to be going out to have this type of full-frontal nudity—and even then it would have only occurred following rounds of negotiations. After a few minutes, he put his hands on my shoulders and did the patented 'Downtown Nudge,' which no one likes. Myself included. Wasn't it enough that I allowed him to take all his clothes off? Now he was expecting me to do all sorts of sordid things without so much as a movie and Reese's Pieces Sunday at Friendly's? Nice girls like me didn't play that game.

And so, I casually announced that I had forgotten something outside and that I'd be right back. "What did you forget?" he asked, looking at me confused. "I forgot my sister," was my response, and yes, it made no sense, but I was desperate to get away from the big pervert and didn't have time to concoct a better excuse.

I hopped out of the bed, and rather than racing up the hallway and out the front door to freedom—I opted instead for the garage. It seemed more covert. I imagined that I'd get in there, yank open the door and casually get lost in the crowd that was gathered on Brown's driveway. From there the entire incident would just melt away and we could pretend it didn't happen and chalk it up to too much alcohol.

Sadly, it was an electric door, and despite my Hulk-like attempts to lift it, followed by my inner cry for super human strength (like you see when mothers save their children and overturn cars and stuff), the damn door wouldn't budge.

I tried to get back in to the house, but the door was self-locking. This left me trapped in the garage, which was dark because I'd forgotten to turn on the light switch. With nothing left to do, I began banging on the garage window trying to get the attention of the stoned masses standing on the other side of the door.

I was yelling "Help!" and "Get me out of here!" when I finally got the attention of about ten stoned guys who thought my appearance at the window was baffling. In their pot induced haze, they had lost the ability to think and every time I yelled, "Get me out of here!" they'd ask, "But why are you in there?"

This went on for like five minutes until I finally just blurted out, "Matt wants a blow job and I'm not giving him one!" Just as the words left my mouth—the door opened, the lights flicked on, and there was Matt standing in the doorway, naked and confused. The guys at the window started howling with laughter, this prompted more onlookers and soon all eyes were on the row of garage windows. It was, as they say, awkward.

Perhaps a more dignified person would have handled things better but I decided to channel Florence Griffith Joyner and run . . . I ran past Matt, then I ran out of the house, and down the driveway, (while everyone cheered I might add), and I continued to run, all the way to my house (two miles away) where I spent the rest of the night trying to figure out how I could transfer to a different high school.

Kristen Buckley
Northern Highlands Regional High School, Class of '86
Author of *Tramps Like Us: A Suburban Confession*

EGGS OR VENGEANCE

As Dave delivered the last pizza of the night, we killed the lights, locked up the doors, and headed up to the CircleK. Apparently, the cashier had as much enthusiasm for his job as we did ours. He didn't even look up from his comic to ask why we needed 10 dozen eggs.

Earlier in the evening, Ken, my fellow pie builder, had finally gathered the courage to ask Jenny Stevens out. He had been sweating this forever. She'd never go for it. She was hot. He was not. Of course, she politely declined and said she was going to stay home and look after her sister. Maybe some other time. Thanks, but no thanks

She was later spotted by Dave while on a delivery to a party. And she was with a guy. It wasn't so much that she was out with a guy. It was just that she made up a story to let Ken down easy. He got kinda steamed.

So we rolled up quietly and the three of us took positions in front of her house. We then proceeded to toss eggs in all directions. Their dog was barking. Lights came on. We ran.

But not as fast as the old man in his underwear behind us.

As we dove into Dave's car, we were simultaneously extracted from Dave's car. Jenny's dad was an ex-Marine. We were high school ▶

losers. He marched us back up to the house, leading Ken and Dave by their ears and kicking me in the rear to urge me along.

The whole family was there to greet us. Mom, little sister with her broken leg, and there she was—Jenny, standing behind her. As we were sitting in the police car a little later, Dave explained to Ken that the Jenny standing on the porch wasn't the Jenny at the party. He should have kept that info to himself. We both started beating the crap out of Dave in the back of the cruiser. Jenny's dad was nice enough to let us go without pressing any charges, but we had to come back the next day and clean the house, driveway, garage, and lawn. We made Dave wash the dog.

Grant Murray
Washington High School, Class of '88

GOAT'S HEAD SLIP

It's super hard being foreign. The daily taunts from Tom Stone, "Why don't you go back to your country on your camel?" or Rhonda Clay and Jenny Appleby trying to get me to date Raj Patel, a tall Indian Gujrati guy who I couldn't have married even if I had wanted to because Muslim and Hindu fraternization was total honor killing material.

Then one day, it got worse. Jason Schweiber, a Jewish kid whose father was a surgeon and general golden boy of the 6th grade asked me, "Do you sacrifice goats?"

I said "no" because I didn't think I did. We actually do on a holiday called *baqra eid*—

What had tragically happened was that mom and dad had decided that fresh goat was where it's at so they killed a goat in our garage on Deerwood Lane. My neighbor, Stephanie, a girl whose hair was as bright and flaming as a June morning, had found a goat's head that my parents had disposed of in the trash. Her cocker spaniel, which had a habit of leaving its business in our backyard, had brought the neighbors a "surprise," so to speak.

And so, a haunting and disturbing myth of the Qureshi family doing unsavory, un-PETA activities in the backyard followed me throughout my time at Carlisle School.

Mariam Qureshi
Carlisle School, Class of '02

DAUGHTER'S LITTLE HELPER

I was a late bloomer. For most of high school I weighed around 90 and I barely hovered around five feet tall. Many of my classmates initially assumed I was a child prodigy—which would have been amusing if I'd had the grade point average to back that premise up.

When I was 15 my mother approached me and said, "Honey, if you ever find yourself pregnant or in trouble with a boy in any way I hope you'll come to me." I shut myself in my room for the rest of the day. I was baffled by my mother's words. A boy hadn't so much as called the house since the seventh grade. I was *always* home. Was it possible that my own mother was making fun of me?

When I was 16 I found a reason to leave the house. My friend Donna's single mother got a serious boyfriend, and Donna began having "get togethers" nearly every night of the week, while her mother was out.

One evening my friend Suzanne showed up at Donna's with some valium she'd stolen from a friend's mother's medicine cabinet. I, of course, was ignorant of the properties of Valium, but Suzanne talked me through it. She recommended we grind the Valium up in the bathroom and snort it, because according to Suzanne, Valium was more effective that way. Suzanne had spent time in juvenile detention centers and had a wealth of drug knowledge, so I knew I was in good hands. After we'd snorted the pills, Suzanne suggested that we have a beer. "Valium plus beer is one of the best buzzes ever," she said. We grabbed two beers and settled ourselves on the couch.

I felt sophisticated and worldly, there in Donna's living room. I'd partaken of mother's little helper: The Rolling Stones wrote songs about women like me.

I was most of the way through my beer when I was overtaken by tears. I don't mean a few stray tears rolled artfully down my cheeks. I mean I burst into uncontrollable sobs accompanied by childish wailing. Suddenly all eyes were on me. I didn't understand what was happening, but I knew that my behavior was not going to win me any popularity awards.

I grabbed for Suzanne, who had a grin stretched across her face and was the only one who hadn't yet noticed my predicament. Suzanne barely weighed more than I did, but was somehow not only in possession of a womanly figure, but an incredible tolerance for substances.

"What's wrong?" Suzanne asked. "Aren't you having a good time?"

I couldn't stop crying. An apish, chubby, red-headed guy who went by the nickname Whitey attempted to comfort me on the couch. I buried my head in his shoulder and continued to cry. "Shhh," he said. "It's okay." He stroked my arm and then moved in the direction of my nonexistent breasts.

I leapt up from the couch and made my way to the front door. The crowd I'd drawn followed. I staggered down the steps of Donna's apartment complex and into a grassy area, where I went down on my knees.

I was sure I could pull myself together if I could just get a moment to myself. ▶

Selections from the *I Love You, Beth Cooper*
Agony/Ecstasy Contest *(continued)*

"Amy."

Somehow, my stepfather was standing before me. As soon as he appeared my audience receded back into the apartment, and in seconds we were alone.

Instead of questioning me my stepfather gathered me up and carried me to the car. I cried the whole way home. I couldn't think who could have possibly come up with the bright idea of calling my parents—certainly not Suzanne—but I supposed it was better than calling an ambulance. Maybe.

Once home, I locked myself in the upstairs bathroom. My mother knocked on the door. "Honey, is everything all right?" I cast around for something to say other than "I think it's the valium!"

"Someone hurt my feelings!" I shouted through the door.

"Frances, she's *on drugs!*" I heard my stepfather say. "She could barely walk from the car to the front door!"

I sobbed out a story about a boy I liked—a boy I *thought* liked me back. I told them that he had rejected me tonight, and now I felt awful.

"Poor thing," my mother said. "Open the door."

I would not open the door.

My stepfather was having none of it. "She's *on drugs!*" he insisted.

Finally my parents retreated to their bedroom and I retreated to mine. The next day, my mother made me a cake to cheer me up, and my stepfather grudgingly dropped the subject.

I called Donna to find out when she was having people over next. I was sure I would do better next time.

Amy Bryant
Herndon High School, Class of '88
Author of the novel *Polly*

SCHOOL SPIRIT

I was on the swim team in high school. I was a member of the Junior Varsity team for 9th grade. However, I made Varsity in my sophomore year.

Unbeknownst to me, or anyone other newly made varsity swimmer, the current varsity members had an "initiation" ritual for all the new members. They called all the parents and swore them all to secrecy. Once they knew that the initiation was going to be kept a secret from all us newbies, they began explaining their grand plan to the parents. So, on one warm fall evening, I kissed my mom and dad goodnight and I went up to the second floor of my house to go to sleep.

Now, growing up, my parents didn't have a lot of money. I was the youngest of 6, and my mom was a stay at home mom. Any "extra" money that we had went for such luxuries as new socks and/or underwear. We did not have air conditioning. So naturally,

I slept sans sleepwear. In the middle of this particular night, at about midnight, my bedroom lights went on and my covers ripped off of my body. Not knowing who or what was in my room, I stood up trying to focus in on the group that was currently standing in my room.

It was the entire girls' Varsity team. They had come to "kidnap" me for the night. That alone would have been okay, but as I turned around to grab a blanket to cover myself with, I looked out my bedroom window.

There, in my now completely toilet-papered yard, was the entire boys' Varsity team looking right up into the only lit room in my house.

At least they were cheering.

Beth Cooper
Parma Senior High, Class of '89

MYSTERY MEAT

I was basking in the afterglow of my successful spin about town in the ungodly huge Driver's Education car with the principal/teacher and a few other students. I think the car was big enough to hold at least 15 students. I parked successfully and entered the building, taking my time getting to my locker.

Then the strange rumblings began.

Whatever I had eaten for lunch, it could have been the mystery meat, or the beets/peas/celery stick with cheese medley, something was apparently growing in my stomach. There was a pressure building, and I began my slow trek to the boy's bathroom, suddenly feeling the need to hurry up.

The sweat began to pour and I began to run.

About the time I hit the door, my stomach felt as if it actually exploded into my then-fashionable double knit faux blue jeans. As I made it to the stall (of course there were no doors on said stalls), I dropped to the seat and lowered my pants to find myself covered with, well, shit—down the back of my legs, in my underwear, in my socks and slowly pooling in my shoes.

There I sat; I couldn't get up because I was dripping everywhere. Of course, who walks in but the principal and another teacher, wrinkling their noses and commenting about that terrible odor, supposing the sewer must be backed up. I just lowered my head and prayed they would leave and take no notice of me.

I sat there awhile longer and knew time was ticking away and that I had to do something before the bell rang and the bathroom got busy. So I wiped my butt, body, legs, socks and shoes the best I could and decided I should make a break to the office to call my mom. Now this was probably in 1973–1974 and of course there were no cell phones ▶

**Selections from the *I Love You, Beth Cooper*
Agony/Ecstasy Contest** *(continued)*

or this would have been a lot easier. No, I had to walk to the office,
covering my backside as best I could, making sure no one was behind
me and made a mad dash in to the office and started dialing my mom
at home.

The secretary was in the principal's office and not at her desk by
the phone, fortunately, but even in there, she got a bad look on her
face and said, "wow, what is that smell." I talked as fast as I could
and said, "momcomegetmeihadanaccidentandwassickatmystomach
andmadeamessandihavetoleaveassoonaspossible." Mom said she
would get to the school as soon as she could. I sneaked to the front
of the building and hid behind a tree waiting for her. She finally
arrived in the old blue pick-up and made me ride in the back all
the way home due to the smell.

The spiffy knit blue jeans were burned.

Richard N. Hudson
Big Sandy High School, Class of '75

I WANNA HOLD YOUR HAND
If you tell somebody in the know that you graduated from New Trier
High School in suburban Winnetka, Illinois, circa 1984, 52% of the time
they'll think, *You must be a rich-ass North Shore of Chicago snotface.*
(The other 48% is divided between *Don't you mean Jew Trier; you
hairy-armed Christ-killer,* or *Hey, that's where my coke dealer goes.*)

Sadly, that 52% is probably right. You probably were a child of
privilege. You probably had a state-of-the-art 386 PC, your very own
tricked-out AudiBeamerBentleyFerrariPorche, and a trampoline next
to your backyard swimming pool. My first real girlfriend was a child
of major league privilege. (Yes, my high school girlfriend had a
trampoline in her backyard. And don't get excited. It wasn't nearly
as much fun as it could've been.) I was a child of Double-A privilege
at best. Girlfriend's family was the upperest of the upper class. My
family was the middlest of the middle. Now I'm not making any class
judgments here. I'm just setting the scene. Plus who can resist the
opportunity to make a trampoline joke.

At any rate, I *so* didn't want to go to our senior prom, partly
because I was an unromantic slug, and partly because I was a
cheapskate Jew who didn't want to pay for the dinner, the prom
cover charge, the tuxedo rental, my portion of the limo, flowers,
a haircut, or toothpaste. But Girlfriend badly wanted to go, so
she said she'd pick up the tab for the food, the transportation,
and the party. Sounded fine to me, but I still wanted to keep
my costs as low as possible, so I blew off the haircut, I busted
out the tux that I wore for our orchestra performances—yeah,
I was a band dweeb, are you surprised?—and dug an old pack

of Wrigley's Spearmint Gum out of my parents' junk drawer to quash any potential breath issues. My contribution to the cause: $15.81 for a corsage.

So prom night rolls around, and I'm all duded up in my cheesy half-tails, and my feet are squished into a pair of eerily shiny dress shoes, and I'm completely, utterly, wholly unpsyched. The only positive that could come out of this night could be a brief touch of boob, but Girlfriend and I have been dating for almost three weeks, and I've been thwarted on several attempted trips to her chest area, so I'm not holding out much hope.

Girlfriend's limo pulls into our middle class driveway (no class judgment), and she steps out looking gorgeous in her three-jillion dollar dress (no class judgment), and her Harry Winston-ish ear and neck bling (no class judgment). I wrap the $15.81 flower around her wrist, my parents cluck about how cute we are, they snap off a few shots with the Kodak Instamatic, then Girlfriend takes my hand, and we skip off to the limo.

On the way to our dinner spot, an unbelievably expensive steakhouse (no class judgment), we pick up the other half of our double date: One of my fellow band dweebs and his squeeze, who just happens to be a semi-hottie that I used to semi-go-out-with. That wasn't awkward for me in the least. Really. Honestly. It's not like a few weeks before, Fellow Dweeb asked me, "Do you mind if I ask Semi-Hottie out? It's not like you even got to second base with her or anything." Okay, that's exactly what it was like. And it was awkward as hell.

After a dinner filled with stilted conversation and declarations of how prom's gonna totally rule, Girlfriend pays the entire bill with her fancy-schmancy, infinite-credit-line-having Platinum AmEx (no class judgment), then she takes my hand and we toodle off to the North Shore Hilton in beautiful downtown Skokie. It's your typical prom stuff: Lame cover band, bad hair on the guys, awesome cleavage on the girls, incongruous theme that I can't recall, blahblahblah—I'll spare you all the details.

Girlfriend still has my hand, and since she's in better shape than I am, she easily drags me onto the dance floor, which sucked, because I was a crap dancer—still am, really. With her sexy, expensive dress and her funky, funky steps, she looked damn good. With my thrift-store-looking tux and my heinous pseudo-disco bullshit moves, I looked damn stupid. Again, I'll spare all you the details. Except for one. Regardless of the song's tempo or content, Girlfriend will not let go of my hand. She holds my hand through Styx, and Prince, and Stevie Wonder, and KISS, and Gary Numan. And she holds it hard. Zero chance of escape. *Zero.* I stroll over to the drink table, and she holds my hand. I wander off to talk with some of my friends, ▶

**Selections from the *I Love You, Beth Cooper*
Agony/Ecstasy Contest** *(continued)*

and she holds my hand. She wanders off to talk to some of her
friends, and she holds my hand. On the way to the john, and she
holds my hand. If they would've let her into the little boys room, she
probably would've kept holding my hand while I pissed, which would've
been a drag because I'm piss shy, an affliction that caused a number of
problems during high school (and beyond).

After a couple more hours of this hand jive, I manage to extricate
myself from her G.I. Joe kung fu grip, and head outside to get some air.
In the far corner of the parking lot, a crowd of about 20 tuxedoed slobs
surrounds one of the many limos. The longer I stay outside, the longer
I get to have my hand to myself, so I head on over.

One of the clarinetists from my symphonic band is hanging on the
perimeter. I ask him what's up. He gives me a weird look, then tries to
guide me away from the crowd. He says, "Dude, you don't wanna look.
It's ugly" I say, "Hell yeah, I do. I have no circulation below my wrist,
my tux makes me look like I should be playing some Shostakovich, and
I suspect I won't be getting any tit tonight. I deserve some ugly."

He shrugged. "Don't say I didn't warn you, man."

The sea of bodies parts. Several people pat me on the back as I head
towards the limo. I peer into the window, and there's Semi Hottie giving
what looked to my virgin eyes like an expert blow job to Fellow Dweeb.
My brain says, *Avert your eyes, avert your eyes.* My eyes say, *Screw
you, brain, we're masochistic bastards, so strap on in.* My johnson
says, *I am so frigging jealous, it's not even funny.* My hand says,
We'd have been better off staying with Girlfriend, you dumbass.

Epilogue
After the dance, Girlfriend, Semi-Hottie, Fellow Dweeb, and I jump
into the offending limo and made our way to a party at somebody's
monolith of a house on Lake Michigan (no class judgment). Girlfriend
and I make out for a while—pretty passionately, actually—then
I pathetically fell asleep in the basement around 4:00 AM. Had
I managed to stay awake, I might well have gotten myself an
expert blow job. Two days later, Girlfriend dumped me.

Alan Goldsher
New Trier High School, Class of '84

Author of *Modest Mouse: A Pretty Good Read* and *Hard Bop Academy:
The Sidemen of Art Blakey and the Jazz Messengers,* as well as
the novels *The True Naomi Story, Reality Check, Jam,* and *The Record.*

A BAD DATE
I'd spent my freshman year exposing my midriff to a young man
I'll call Joe. Joe was twenty-one, deeply religious, and worked for my
mother. We saw each other every day because working with my mom

was my after-school job. Come summer, I redoubled my efforts to get his attention. He broke down and asked me out to dinner. My mother knew Joe to be a really decent person. Still, I can imagine her panic at her fifteen-year-old daughter dating a twenty-one-year-old man.

Joe was a virgin on a serious wife-hunt. His twenty-five-year-old brother had recently married/adopted a high school junior. They married young in his family. And they wanted virgins. I was a virgin. I wasn't looking for a husband that year, but as dating prospects went, at least Joe wasn't just trying to get laid. He wanted to *talk* to me. I studied anatomy with him for his upcoming EMT exam. He tried to get me to like Randy Travis, I tried to win him over to the stylings of Boyz II Men. We quoted the Bible at each other—I'd marinated in Catholic school long enough to hold up my end of the conversation. We debated the appropriateness of church music: his church was strictly a capella, I argued that musicians were entitled to use their talents to praise God as much as singers. He said he'd never thought of it that way. This continued for a couple of months.

One day he invited me to his grandmother's eighty-third birthday. I accepted. I wore my most modest dress which, as it turned out, was the dress I'd worn to my grandmother's funeral six months before. Catholic school does odd things to a girl's wardrobe. She ends up with ten pairs of ripped jeans, eight tank-tops that end just above the ribcage, three gitchy-ya-ya dresses, one black dress suitable for weddings or funerals, and a plaid jumper. "You look nice," he said when I opened the door. He had on blue dress pants, a crisp white shirt and a tie. This, I thought fondly, is what he wears to church.

"You, too."

"No kissing in front of my family."

"Okay."

This struck me as terrifically weird. I'm Latin-American. In my family, one was scolded for *not* kissing everyone in the room upon entering or before leaving—and couples were openly affectionate. But I liked Joe. A lot. I would not embarrass him on purpose.

Soon we were in a Knights of Columbus hall, festooned with hand-made banners wishing Joe's grandmother a happy birthday. It felt like a school dance, only I had a date and I was the only Catholic in the room. And the only brunette. This must be, I thought, looking at all the real and simulated blondness around me, how a mouse feels when he walks into a room full of hamsters.

"So," Joe's mother approached me with a down-home smile, "You must be Jennifer." We shook hands. It was the first time I ever felt a strange woman's eyes dress me in white organza and calla lilies. Her smile was from the future. And not only hers. His entire family was, ▶

in fact, weighing the potential impact of my pigmentation on their gene pool. I was frightened. There was but one guest missing from the company. One person who'd yet to study my darkness and either nod their approval or disapproval at Joe. The guest of honor had not arrived.

"Joe, Joe," called Joe's mom meekly from across the room. We were immediately at her side. I'd become Joe's shadow. At least, I berated myself, I'm dressed for it. "Joe, Honey, can you pick up your grandmother? She's not answering her phone and she should have been here an hour ago."

"Sure, Mom." He turned to me, "You want to come with me, or stay? It's just around the corner. I'll be back in ten minutes." His mom looked at me again with her white organza fantasy. I could see her fussing with the lilies in my hair, coaxing a stray bloom into place. Please, I whispered with my eyes, don't leave me here. "Jen's coming with, if that's all right."

"Go ahead," the fantasy shut down, "you two probably want to be alone." Oh, that last word, "alone." There was brimstone in it. I'd gone from white organza to slut in one word. He didn't say anything when we got in the car, but when I reached for his hand he gave mine a squeeze. Okay, I soothed myself, he's not so much of a momma's boy that he's mad at me.

We pulled into the assisted living complex. His grandmother's apartment was on the third floor. We rang the bell five, six, seven, ten times. No answer. He knocked on the superintendent's door. The super got the key and let us in. His grandmother was in the kitchen. She was quite dead.

Joe tried to resuscitate her, but she was extremely dead. Cold. Curled up next to the oven as if she'd planned to pull her own birthday cake out of it. Joe started to cry. I'd never seen a man cry. And I'd certainly never had one sobbing into my lap, wetting the dress I'd worn to my grandmother's funeral; making me think, Damn, I'm burning this dress when I get home. I stroked his hair and made the kinds of noises my mother made when I was six and had fallen out of a tree.

The super called Joe's mother. Five minutes later everyone from the party clotted in the grandmother's hallway; moaning and weeping. I'd gone from conspicuous to invisible. There was no sensitive way to tell Joe I had an 11 o'clock curfew and that it was 10:45. I sat in a corner for hours, like a floral arrangement—or an urn.

He drove me home in monastic silence at 2 a.m. He walked me to the porch and returned quickly to his car, not waiting for my mother to open the door. All my mother knew was that Joe had kept me out way after curfew. She turned to me, "You'd better have a damned good reason for being so late and you're grounded for two weeks either way."

"Mom," I spoke in monotone, "his grandmother died and he and I found her body. Sorry I'm late."

Later that week, Joe broke up with me.

Jennifer Companik
Cardinal Gibbons High School, Class of '96

PIG PARTY

When I was in high school, I was the class slut. Okay, I wasn't the class slut, but I really, really, really wanted to be. Carol McBee was the official class slut. She decorated her room in black and had sex with Steven Levine in sixth grade. I know this was true because Steven told me himself.

Meanwhile, I spent years trying to win her crown but never got very far, probably due to the thick eyeglasses, braces, and palatial expander (headgear) that I wore from time to time at school because I thought it made me look cool. Looking back at my eleventh grade class photo (in which I wore it), I think it did.

By senior year, my greatest desire was to get laid by Stanley Steele. Stanley was the class hero—gorgeous, football star, student council vice-president, cheerleader dater—I could go on and on, but you know the boy I mean. Every school has one. Naturally, he didn't know I existed.

In the spring, to my great surprise, I was invited to a make-out party hosted by Kelly Davis, a football player—need I say more? I practically tinkled in my pants in anticipation. Okay, I did tinkle, but only about a teaspoon. My mother bought me a new outfit for the party—a polyester beige pants suit with matching shoes from Pappagallo. Pants suits for girls were new at the time, especially machine washable ones.

Upon arriving at the soiree, I knew something was amiss. First, Kelly's parents were "out of town" so there were no chaperones. Second, every boy there was cool and popular, while every girl was a gawky loser (except for me). Finally, and most disturbing, when I arrived, Sheldon Whitehead said, "Welcome to our pig party." I asked him what a pig party was and he explained it was when the cool guys invited all the ugly girls over. We were supposed to be so grateful for the attention that we would have sex with them. I don't think Sheldon was supposed to tell the girls that this was a pig party, but he was about as thick as tar.

I was hurt, but figured it was my only chance to win over Stanley Steele. I tracked him down by the ice and beer filled bathtub and asked if he'd like to get it on with me. He said he would, but only if I would remove my headgear. So I did. We went down to the basement. Stanley turned on the black light. To this day, anytime I see a man's teeth ▶

Selections from the *I Love You, Beth Cooper*
Agony/Ecstasy Contest *(continued)*

glowing in the dark, I am transported back to that moment in Kelly
Davis' basement.

After we took our positions on Kelly's make-out mattress, Stanley
suggested we get naked. I thought if I went all the way with him, he
might fall in love with me and ask me to wear his silver ID bracelet.
Then we could become a couple, maybe even homecoming king and
queen. So I stripped. He did too. We began making out. It was my
first time, but Stanley knew what he was doing. With his guidance and
my raging teenage hormones, I just about lost every inhibition I had
along with my virginity. As we were about to do the deed, I heard the
unmistakable toot of an ass breaking wind and the sound of nervous
teenage boy giggles. I looked up and saw the whites of twenty eyeballs
glowing in the dark.

That's when I knew Stanley was using me. You have to understand
that I was retarded in the ways of love. With all the dignity I could
muster, I dressed, put my headgear on, and left. When my mother
asked me why I came home early, I feigned severe heartburn.

The next week, rather than face the gossip at school, I skipped
classes every day and went to the anti-war demonstrations taking
place at the university in our town.

At my twenty-year high school reunion, I learned that Stanley was
pumping gas at the Texaco station on Lanier Drive. He was mostly bald
with a few errant scraggly hairs. His face had that red, bloated face of
a guy who drank too much. I can only surmise that God punished him
for being such a schmuck. When I said hello to him, he didn't
remember me.

Karen Quinn
Anderson High School, Class of '74
Author of *Wife in the Fast Lane* and *The Ivy Chronicles*

EAT OR DIE

I went to an all-boys high school in North Hollywood, so it took a
summer abroad for me to find the kind of elation/humiliation that
only first love brings.

Because—like all sixteen-year-old boys—I was a complete pain in the
ass, my parents jumped at my Spanish teacher's suggestion of sending
me to Spain on an exchange program. And because—like all parents of
sixteen-year-old boys—my mother and father were complete pains in
the ass themselves, I shared their enthusiasm.

After a redeye from L.A. to Madrid and an agonizingly slow train
ride, I arrived at a little town in the province of Valladolid (the last "d"
is pronounced with a distinct lisp). My bullfighting-obsessed host father
(he'd been gored three times and was reduced to walking like a crab),
picked me up at the station and drove me directly to his favorite bar.

It soon became apparent that my rudimentary Spanglish was not going to be of much use. Not only did I fail to understand a word the host father was slurring, but when I tried to order a bottle of *agua*, I end up with a glass of rosé. The bar quickly filled up with other host families and exchangees suffering similar linguistic hurdles, and I caught the eyes of an equally bewildered girl from New York who was nursing a beer after failing to order a Diet Coke. She had on a tight pink T-shirt and a frilly white skirt that contrasted sharply with her "You touch me, and I will castrate you" NYC expression. It took a couple more *copas* of wine, but eventually I gained the *cojones* to approach her with my patented pickup line, "Excuse me, but do you know where the restroom is?"

To put it simply: I was sixteen, she was fifteen, and we were drinking. I fell madly in love with . . . Well, to protect her identity, I'll simply call her Scarlett Johansson.

My host family was, at least initially, quite supportive of my flowering love for Scarlett, especially when I explained that she was my *novia* (which I took to mean "girlfriend" and they took to mean "fiancée"). They invited her along to the various bull-related festivals occurring in the surrounding towns and plied her with the same continuous flood of vino that I'd quickly come to enjoy. That is, until one evening a local kid introduced us to the magic of gin and tonics, and we proceeded to drunkenly make out in the town's central plaza.

Now I will admit that in our youthful ardor we might have actually been lying down on that park bench, and that perhaps our hands were roving a mite freely, but WE DID NOT HAVE SEX IN THE TOWN SQUARE. I know this for a fact, because we'd already had sex up at the old abandoned castle just an hour previously. Thus, I was shocked the next morning when I awoke to find the family's modest apartment crammed to capacity with whispering neighbors—including the rather intimidating father of Scarlett's host family. The American schoolteacher who headed up the exchange program muscled through the crowd and dragged me out into the hall.

"Did you . . ." She was a religious Texan and had trouble getting the words out. ". . . Did you have sex with Scarlett?"

Of course, I was guilty as charged, but attempted to equivocate with the same technique that Bill Clinton would so ineffectively use years later.

"Define sex."

"Did you have sexual congress in the main square last night?"

"No," I carefully chose my words. "I did not have sex . . . *in the main square*."

"They saw you!" She waved back at the people in the apartment, seeming to imply that all fifty or so of them had seen me. ▶

Selections from the *I Love You, Beth Cooper*
Agony/Ecstasy Contest *(continued)*

My first thought, of course, was of poor Scarlett. I'd read some
of the Cliff Notes for *Don Quixote* and a smattering of Hemingway,
so I knew that Spain was a deeply religious country full of highly
unrealistic virginity demands. I was far from Scarlett's first—she
was from New York City, after all—but of course, the townspeople
didn't know that. Would they brand her as a whore? Ship her off
to a convent? Or . . . Oh God, they weren't going to try and marry
us, were they?

"I swear, we were just making out," I pleaded.

Unfortunately, this statement somehow only managed to confirm in
the mind of the program director that I'd had sex in the plaza.

"I'm sorry, but you're on your own with this. They've already sent
for a car." She shook her head.

"A car? For what?"

She shrugged and started for the stairwell.

"You can't leave me!" I called after her. "I don't even speak
Spanish!"

"You should have thought of that before you decided to fornicate in
public."

"It wasn't in public!" I shouted, but she'd already disappeared.

Before I could slip back into the apartment, the host mother burst
through the still open doorway in tears and gave me a bear hug. She
was the kind of woman with meaty forearms who could really crush
your floating ribs.

"*Espehasnobkosthchuthasdemorglahodadeconyoeheeto,*" she
whispered soothingly in my ear.

Just as I was starting to pass out from the bear hug, the host father
crabwalked into the hall rolling a giant wheel of cheese.

"*Vamanos!*" Close to tears himself, he clapped a drunken hand on
my shoulder and directed me towards the stairs.

———

Minutes later, I found myself wedged in the back seat of a minuscule
seat with the giant wheel of cheese. The drunk father drove, while
the mother sat in the front passenger seat furiously wearing out
rosary beads. We made our way through the crowd of townspeople
who (unable to fit in the apartment) had mobbed the streets to see
us off, and began driving out of town on an old overgrown pothole-
ridden road.

As we continued to drive for over an hour along what gradually
turned into a dirt trail, my thoughts shifted from Scarlett's fate, to
my own. Peering out the grimy window, all I could see was rocky
pasture land and the occasional flock of sheep. Where were we going?
And what the hell was up with the giant wheel of cheese?

"*Adonde vamos?*" I asked in my best Spanish. But as usual,

the host mother failed to understand my question, and simply passed back the bottle of Fundador brandy the father had been swigging.

Eventually we reached a village of maybe twenty dilapidated whitewashed houses—several with actual mules tied up in front. The father wrestled out the wheel of cheese, and the mother led me into one of the houses. There I was introduced to a very small old woman in traditional garb who I took to be grandma. Grandma crossed herself a few times against my recent fornication, and then directed me over to an ancient medical scale conspicuously standing in the middle of the living room. I was carefully weighed, and then repeatedly pinched about the midriff as grandma used her fingers as calipers to precisely measure my fatness.

There was a lengthy discussion (of which I understood not a word) and more tears and bear hugs from the host mother. Eventually I was seated alone at the head of the dining room table. Both ma and grandma disappeared into the kitchen, only to reappear moments later with platters of food. They placed the food in front of me, and then mimed for me to start eating.

And ate I did. For at least two hours straight. Everything from ham to chorizo to squid to lamb brains. I've never been a picky eater, and grandma's cooking was DELICIOUS. The host father returned sans cheese wheel to join ma and grandma, and all three of them watched with increasing delight as I shoveled in the chow. When finally I could eat no more, they had me waddle over to the scale and weighed me again. I'd gained 2.5 kilos (or roughly five and a half pounds). Based on the cheers that went up in that house, you would have thought Spain had just won the World Cup.

Without explanation (not that I would have understood an explanation, had one been offered), we got back in the car and rushed home along the potholed road—me trying desperately trying not to puke. The crowd still was still waiting for us in front of the apartment building, and when the host mother announced to them my astonishing weight gain, they too cheered. For the next few days, I even found myself inexplicably to be something of a town hero.

———

I imagine the question you're asking yourself is "Huh?"

Well, I was stuck asking myself the same question for at least a week, before the head of the exchange program calmed down enough to start speaking to me again. Apparently the stress of my fornication scandal had caused her take up smoking again.

"They thought you were dying of tuberculosis." She sucked at her Marlboro.

"What?" I thought about this a minute, then added, "What?"

"I'm serious. The whole town believes that boys under the age of ▶

**Selections from the *I Love You, Beth Cooper*
Agony/Ecstasy Contest** *(continued)*

eighteen who have sex die of tuberculosis. Even the doctor. It's like
they're living in the Middle Ages."

"That doesn't make any sense."

"Of course it doesn't make any sense. They're *Catholics*." Her Texas
accent kicked in with extra force on the last word.

I couldn't see how being Catholic had anything to do with it, but
then like all Hollywood natives, I'd been raised Hedonist.

"They think I'm dying?"

"Not any more. That's why they force-fed you. Apparently, they also
believe that people with TB lose weight. When they proved that you
had actually gained weight, it signaled to the town that you'd been
miraculously 'cured.' "

"I . . ." As a sixteen-year-old, my powers of comprehension pretty
much stopped there.

"*Catholics*." She leaned her head back and exhaled a cloud of smoke
at the sky.

————

Scarlett and I managed to continue long-distance dating for at least a
year after we returned to the States, although in the end she admitted
that she'd been cheating on me pretty much from the start.

Oh, and I never did figure out what the deal was with that giant
wheel of cheese.

Jonathan Selwood
Harvard-Westlake School, Class of '89
The utterly dissolute author of *The Pinball Theory of Apocalypse*

*If you have a magical/horrific high school story—and c'mon, of
course you do—we're giving away more crappy prizes. For details,
go to www.iloveyoubethcooper.com.*

....